The Night Dancers

A Twist Upon a Regency Tale
Book 12

By Jude Knight

DRAGONBLADE PUBLISHING, INC.

ARE YOU SIGNED UP FOR DRAGONBLADE'S BLOG?

You'll get the latest news and information on exclusive giveaways, exclusive excerpts, coming releases, sales, free books, cover reveals and more.

Check out our complete list of authors, too!

No spam, no junk. That's a promise!

Sign Up Here

www.dragonbladepublishing.com

Dearest Reader;

Thank you for your support of a small press. At Dragonblade Publishing, we strive to bring you the highest quality Historical Romance from some of the best authors in the business. Without your support, there is no 'us', so we sincerely hope you adore these stories and find some new favorite authors along the way.

Happy Reading!

CEO, Dragonblade Publishing

Certain that the Marquess of Teign is behind her cousin's disappearance, investigator Melody Blackmore enters his mansion disguised as a man. Teign hires her to discover how his sons are leaving their tower prison or having food and other items brought in, and she soon realizes that the sons are also the marquess's victims. As her interest in the eldest of the brothers grows, she joins them all in a campaign to bring Teign down.

Allan Sheppard, the Earl of Kemble, is the eldest of Teign's ten sons. He is weighed down by his frequent failures to protect his brothers from Teign's beatings and abuse, but determined to keep them as safe as he can until his youngest brother is no longer under Teign's guardianship.

All they must do is fool the most recent investigator sent to find out their secrets. But Mel Black is not like the others, and Allan finds that an alliance with her gives the brothers the chance to not only survive, but to thrive.

However, Teign will stop at nothing to punish his sons for escaping him. Only Allan's and Melody's growing commitment to one another keeps them steadfast as they uncover evidence of unspeakable crimes and evil beyond imagining.

Content Warning: this book contains mention (but no graphic scenes or descriptions) of certain unspeakable crimes against women. Please be advised!

FOREWORD AND WARNING

This book is perfect for holiday reading. It was inspired by the fairy tale *The Twelve Dancing Princesses*, and pays tribute to the song The Twelve Days of Christmas, which are the days between the feast day of Christmas and the feast day of the Epiphany.

Dear reader, this book has one hero and one heroine, and is told from their points-of-view, turn and turn about. But the story that inspired it had romances for every princess, so inevitably, the hero's dancing brothers also need to find love. Since I cut them back to ten, and made two of them rather young for marriage, that meant I only (**only**!!) had an extra seven marriages among the brothers. In addition, my heroine has a sister and my hero has a brother-in-law, and they are also in love. This means my story gives happy endings not just to Allan and Mel, but to seven of Allan's brothers and to Mel's sister.

At one point, a troupe of aristocrats becomes involved in fighting the villain, introducing more names into a name-heavy book, but their names are not particularly important. They are just there to throw a bit of power and influence in the direction of my hero and his family.

Fair warning, dear reader: to make the cast of characters even more confusing, for part of the story the brothers and their heroines are in disguise and using code names. The things my plot elves do to me!

I've tried to help. I named the brothers in alphabetical order by age, and their code names have the same initial letter. And I've tried to avoid naming people who don't play an important role in the story.

Just keep track of Allan and Melody, dear reader, and the

story will make sense. Or, if you prefer to place everyone, bookmark the list of characters that follows this foreword so you can refer back to it. If a character is named in the text but isn't in the list, you only have to remember them for the single scene in which they appear. They're not coming back.

Evil villains and their crimes

Please note that Teign is evil beyond words. Teign's crimes are crucial to the story, but are mostly described by characters, with only the mildest appearing as action on the page. And my promise to you is that justice prevails, and the good reach their happy after ever. If even the mention of certain unspeakable crimes against women bothers you, proceed with caution.

In real life, sadly, there are people like Teign. Even those who turn a benign face to the world can perform unspeakable evil behind the scenes, and when they achieve enormous wealth, power, and status, they believe nothing can stop them. In their minds, other people have no reality, and the sufferings of others are merely proof that they are invincible.

Such people are not born that way. Upbringing plays a crucial role, but I believe choice is also vital. And above all, the choice to regard others as pawns in one's own story. What made Teign the man he becomes? Since he was already a mature man when he first married, Allan never knew, and nor, probably, did he care. I suspect it began with a father and mother soured by their lack of title and status, who raised their son to believe he had a grievance against the senior line of the family, and always took his part and praised him no matter what he did. But this is Allan's and Melody's story, not Teign's.

Characters in *The Night Dancers*

The heroine and her family

- Melody Blackmore, known as Mel Black when in disguise as a man, and as Lady Mnema at the Golden Adonis
- Harmony White, her sister, a widow

- Mel's daughter Harriet
- Harmony's son Benjamin, known as Benjie

The Sheppard Brothers, sons of the Marquess of Teign

Sons of Teign's first wife:

- Allan Sheppard, Earl of Kemble: heir to the Marquess of Teign and eldest brother. Known as Lord Apollo at the Golden Adonis.
- Baldwin Sheppard, second son, twin to Cornelius Sheppard. Known as Boreas at the Golden Adonis
- Cornelius Sheppard, third son, twin to Baldwin. Known as Chiron at the Golden Adonis

Sons of Teign's second wife:

- Donald Sheppard, fourth son. Known as Dionysus at the Golden Adonis
- Ernest Sheppard, fifth son. Known as Eros at the Golden Adonis
- Francis Sheppard, sixth son, called Frank by his brothers. Known as Faunus at the Golden Adonis
- Gerard Sheppard, seventh son, twin to Hudson. Known as Ganymede at the Golden Adonis
- Hudson Sheppard, eighth son, twin to Gerard. Known as Hermes at the Golden Adonis

Sons of Teign's third wife:

- Isaac Sheppard, ninth son. Known as Iakkhos at the Golden Adonis
- Jerome Sheppard, tenth son. Known as Zephyros at the Golden Adonis

Love interests of the Teign brothers

- Amber Spense, beloved by Gerard. Known as Aedas at the Golden Adonis, where she works as a ladies' maid

- Clara, Mrs. Wickham, a widow beloved of Baldwin. Known as Lady Melissae at the Golden Adonis
- Parthena, beloved of Hudson. Known as Thisbe at the Golden Adonis
- Rosina, beloved of Ernest. Manager of the Golden Adonis, where she is known as Thalia
- Thomasina, Lady Cornelius. Known as Lady Opora at the Golden Adonis
- Verity, beloved of Donald. Known as Hestia at the Golden Adonis
- Winifred Querrendale, daughter of Dr. Querrendale, beloved of Frank. Known as Lady Andromeda at the Golden Adonis

Also at the Golden Adonis

- Madame Hera, proprietress

Family members of the Sheppard brothers

- Alberta, Allan's deceased wife
- Lydia Sheppard, Allan's daughter. Known as Lydia Eastwood.
- Phineas, Allan's brother-in-law. Known as Phineas Eastwood.
- The Earl of Nottwick, Phineas's older brother
- The three French aunts of Thomasina, Lady Cornelius
- Elias, son of Cornelius and Thomasina

The archvillains

- The Marquess of Teign
- Farnham, Teign's steward and henchman

Servants at Teign Tower

- Teign's butler (known only as "the butler")
- Mrs Palmer, the Cook
- Jenny, Cook's assistant

Prospective brides selected by Teign. Also their mothers

- Patrice and her mother Lady Atkinson
- Lady Felicia and her mother Lady Farringford-Smyth
- Imogen and her mother Lady Spurfold

Allies of the Sheppard brothers in alphabetical order by surname or title

- Mr. Beauclair, a minister of the Church of England and a specialist in spiritual healing
- Mr. Blasingstoke, another minister
- The Duke of Dellborough (the head of the Versey family, who appears in a few of my books) and his wife Aurelia, the duchess
- Felix and Adaline, The Duke and Duchess of Kempbury (hero and heroine of *The Lyon's Dilemma*)
- The king, who at this time was George IV, formerly the Prince Regent
- The Bishop of London
- Mrs. Moriarty and the bodyguards who work for her in the firm Moriarty Protection. I name some of them at one point, but their names don't matter for the story.
- Chris and Clemmie Satterthwaite (hero and heroine of *The Secret Word*)
- The Earl of Somerville, who married Kempbury's widowed sister-in-law in *Thrown to the Lyon*
- The Marquess and Marchioness of Thornstead (Garry is heir to the Duke of Dellborough)
- Lord Alexander Winderfield (Alex), fourth son of the Duke of Winshire

Pets

- Zero the cat
- Benjie's pet mice

Chapter One

London, late in 1824

THE HOUSE KNOWN as Teign Tower felt oppressive from the moment Melody Blackmore entered. Perhaps it was just that she knew the owner's reputation. Rumor ascribed all sorts of wicked deeds to him, including the murder of the cousin who had preceded him in the title, and that cousin's entire family.

No doubt the sons she was here to investigate were just as bad, though the rumor mill was less informative about them. *Well. Time would tell.*

The footman who opened the side door at which she had been told to present herself asked her to wait in the entry hall and disappeared along a passage to the right, leaving Mel with the hair rising on the back of her neck and the sense that something nasty was watching her from the shadows.

By the time the marquess sent for her, twenty minutes later, she had almost talked herself out of staying. *None of that. Thomasina needs you. If she still lives.*

Keeping her goal—and her missing cousin—firmly in her mind, Mel followed the footman.

"Mr. Black, my lord," he announced, as he ushered her into the room.

The impression of menace and evil was stronger here, and centered on the man behind the desk. He did not stand, but then, she was dressed as a man and was there to do a job. Such a courtesy could not be expected.

She knew the marquess was in his seventies, but would not have guessed it by his appearance. He was still tall, burly rather than stout, and clearly physically fit. His full head of iron-gray hair added to the illusion that he was still in his prime, as did the domineering presence he projected.

The way he looked at her as though she was something unpleasant he had found on the heel of his boot said everything that needed to be said about his character. If the investigation he wanted her to undertake had been the real reason she was here, she would have found some excuse and left without further ado.

Although, from what he was saying, it was already too late. "You will move in immediately. You have one week to complete your investigation. At the end of that time, if you have not discovered my sons' secret, my men will take you out, beat you, and hand you over to the navy press gang."

This was a further escalation. Of the previous four investigators, the first had been dismissed, the second dismissed with a buffet or two from footmen, and third and fourth beaten each more heavily.

She would not give him the satisfaction of a reaction. "Two weeks, as written in this contract." She handed it to the bullying lord. "You will see that my daily charge is five guineas, plus expenses. Since you expect me to live in, you will be responsible for my keep for the fortnight. And, of course, we have yet to discuss my success fee."

He stood and leaned on the desk, looming over her as she sat facing him. "You are not in a position to dictate terms, Mr. Black."

"And yet you need my skills, Lord Teign," Mel pointed out, maintaining her calm facade. "My success rate is second to none. And you have discarded so many investigators so violently that word has gone out in the fraternity. It is me, or no one."

The argument got through to him. With a visible effort, he

subdued his rage and sat down. "You are an arrogant young man," he accused, with a hint of surprise that said volumes about how seldom anyone opposed him.

Mel accepted the accusations without a blink. She was not a man and not particularly young, but she owned to a degree of arrogance. She had earned the right. Her disguise had passed muster. No one saw past the short-cropped hair, a specially designed corset that flattened her breasts and was padded to disguise her waist, a male stride and other mannerisms, and a deeper voice than was natural for her.

She had been lying about her identity since the day she donned men's clothes years ago to undertake her first investigation, and that lie, at least, no longer bothered her. She replied, "My arrogance is justified. Within a fortnight, my lord, you shall have an answer. If we come to terms. Otherwise, I shall leave, shooting my way out if necessary."

The last statement got his full attention. "Shooting? Damn it, man. I am a marquess. You'll not get out of here alive."

"My reluctance to shoot you, my lord, is not as great as my reluctance to be beaten and pressed. And if you are dead, you shall not be able to deny whatever story I tell."

Given the reception she was likely to get from the sailors when they discovered she was a woman, she would rather die trying to escape the marquess's house, than perish miserably in a ship's hold after the sailors made a plaything of her.

If those were her choices, she'd be certain to send him down to Hell before she breathed her last. But with two bad choices before her, she'd try for a third way.

"We do not, however, need to be at odds, my lord. You wish to find out how your sons are managing to remain fit and well without adequate food, and going through dancing slippers without any way of leaving their tower. I wish to survive this engagement and be paid for it, so I am highly motivated to discover their secret. That is my only interest, Lord Teign."

"You are remarkably calm," Lord Teign commented, frowning. He pulled the contract toward him and began to read it. Mel expressed her relief in a single long respiration. *In. Out. Relax but remain alert. Remember your purpose.*

Having made up his mind to accept her terms, Lord Teign spent little time reading the contract, and indeed, it was simple enough. He did not haggle over the two-week term, the daily payment, the bonus for success, nor any of the other terms, but simply read the contract through and signed both copies.

With the suspicion that had become second nature to her, Mel wondered if he was so relaxed about the terms because he had no intention of letting her leave alive. It was not a problem. She, too, was merely using the contract to lend verisimilitude to her act—she was not here to investigate the sons, but the marquess himself.

Within twenty minutes, her copy in her pocket, she was following the butler to what he called "the young lords' tower" through a maze of passages—servants' passages, which might have been a deliberate affront.

The butler had searched her bag and her person, missing the false bottom in the bag and most of the weapons she had about her person. He did find the decoy gun she had in her pocket, but not the real one worn in a harness in the small of her back under her coat. Nor did he find the gunpowder and bullets in the heels of her boots.

On the whole, Mel was not dissatisfied. Nor was she discouraged by the butler's pompous recitation, as she accompanied him through the house, about the impregnability of the tower—its thick walls, barred windows, and single door, which was both locked and guarded.

After all, ten spoilt lordlings had been coming and going as they pleased, evading the tower's defenses, their father's servants, and the surveillance of four men who specialized in solving the problems of the *haut ton*, and uncovering their secrets. If the lordlings could do it, so could Mel.

All she had to do was discover their secret, and meanwhile

carry out her real mission.

She and the butler turned a corner and began traversing a long hall with windows that looked out over roofs on one side and on the other, down into a stable yard. Two-thirds of the way to the other end, bars blocked their passage. Two sets of bars, in fact, each containing a gate.

The butler unlocked the first gate, then handed the key to one of the two footmen who had been escorting them through the house. The footman stayed outside and locked the gate. The same process saw Mel and the butler on their own at the end of the hall, with two locked gates behind them. *Clever.* The young lords would not be able to escape even if they overwhelmed whoever came into their chambers.

And yet, they had some way to either leave or to bring in supplies. Mel's respect for them went up a notch. Perhaps they were not so contemptible after all. It didn't matter. They were not her main purpose here.

Next came a door, which the butler also unlocked. It opened into an antechamber. The butler handed Mel his lamp and said, "Ring the bell and wait here for Lord Kemble." She heard the key turn in the lock after he shut her in.

Bell. There it was, a large handbell, on a table against the side wall of the chamber. There was a door opposite the one she'd entered by, and another table on the fourth wall of the room. And that was all. Just bare stone walls and a wooden floor, a plain ceiling, the two tables, the two doors, and the bell.

Very well, then. Time to meet the sons of the Marquess of Teign. Apples did not fall far from the tree—no doubt they were as vicious and evil as their father, so Mel would need to be very wary. She put down her bag on the floor and the lamp on the table.

What would they say when she told them why she was there? She intended to confess she was an investigator, for she would learn from their reactions. She'd not tell them everything she was here to investigate, of course. Just their part of it.

There was one sure way to find out what they'd do. She picked up the bell and rang it.

⊁⊰

ALLAN WAS PLAYING chess with his brother Frank when the notification bell rang.

"What's happening?" Frank wondered. "It is not yet time for our meal."

The meal was always delivered at seven in the evening. If you could call it a meal—bread and water, and barely enough for three grown men, let alone ten. On days their father allowed some of them out, the cook often managed to slip them food, and those of them required to attend events could hope for a good supper.

However, their father's plan was to starve them into compliance, so he usually found ways to block these other sources of food. Had it not been for the secret, Allan didn't know how he could have held out, or his brothers either.

"Another investigator?" Donald wondered, looking up from his drawing. Those brothers who had not already been in the central space had emerged from the surrounding chambers, all looking toward the entrance. "His lordship is not due for another rant."

"There's a simple way to find out," said Jerome. He was the youngest of the brothers, and occasionally impetuous—but in this case, he was correct. Allan looked up at those hanging over the balcony to the gallery that circled the room and gave access to the upper tier of rooms. Hudson was closest.

"Hudson, check who is there," he said. Hudson disappeared from view. In his imagination, Allan visualized his brother pulling back the carpet, lifting the trapdoor that they had laboriously made in the thick oak floor, and peering down into the antechamber below.

After a long moment, Hudson was back at the balcony. "It is one man," he reported. "Not one of the servants."

Almost certainly another investigator. Poor chump. According to the butler, the previous one had been badly beaten and thrown into the street. "Let him in," said Allan to the brother nearest the door. He could not afford to sympathize with the man, who was, after all, working with the enemy. They would need to treat him as they did the others: Drug him to sleep at night and run rings around him in the daytime.

The investigator entered, looking around the room with interest. For some reason, he chose to bow first to Allan. What made the man think Allan was the eldest? They were all there, and though the younger brothers were clearly only in their twenties, Baldwin and Cornelius, the first set of twins, were a mere two years younger than Allan.

"Do I have the honor of addressing Lord Kemble?" the man asked, in a light, pleasant voice that was more cultured than his mediocre appearance suggested.

"And you are?" Allan replied.

Another bow. "I am Mel Black. I am an investigator, and your father has hired me to find out why he is failing in his efforts to bully and intimidate you into obedience."

Around him, his brothers stilled in shock at the investigator's honesty.

There had been four before this one, sent to discover how the brothers were managing to hold out against the marquess's strictures. Two had claimed to be valets, one a footman, one a drawing master, of all things. As if jailers sent drawing masters to those they were trying to starve and subdue.

None before had stated the marquess's true purpose in sending them. This man was audacious, to say the least. This boy, rather, for his shoulders were narrow and his cheeks showed no signs of a beard, even close up—this boy had a plump gut but thin wrists, like a youth that had just begun a growth spurt. Perhaps Allan should offer him a way out.

"Has his lordship told you the price of failure?" Allan asked. "They will beat you, and possibly kill you. I can smuggle you out tomorrow when the gates open, if you wish to escape."

"I am tougher than I look, Lord Kemble," said Mr. Black. "The marquess has told me that, if I do not uncover your secrets, I shall be beaten and given to a press gang. I have a strong incentive to win. I am sorry that we are on opposite sides, but I think it best to be honest."

"One has to admire Mr. Black's cheek," said Baldwin. "I am Baldwin, Mr. Black. Allow me to present you to my brothers." And he went around in age order, to his twin Cornelius first, then Donald, Ernest, Francis (whom they all called Frank), Gerard and Hudson, who were the second set of twins, then Isaac, and finally Jerome.

Mr. Black bowed to each of them, his bright eyes taking everything in. Allan had the feeling he was cataloguing, not just the ten brothers and their individual differences, but also this central room of the tower, from its floor to the top of the dome nearly forty feet above their heads.

He gave himself a mental shake. The young man's confidence was misplaced. By his appearance, Black wasn't out of his teens. Where older and more experienced men had failed, this one would be no match for the ingenuity of the Sheppard brothers.

"Baldwin, show Mr. Black where he will be sleeping," he said. "Also, tell him where the necessary is and anything you think he needs to know about conditions here."

Baldwin nodded, and led the youth away. Allan went back to his game, but his concentration was divided between countering Frank's chess moves and keeping track of Mr. Black's movements around the tower. He seemed to be going in and out of every room—always with one of the brothers. What was he up to?

Allan found out when Frank put him into checkmate. The young investigator approached their table. "My lords, your brothers have been kind enough to allow me to visit every room in your tower except for your own. Lord Kemble, Lord Francis, may I see your bed chambers, too?"

"For what purpose?" Frank asked before Allan could do so.

Black's lips curved as he regarded Frank with amused eyes. "So that I can ferret out your secrets, of course, my lord." He chuckled, and added, "To be serious, checking the bounds of my environment is an old habit. If you prefer me not to see your room, then I shall stay out of it."

Frank pushed back his chair and stood up. "You'll find no secrets in my chamber. This way." He limped off, not looking back to see Black following him, but Allan watched the youth until he disappeared through Frank's door.

Donald had gone back to the diagram he had been drawing when Black arrived, but was now considering Allan with his head on one side.

"What do you think of him?" Allan asked.

"He has a good memory for names and faces," Donald answered. "Baldwin introduced him around, and he has addressed us all correctly since. He has not even been confused by Baldwin and Cornelius, though they are dressed alike today."

"He has charm," Baldwin said. "I suspect he uses it to hide how clever he is. We shall have to be careful tonight."

Coming from Baldwin, who also used charm to deflect attention from his intelligence, it was a warning worth noting. "We shall be careful," Allan said.

"He recognized my drawings," Donald commented. "The ones of the Trevithick locomotive."

Allan could feel his eyebrows twitch upward. Donald had been interested in the innards of the machine rather than its external appearance. The diagrams in question looked to Allan as if an anonymous engine had exploded across the page.

"Also," Donald added, "Zero likes him. He accepted a pat from him."

Surprising! Donald's scarred old black tomcat didn't like anyone except Donald. If Black's charm worked even on Zero, it was a formidable force indeed. He was an unknown quantity, and they would need to be even more cautious than usual. Perhaps they should call off tonight's excursion, but Allan was reluctant. It was nearly Christmas, and the ladies of London—those who had the money and the independence to be useful to the Sheppard brothers—were in the mood to spend.

Perhaps he would conduct Black on a tour of his own room and see if he could find out how long the marquess planned to give the boy for his investigation. If it was only a week, that would still give them another week until Christmas without an intruder watching.

Yes. He would show Black around and see what impressed both Baldwin and Donald—two personalities as different as brothers could be. Allan waited by the door of his room for Frank and the investigator to emerge.

It was at least another ten minutes. Interesting. Frank was cautious with strangers, and tended to keep even the maids and his brothers out of his room.

"You wanted to see my room," Allan said to Black when the youth emerged back into the central space. "Come." He opened his door and led the way inside. The appointments were spartan—his brothers had brought in items to furnish and decorate their own spaces, but Allan had kept to the bare necessities, unwilling to spend energy, money, or thought on anything that did not contribute to their escape.

Indeed, the very plainness of the room reminded him that the luxury in which he had encased for as long as he obeyed his father had been no protection against the evil man's whims, nor had it saved his wife or her second child.

Black strolled around the room, pausing briefly to touch the one personal item it contained—a painting Cornelius had made of Allan's daughter when she was no more than a toddling infant. He often spoke to it, telling his little girl what he was doing, wishing he could see her again.

"Is this your daughter?" Black asked.

"That is not your business," Allan snapped back, his jaw set against the pain, his hands clenched against the urge to forcibly remove the hand that was violating the frame of the painting.

Some of that must have conveyed itself to Black, for he snatched his hand back, and said, softly, "I am sorry for your loss, Lord Kemble."

He stepped to the window and looked out over the courtyard, the perimeter wall, and beyond at the glimpse of street and the untidy cluster of roofs and chimneys. Did he stay silent to allow Allan time to compose himself? Perhaps.

Certainly, it was several minutes before he said, "Thank you. I appreciate your forbearance." And he left the room.

Baldwin came in a moment later and shut the room behind him. "I am ready," he said. "We have soup simmering on the fire to go with tonight's allocation of bread. I suggest we put the potion in Black's bowl, and then serve everyone from the same pot."

"Good thinking." That should work. Allan had been wondering how to administer the sleeping draught that had served them so well with the other investigators. This one was smart enough to refuse to drink, or even to pretend to drink but stay awake to find out their secrets.

They could not let that happen. Whatever the consequences to Black, they had to succeed in bamboozling the man, for the marquess must not discover what they were hiding.

THE EVENING MEAL was delivered at seven o'clock—merely bread and water, as the previous investigators had told her. But, as they had also said, the brothers produced wine from somewhere. The pot of soup, too. It had been simmering on the stove all afternoon, but disappeared when the bell rang to announce the arrival of the bread, leaving nothing behind but its enticing smell.

It was magic, two of the agents had claimed. It was collusion with the servants, another hypothesized. The fourth had been too badly beaten to express an opinion, and it would only have been an opinion, for none of the investigators had discovered any evidence.

The marquess had found no wine nor any food when he had had the tower searched after each investigator reported. Indeed, many of the items she had seen in the bedchambers had apparently disappeared between when the other investigators saw them, and when the searches were made.

Magic was unlikely, in Mel's opinion. She'd certainly never seen objects appear and disappear in a way that defied nature. The tower must have hiding places that the marquess knew nothing about, and if it had hiding places, it might also have hidden ways in and out.

Though if that is the case, why do the marquess's sons stay? Why do they not just leave? Almost all of them are of age.

Mel accepted a glass of the wine, but made certain to spill it discreetly, for the other investigators must have been drugged somehow, no matter how they denied it. The soup was served from a common pot, so should be safe enough.

Mel returned to her room after dinner, and drank sparingly from the water she had brought with her. She then sat in the chair by the room's little fireplace, for her intention was to remain awake and thoroughly search at least the public rooms once the brothers had all gone to bed.

Although I am feeling remarkably sleepy. That was her last conscious thought.

When she woke up, her head ached and her thoughts moved sluggishly, as if through a fog. Light was filtering in around the edges of her drapes, and she could hear the muffled hum of conversation.

She forced herself to sit up, hoping it would help. Pain stabbed at her temples, and the room seemed to reel around her for a dizzying moment, but then stabilized. In the dim light, she could see this was not the room at her sister's house where she lived between assignments.

Oh yes. The tower. The marquess's sons. They must have managed to drug her, despite her precautions! Well, then. From now on, she'd eat only what she had managed to bring with her in the hidden compartment of her bag, and drink only water.

She pulled back the curtain nearest the bed. From the light, it was early morning. What were the brothers doing out of bed?

Mel wasn't at all certain she could walk across the room, so she crawled, and opened the door just a crack. Not enough to see, but enough that the voices from below floated up to her ears.

"Ought you to check on Black?" That was Lord Kemble.

"I won't disturb him. I gave him enough of the drug to knock him out for the night, but he could be stirring about now." That was Lord Baldwin—the one with medical textbooks and herbals on his bookshelf. "If we leave him alone, he might sleep as late as we do."

"Then let's all go to bed," Kemble said. "A good night's work, brothers."

A night's work doing what?

Footsteps on the stairs to the second level had her closing the door quickly. Presumably, the Sheppard brothers were all heading to bed. Let them. Then Mel would be able to examine the tower's public spaces. Meanwhile, her head was spinning. She had better not lie down lest she went back to sleep. But surely it would not hurt to sit down again for a while?

Chapter Two

T HE NEXT TIME Mel woke up, it was full day, though she couldn't tell what time. Sound drifted through the door. Someone was playing music—at a guess, using a violin and a clavichord. Probably the two younger brothers. Lord Jerome had a violin in his room, and Lord Isaac had a stack of sheet music.

She rose, moving her neck to ease the ache caused by an awkward sleeping posture. There was no point in castigating herself for falling for the Sheppard brothers' tricks, or for falling asleep again. In her adult years, she had learned that self-blame achieved little. One could only learn from a misstep and move on, trying not to make the same error again.

She needed washing water, a change of clothes, and something to drink to remove the disgusting taste in her mouth. She straightened her rumpled clothing and went out onto the gallery that acted as a passage for the chambers on this upper level.

She had watched the marquess's London house for several days before approaching him. She had circled it twenty or more times, checking it from every possible angle. Knowing that the sons were confined to the tower most of the time, she had given it particular attention. It was octagonal and separated from the house. A closed-in bridge from a back corner of the house joined it to the tower on the fourth level.

The tower rose one floor higher than the bridge, and then terminated in a cupola as high again, with an eight-sided ring of windows forming the base of the cupola. An octagonal skirting of roof sloped from the base of the windows to the outer wall of the tower. There were neither doors nor windows at ground level, and yesterday she had seen no way to access the lower levels from the brothers' apartment.

Surely, though, there must be some way into those rooms? The tower had secrets, and she was determined to discover them.

Crossing the gallery to the balustrade, she looked up into the dome, and then down into the living room. From the living room floor to the top of the dome must have been at least thirty-six feet.

Lord Kemble was below, casually dressed, as he had been last night, in pantaloons, shirt and waistcoat. He had his face turned up and their eyes met. In appearance, he was a copy of his father, as the man must have been when he was in his prime. Was it apprehension that made her shiver?

Surely not. For one thing, he did not have the same aura of evil. For another, she had faced off against villains much more dangerous than an aristocratic heir who, at the very least, stood by while his father bullied his wife, and who did not even have the gumption to leave home. But if it was not fear, then why was she breathless? Why did she feel suddenly weak at the knees?

Mel rejected the obvious answer. An unwanted attraction to Kemble could be ignored. It was not relevant to the investigation. More to the point, neither the tower nor the brothers set her skin creeping and her nerves jangling. No aura of evil. No sense of immediate danger.

Eight wedges made up the outer ring of rooms at both levels of the tower occupied by the marquess's sons. On this level, seven of them were bed chambers and one contained the stairs to the lower level. She strolled downstairs, where there were four more bedchambers, a book room, and a double space, open to the living room, that had a table and a dozen chairs. The soup had been heated on the stove in one corner of that part of the room.

On the outskirts of the central chamber, the upstairs gallery formed a ceiling over more intimate spaces, and Lord Isaac and Lord Jerome were in the one that held the clavichord she had noticed yesterday, which Lord Isaac was playing while Lord Jerome played the violin. Seated as they were, Lord Jerome's lameness was not obvious. Was it some sort of family trait? Lord Francis, too, had a limp, though not as bad as his younger brother.

The other brothers were also scattered around the chamber, but Mel's gaze was drawn to Lord Kemble, who beckoned her to him. "There is bread, Mr. Black, if you would care to break your fast."

More than bread. The aroma of freshly brewed coffee was unmistakable. A little cheek was called for. "Do I smell coffee?" Mel said. "My information is that you use magic to supplement what the marquess's household provides. I deduce that coffee is not beyond the capabilities of your good fairy."

Lord Kemble's lips twitched and several of the brothers laughed outright. "I shall pour you a cup," offered Lord Baldwin.

"Preferably without whatever Lord Donald gave me in last night's soup," Mel suggested.

"You are our uninvited guest, Mr. Black." Lord Kemble's voice was as arctic as his expression. "Here to pry into any secrets we may or may not have. I advise you not to challenge us."

"Circumstances have put us in opposition, Lord Kemble," Mel commented. "My health and wellbeing are on the line. Perhaps my life. Probably my life. Unless you give up your secrets willingly, I must pry."

"How do you take your coffee?" asked Lord Baldwin. "Cream? Sugar?"

"Black, thank you," said Mel.

"I can arrange for you to leave," said Lord Kemble. Some warmth had returned to his voice and his expression. "Escape this place, Black, while you still can."

"And what?" Mel asked. "Hide? Change my name and my identity? Do you think the marquess will let me disappear without seeking me out to punish me for failing him?" Come to think of it, that was as good an explanation as any for why the brothers didn't leave.

"If you know what he is like, why are you working for him?" Lord Donald demanded. "You should never have taken the job. If you do his bidding, you are as bad as him."

If you know what he is like and what he has done, why have you not given evidence of his crimes to the authorities? You are complicit, at the very least. All of you, and especially the older ones. Mel kept the words behind her teeth. They skirted too close to her real motive in being here.

"Your coffee," said Lord Baldwin, handing her a cup around which the fragrant bitterness of the beverage perfumed the air.

"Thank you, my lord," Mel said, and took a sip. The taste fulfilled the promise of the smell. She sighed in satisfaction. That would finish the job of waking her up.

Except for the two musicians, the brothers had stopped what they were doing to watch the exchange between her and Lords Kemble and Donald. As Mel focused on her coffee and Lord Donald turned his attention back to the drawing before him, the others returned to their own activities.

Not Lord Kemble. He was frowning thoughtfully as he watched Mel. Once again, she shivered, as if his gaze was a gentle touch. What on earth was wrong with her? He was a suspect—and if not an accomplice to his father, at least a careless bystander.

At the clanging of the bell, he turned his attention to the antechamber door, and Mel's relief was oddly mixed with loss. She was not attracted to the brooding earl. Or if she was, it was just a physical reaction. And a ridiculous one, at that.

One of the brothers had run upstairs while she was distracted by her uncomfortable thoughts. The others were all alert and waiting. Even Lord Isaac and Lord Jerome had stopped playing.

"The butler and a crew of maids," reported the brother who'd gone upstairs.

"You all know what to do," said Lord Kemble. "Mr. Black, the maids are coming to clean and the fairy you mentioned is going to prepare the place for them. Please take your coffee to your bedchamber, close the door, and wait for my signal to return downstairs."

There was no question of refusing. Several of the brothers stood ready to enforce Lord Kemble's request, and the earl himself was probably capable of carrying her upstairs without assistance. "Certainly, my lord," she said.

She looked over the balustrade once she was upstairs. The brothers were collecting books and other items to load into two large baskets. The coffee pot had disappeared. Lord Kemble looked up at her. "Mr. Black," he said.

Mel tipped her head in acknowledgement of his unspoken command. "Bedchamber, right." Cooperating now was more likely to bring results than sneaking a peek to see where the hidden spaces were and how they were accessed, particularly since she was likely to be caught.

Sure enough, footsteps on the stairs indicated that the brothers with rooms upstairs were heading in her direction. She shut herself in her bedchamber. Perhaps searching this room, bare that it was, would give her some clues. If she could find the catch to a hidden door here, the likelihood was that others in the tower would have a similar mechanism.

She had searched one wall when a knock on the door proved to be a pair of maids with a pail of water, wash cloths, a duster and a broom. "We're to clean your room, sir," said one of them. "And Lord Kemble says he would like to see you downstairs, sir."

Lord Kemble wanted to tell her that the marquess had ordered her to be confined in the tower today. "The butler brought today's orders," he said. "Three of us are commanded to appear for inspection by callers. Everyone else is to stay confined today, and that includes you, Mr. Black."

Having said that, he went into his bedchamber. *Inspection by callers*? An odd way to put it. Another pair of maids came out of Lord Kemble's chamber and disappeared into the next one. A minute or two later, a third pair moved between chambers further around the room.

"They clean once a week," said Lord Francis, coming to sit in a chair near Mel. "We never know in advance the day or the time, so it might be ten days between cleans or four, first thing in the morning or late in the evening. But Allan says it could be worse. At least they do come and clean. We are permitted bath water once a week, too. I daresay other prisons are less comfortable and much smellier."

They were. Mel had visited a few prisons in her time, and this was a palace by comparison. "Loss of freedom bites hard, no matter how comfortable the cage," she commented.

"Freedom?" Lord Francis sighed. "For the sons of the Marquess of Teign, freedom is a distant dream."

"You are of age, are you not?" Mel asked. "What can he do to you?"

In the look Lord Francis gave her, incredulity mixed with a bitter amusement. "Anything he wishes. Did you not say it yourself?" He quoted her earlier comment. *"Do you think the marquess will let me disappear without seeking me out to punish me for failing him?"*

"I did say that," Mel acknowledged. "You are his son, though," she pointed out.

Lord Francis shrugged. "He has other sons. Indeed, if he had grandsons, we would all be superfluous to requirements. He prefers his heirs young and manageable."

"Frank. Enough." The warning came from Lord Kemble, who emerged from his bedroom immaculately dressed, from polished Hessians to spotless white cravat. His cream pantaloons hugged his form, as did the green coat he wore over an ornate waistcoat. The green stone in his cravat pin must have been an emerald, given its brilliance.

If he was appealing in undress, he was stunning in formal

daywear. Mel's mouth dried. This untoward lust toward a suspect would not do. She swallowed hard.

"Never was a prisoner so richly dressed," she commented.

That remark was met with a thin smile and the wry comment, "You have not yet seen Baldwin or Ernest."

"What does your father hope to achieve?" Mel asked. While the near imprisonment of the ten lords was a poorly-kept secret among the ton, no one with whom she had spoken knew the reason for it. They had defied him in some way, people assumed. But over what?

"Did your audacity not extend to asking him?" asked Lord Donald.

Mel regarded him for a moment. It was a fair question, and the hostile tone was forgivable, under the circumstances. "I did ask. He told me it was not something I needed to know."

"You have your answer then," said Lord Kemble.

No. She didn't. But Mel was beginning to think she needed it. The brothers' anger at their father was barely veiled, and if they were not her enemies, perhaps—despite her earlier assumptions—they could be her allies.

Lord Baldwin and Lord Ernest came down the stairs from their bedchambers, each as richly dressed as Lord Kemble. The maids must have finished their cleaning, for eight of them were gathered around another woman servant, this one better dressed and not wearing a mob cap. A housekeeper, perhaps.

"We are done, Lord Kemble," this woman said.

The earl nodded, and one of the brothers unlocked the door and rang the bell.

From where she was sitting, Mel could see the footmen opening the gates, and letting out the first four of the maids, then the housekeeper and the other four maids.

It was the reverse of the process by which she had been brought inside—the furthest gate opened and a footman left inside to open the nearest gate, which he locked again once those leaving had come through. Only then did the outer footman open the furthest gate and let the group out.

"Take care," said Lord Donald to those brothers who waited to leave.

"Lock the door behind us," said Lord Kemble. "Keep an eye on our Mr. Black." And he gave her a wintery smile.

Chapter Three

ALLAN AND HIS two brothers went downstairs together. They were early. The ladies being brought to inspect them would not be here yet. But the marquess would not bother to monitor their movements, since he held seven hostages to ensure they turned up in the parlor at the required time, and performed creditably while under his eye.

They would be searched before they were permitted back into the tower, but if they could beg a sandwich each from Cook, or slip outside to buy a pie from a street vendor, there'd be that much more for the other brothers to eat. Black, too. Last night, the bread allowance had not been increased to allow for the investigator's presence.

Young Mr. Black was an enigma. Much more mature and confident than his apparent age would suggest. With a charm and a cheek Allan could enjoy if the man was not the marquess's pawn. Or perhaps it was more appropriate to compare Black to a knight, with his conversational leaps and unexpected changes of direction.

The man fascinated Allan. Why, he could not understand. If Black had been a woman, he'd have a name for his reaction to the young man. As it was, he was both mystified and uncomfortable.

The cook had heard they'd been released and had a good feed

ready for them. Three quarters of an hour later, their hunger satisfied, they were back in the drawing room and in the marquess's presence. They had timed it well, for the old man had no time to berate them before the first group of visitors was announced.

They had met all three families before. The marquess had been promoting these matches for weeks. Allan had trouble remembering which skinny blonde fashion doll of the three proposed brides was which, but he recognized the mother of the one intended for Ernest—she was one of those who didn't bother with a mask for her nighttime revels. Allan knew her as a harpy with vicious lusts and a bad temper.

Was the daughter like her mother? It didn't matter. Even if the girl was a saint with the temperament of an angel, none of the brothers wanted to bring another bride into the family. Not after what happened to Allan's wife, or Cornelius's.

The second and third group arrived, the girls all spoilt princesses confident they were about to marry into one of the foremost families of the realm, the parents all false smiles and fake good cheer. All of them directed their attention at the marquess. Everyone knew that Lord Teign held all the power in the room, and that his sons didn't need to be courted.

Even so, each brother had an opportunity to speak to their prospective wife when the marquess ordered his sons, "Sit beside your young lady and be charming." Allan held back until Baldwin and Ernest had seated themselves. Presumably, the remaining young lady was the one intended for him.

"You should be aware," he told the woman, "that the marquess is the one pushing for this marriage. I am old enough to be your father, and have no interest in marrying a child, but he will beat my younger brothers until I agree. You may think he is old enough that you shall be soon be a marchioness, but I assure you, living in his household is hell on earth, and he is likely to live another twenty years. His father died in his nineties."

The foolish chit giggled. "Lord Kemble, your father told mine you would tell me fables to try to persuade me to give you up. Papa says all men are afraid of marriage, but I am certain you and I shall be very happy."

Unlikely in the extreme. The chit could not be more than six years older than Allan's daughter! Thank goodness his Lydia was being raised by someone who could teach her some sense. "I very much doubt it," Allan said. "If I am forced to marry you, do not hold me responsible for your misery after we wed."

They were interrupted by the girl's mother, who wanted to twitter on about what a handsome couple they were, and what lovely babies they would make together, and then the marquess gathered the three young ladies around him, two on one side and one on the other.

The parents looked on indulgently, assuring one another it was a pretty sight.

While the would-be daughters-in-law were serving the marquess's tea and establishing his preferences regarding the display of baked treats, Allan told his two brothers what he'd said.

"I told Lady Patrice that it made no difference to me whom I marry, since the marquess would be the one bedding her," Baldwin reported in an undertone. "Either she doesn't believe me, or she doesn't care."

Ernest whispered, "I told Lady Imogen that my sister-in-law Thomasina ran away because he had her whipped when she refused his attentions. Look at the silly goose making up to him. Does she think being whipped is a pleasant little tickle?"

Patrice and Imogen. Which meant Lady Felicia was the one who had giggled at him and was certain they would be happy.

Pathetic little fool. She would soon find out her mistake if Allan couldn't stop the weddings.

The parents were discussing wedding dates. In the new year, they all agreed. Preferably not until March or April, when Society returned to London for the Season. The mothers wanted to make a show. The fathers had not finished maneuvering for advantage in the marriage agreement negotiations. The brides, as one of them had the cheek to say, saw "no point in marrying if my friends are not here in London to be jealous."

"No need to wait," the marquess said. "We can acquire a license for each of them, and hold the weddings immediately after Christmas."

Allan's gut lurched, but as his mind raced to come up with a stalling tactic that wouldn't see one of his brothers beaten or otherwise tormented, the families broke out into a chorus of denials and complaints. It was too soon. The girls would need new gowns. They must invite family members and friends to see the triumph of an alliance between them and the marquess's family. The marquess must accept that a mere week was impossible.

If the families thought that the marquess would accept anyone's opinion other than his own, they were very much mistaken.

No one asked Allan's view, nor Baldwin's nor Ernest's. They were ciphers in this entire transaction. Not that the transaction would ever be completed. If need be, the brothers would all escape tonight.

It would be awkward. For one thing, they had not yet saved enough money for all ten of them to travel beyond the marquess's reach. For another, Jerome was still under his lordship's guardianship, so the marquess would have the law on his side in any pursuit—at least until May, when Jerome reached his majority.

No matter. They were all agreed that no more innocents would be brought within the marquess's reach, so the marriages could not go ahead. They would have to manage. Somehow. The younger brothers could take ship, and the older ones could stay and distract his lordship's attention.

But wait. One of the mothers had brought up a name that gave pause even to the Marquess of Teign. "My daughter Patrice cannot possibly be wed without the presence of her godmother, the Duchess of Winshire," said the woman. "She is in Shropshire for the Yuletide season."

"Yes, she is godmother to my Felicia, too," said another. "We must write to her and find out when she will be back in London."

Lord Teign ceased his adamant objections. "Winshire? Hmmm. I see. Very well. Write to Her Grace. We shall hold all three weddings on the first day that is suitable for her."

A reprieve. Perhaps not a long one, but it would help.

IT HAD BEEN an informative afternoon. Mel, after an intensive search, had discovered a trapdoor in her floor that opened into a hiding space. It was partially under the bed, completely covered by the floor rug, and almost invisible to the eye.

The cracks running straight across several floor boards were her first clue, but she could see no catch, no way of opening the hatch, if it was a hatch. Then she found a knot in the wood that, when poked with her dagger, rose up out of the floor.

It proved to be the key to the mechanism. She pulled it, and nothing happened. But when she twisted it, the hatch popped up, and after that it was easy to open the rest of the way. She was disappointed to find it empty, but at least she had confirmed that such hiding places existed.

After that, she wandered around the tower, striking up conversations with the brothers. She helped Lord Isaac to dry the dishes and put them away. She offered a hand to Lord Cornelius, who was mending a chair and needed someone to hold a plank while his own two hands were busy trimming it to shape. She played a game of chess with Lord Frank. She assisted Lord Gerard in folding some dry washing.

Some of the brothers were guarded in their replies to her conversational sallies. Others seemed pleased to have someone new to talk to. Lord Jerome, the youngest of the brothers, was one of the latter. She found him in front of the clavichord, and sat to listen to him play. He had a gift for music. Skill, too, which was all the more surprising, for he'd had little formal training. From what he said, he had been imprisoned in this tower, and not permitted to leave, since he was ten.

"My brothers have been my friends, my tutors, and my family," he told Mel. "One day, though, I should like to walk in the sunlight. I should like to see places that I knew as a child, those my brothers have described to me, and even those where none of us have been."

He had a distant smile on his face. "Allan went to Edinburgh once, and when Frank ran away and joined the army, he made it to Madrid before the marquess ordered his legs broken and had him shipped home."

Lord Jerome narrated that snippet of his brother's story in such a matter-of-fact and offhand manner that the sense of it took a moment to penetrate. Was that why Lord Francis limped? The marquess had ordered it done? And if so, did Lord Jerome's infirmity come from the same source? The marquess was an even worse monster than Mel had thought.

The young lord had not noticed her reaction, as he was still thinking about travel. "I should like to see Madrid. Paris, too, and Rome. All the great cities of Europe. Have you traveled, Mr. Black?"

"Through most of England," Mel admitted. "Also, Scotland and Wales. A couple of times to Ireland. Only once to France, a few years ago, after Waterloo."

Perhaps it was only fair to share something of herself. "I dreamed of travel, too, when I was young. Then, for a few years, it seemed it would always be impossible." She had married, and her husband had kept her in the country, waiting on his whims. Not as much of a prisoner as Lord Jerome, but free only to visit the village shops, the neighbors and the local church. "Then I began my current profession and all my traveling has been in the past eight years."

"You are able-bodied, though," said Lord Jerome, wistfully. "I suppose you ride? I was just learning to ride when I was locked up."

"I do not ride particularly well," Mel said. Her father had been too poor for the sisters to have riding horses, though they had both straddled the old cart horse to be carried around the field while the beast grazed. "But one can travel by carriage or boat. A lame leg will not prevent you from traveling, my lord. Was it a childhood injury?"

Lord Jerome's huff of laughter had no humor in it. "You could say that. I told you Frank had his legs broken, at my father's command, to punish him for joining the army and to ensure he did not do so again?"

"You ran away?" Mel whispered her question, as if the truth of the poor man's injury was too horrible to contemplate.

"Cornelius did, with his wife." Mel froze. This touched on her reason for being here. She had not expected to learn so easily what happened to her cousin. Lord Jerome was gently touching the keys of the clavichord and did not see how his words had affected her.

"The marquess's men brought Cornelius back," he continued, "but my brother would not say where Thomasina was. Later, I learned that he could not. For her own safety, he had told her to find somewhere to hide where even he could not find her."

Then the suicide note and the evidence on the riverbank were fake, just as Mel had hoped and believed.

Lord Jerome shrugged. "The marquess had me beaten and tortured in front of Cornelius to make him talk. And then, as he did with Frank, he refused to let a doctor attend me. My brothers did their best to stitch and bind my wounds, and set my bones. Baldwin apprenticed with a doctor for a while, and is quite skilled. Even so, one leg healed crookedly."

Mel said what she was thinking. "He is a fiend."

"That is why they stay," Lord Jerome told her. "My brothers. They remain for me, to keep my father from killing me. He is my guardian, you see. He has a right to beat me."

"Jerome. Is Mr. Black bothering you?" It was Lord Kemble, glaring at Mel as if he wanted to incinerate her on the spot. Had he had a fall? His face was bruised.

The younger man was not bothered by his brother's anger. "No need to fret, Allan. I'm not giving away secrets. I daresay every servant in the marquess's employ knows how the old fiend treats his sons."

"Mr. Black is not our friend, you young cub." Lord Kemble's irritated tone was laced with affection for his brother. Which didn't mean he could be trusted, but if Lord Jerome's story was true—and it confirmed what she had already heard from other sources—the brothers were the marquess's victims, not his followers.

"Nor am I your enemy," said Mel. It was a risk to trust the man, but how much more could they achieve if they worked together? "In fact, Lord Kemble, we might be on the same side."

Lord Kemble's lip curled. "I doubt that very much. You are the marquess's dog, here to serve my father's purposes. My brother might have forgotten that. I have not."

He might change his mind if I tell him my real purpose here, but on the other hand, he might tell his father. Even disclosing her relationship with Thomasina could backfire, if any one of the brothers decided to use the information to gain an advantage with the marquess. She wasn't ready to be thrown out—perhaps even handed over, as the marquess had threatened, to a press gang.

"I am nobody's dog, and my purposes are my own," she told Lord Kemble.

He didn't believe her. To be fair, neither did she believe him, but she was regarding the brothers with more sympathy than when she had arrived. Especially when she noticed that Lord Baldwin's cheek was marred by a welt from a whip or thin stick, and that Lord Ernest was limping.

"I take it his lordship was not pleased with your performance," Lord Cornelius said to his twin in an undertone. Fortunately, Mel's hearing was excellent. She pretended to be absorbed in looking up at the ceiling, which was painted with a scene of dancing.

"The families of the brides checkmated his wedding plans by wanting to invite the Duchess of Winshire whom he apparently does not wish to offend," Baldwin explained. "He took it out on us once they were gone. Come on, Allan, Ernest. I have some salve in my room."

For the remainder of the day, none of the brothers would talk to her about anything beyond the merest commonplaces. Clearly, Lord Kemble had put out an order.

Mel wasn't in the job to make friends, and was used to working in an indifferent or even hostile atmosphere. The fact she was beginning to like the brothers was entirely beside the point. She kept moving around the public areas, studying the walls and what she could see of the floors.

The gallery must have a peephole in the floor that allowed the brothers to see who was in the anteroom, but Mel couldn't find it with a visual inspection, and anything more detailed would have to wait until she could be certain of privacy.

Perhaps she could check during dinner—another pot of soup was already cooking on the back of the stove that warmed the dining area. Mel took her notebook with her to sit in the dining room, hoping to catch someone in the act of putting a sedative in her bowl or her cup.

"What are you writing?" asked Lord Francis.

"Nothing important," Mel said, and turned the page so he could see. There was no harm in showing him. She wrote her case notes as if they were notes for a children's story about a talking cat.

He looked puzzled as he read, and well he might. "'One mouse gave the squirrel a clue to what happened to her relative. If his story turns out to be true, squirrel cousin might still be alive. The search of the mouse hole continues. The mice that left the hole were scratched by the cat, but they were not badly injured and returned home.'"

While he flicked over a couple of pages, Mel looked around her until a discrepancy caught her attention. The wall. It met the outer wall at right angles, but didn't all the other rooms have acute angles in their outer corners?

The tower was an octagon, with the dividing walls for each outer room radiating outward. A right angle was impossible unless the room on either side also had a right angle—the two walls, now that she came to look at the other side of the room. Or, unless each wall concealed a hidden space.

"It is you," said Lord Francis. "You are the squirrel. My brothers and I are the mice. Who is the squirrel cousin?"

She had underestimated the man. "It is just a children's story," Mel insisted.

Lord Francis gave her a disbelieving look, but at that moment, two of the other brothers came into the dining space— Lord Donald to stir the stew, and Lord Baldwin to put bowls, mugs, and plates out on the bench beside the stove.

She tried to keep an eye on Lord Baldwin, but Lord Francis was continuing to try to decipher her notes, and Lord Donald had come over to see what Lord Francis was doing, getting in her way so she could not see exactly what Lord Baldwin was up to without making it obvious that she suspected him of doctoring either one of the mugs or one of the bowls.

Sure enough, when the three of them left her to return to their own activities, one bowl was placed apart from the others, and so was one mug. Mel bowed her head back over her notes and waited for her opportunity to swap them with the ones she had slipped into her bag when she was putting away the dishes.

Her chance came when the bell rang to announce the arrival of the evening basket of bread and jug of water. While the brothers were distracted, she walked around the table and out of the dining area, making the exchange on her way. Sure enough, both bowl and cup had some thick liquid at the bottom. Mel put them into the slop bucket and threw a cloth over them.

After that, it was just a matter of stumbling up the stairs after dinner, weaving slightly on her way to her bedchamber. Before long, she heard footsteps passing her door. The brothers who had their chambers up here, she assumed.

She changed while she waited. All in black, from head to foot, so she would be hidden against the dark city streets. If her guess about the dining space was right, they'd head downstairs again when they were ready. They did, about half an hour later. She waited until she was certain all six were downstairs, then slipped out her door and knelt to peek over the balustrade.

All ten of them were there below, and sure enough, Lord Kemble was standing by the sideboard, his hands on the carving down one side. While Mel watched, he stepped back, and pulled the entire sideboard away from the wall.

He stepped into the space it had covered, and then the other brothers followed, one by one. When all of them had disappeared, the sideboard rolled back into place, presumably pulled by the last of the brothers.

Mel hurried downstairs and soon found the catch. The sideboard needed no more than a gentle tug to swing out. She opened the low door behind it to disclose what looked like an empty cupboard, but since the ten brothers were not within—and indeed, could not have fitted—there must be a trapdoor. She soon discovered how to open it, and below was a flight of steps.

She was not more than a minute or two behind them, but she could not see any sign of light below. Still, it was more important to take a moment to find out the internal latch. She had no idea what the circumstances of her return might be, and she did not want to be caught on the wrong side of the door because she had not taken the time now to make sure she could get back in.

Fortunately, it was a simple lever on the side wall. Moments later, she hurried down the steps in the dark as fast as she could without disaster, holding tight to the rail and running her hand down the rock wall beside her.

There! A glimmer of flame down below. They were not far ahead. She continued downward, being even more cautious lest a noise had them turning back.

She need not have worried. They were strolling along the

tunnel that led from the foot of the stairs, deep in conversation. It was wide enough that they could walk three and four abreast, and Mel was able to creep close enough to hear while staying in the darkness beyond the reach of the lamps they must have picked up on their way. The floor of the tunnel sloped, so that they were moving downhill, and a soft breeze moved across Mel's cheek, hinting at an opening to the outdoors somewhere ahead.

"So, we shall have to move up our escape," Baldwin was saying.

"That means you will have to go into hiding, Jerome," said Kemble. "Just for five months, until your birthday."

"I think the plan to scatter is best." That was Frank. "If we run in ten different directions, we shall stretch his resources, and reduce the chance of him finding Jerome. If he can find any of the rest of us, he will try to force us to say where the others are."

"Jerome is the only one he has legal power over," argued Ernest.

Cornelius snorted. "When has the law meant anything to the marquess?"

Mel kicked something. A stone, perhaps. It shot away from her foot and collided with the nearest wall. She froze.

"Shush," commanded Jerome. "I thought I heard something behind us."

The brothers all paused. Mel closed her eyelids so that the light could not catch the whites of her eyes. Through the slits, she could see the pale ovals of faces looking in her direction.

After a moment, Lord Kemble said, "I don't hear anything. Come on. The boats should be waiting for us by now."

They walked off, with Mel following. A corner in the tunnel brought them within sight of a large arch closed off by bars. Kemble produced something that proved to be a set of keys, for he opened the gate in the bars, and the Sheppard brothers crowded through.

With them out of the way, Mel could see they were on the bank of the Thames, that watermen waited with their boats, and that the brothers were already greeting them and clambering aboard. Kemble shut the gate but didn't bother to lock it again, and Mel was able to escape the tunnel without attracting anyone's attention.

Now what? If she joined one of the boats, she'd be seen. But she was in luck. There were four boats, but the brothers filled the first three, and as each boat was loaded, its waterman pushed off into the current.

Mel stopped the last waterman just before he started after them. "Wait! Do you see those gentlemen?" she said. "Follow them." And moments later they were floating down the Thames.

Chapter Four

ALLAN LED HIS brothers up the river steps and along the street leading away from the dock. He turned into a mews lane and passed several buildings before opening a gate, nodding to its guard. He crossed a small walled garden and turned through a second gate into a kitchen courtyard, from which he entered a large building through the back door.

They had donned their masks before leaving the tunnel. Only the proprietor of The Golden Adonis knew their identity—not the boatmen, not the other employees of the club, and certainly not the clients.

"Good evening," he said to the kitchen servants, as he passed down the service corridor. "Good evening," again to the lady who controlled the staff on behalf of the proprietor. He knew her as Thalia, for all the servants and employees wore nicknames— the names of Greek gods—to protect their identities. Thalia was the manager, or so the owner called her, though her role combined housekeeper, house steward, secretary and—he often thought—ringmaster.

"Apollo," she replied. "Madam wishes to see you and Faunus. She said to send you up when you arrived."

"Problems?" Allan asked.

"Not as far as I know," said Thalia. "Nothing out of the ordinary."

The brothers went in different directions, some to various card rooms, Isaac and Jerome to the music gallery, the remainder to the ballroom. Allan and Frank mounted the stairs to Hera's office.

Hera was the widow who owned The Golden Adonis, a club that provided wealthy women with all the services that gentlemen normally found at their various clubs and other, less reputable, venues.

Seated behind her desk, she conveyed an impression of power that was justly deserved. Here under this roof, she was the final authority, and even beyond these walls she wielded considerable influence. Her origins were humble—or so Allan had gathered in the eighteen months of their acquaintance. Murky, even. Nobody quite knew where she had come from or how she had achieved wealth and power.

To look at, she was nothing special. Finely, even richly dressed. A little on the plump side but all the more formidable for it. In her middle years, though nudging the upper boundaries of that age span, her hair touched lightly with grey. Yet she dominated any room she was in, and no one meeting her could doubt she was a woman of substance.

"Good evening, Madam," Allan said, and Frank repeated the greeting.

Hera looked up from the papers she was studying. "Ah! Faunus. And you, too, Apollo. Good. Faunus, I have a favor to ask. One of our guests has requested that you be her only escort from now on. Apollo, I know you keep a close eye on your relatives, so I asked you to join our meeting."

Frank tended to become speechless when alarmed, so Allan spoke for him. "Faunus does not provide intimate services," he said.

Their employer shook both one hand and her head. "That is not what Lady Andromeda requires. Faunus has already been meeting with the lady, and all she wants is someone to talk to."

"Lady Andromeda," Frank repeated, with a distant smile. "I am happy to talk with Lady Andromeda."

That was a surprising response. Frank found it hard to converse with people he didn't know, and even most of the people he did. Indeed, he was only comfortable with his brothers, so Allan had arranged for him to work at one remove from the social activities that were the lifeblood of the club. He exchanged money for gambling tokens, paid out money when the lady guests redeemed their tokens, and kept careful records.

"I should like to help Lady Andromeda, Allan—Apollo, I mean," Frank said.

"I did not know you had been meeting the clients," Allan grumbled.

"Lady Andromeda met Faunus on her first night here," said Madam Hera. "She says he was kind to her and helpful. That was the evening he helped in the sitting rooms, because some of the other hosts were absent with that ague that was doing the rounds. Ever since, she has sought Faunus out whenever she visits."

Allan was still uncertain. "What does she need, Madam Hera?"

"Confidence, in a word. Lady Andromeda is uncomfortable with most people, but especially with men. She likes you, Faunus, and that is the first step. Rest assured, however, that she is not a customer for our more intimate services. Lady Andromeda is an unmarried miss, and an innocent."

Feeling easier in his mind, Allan asked, "When is she expected, Madam? I shall arrange for one of my other relatives to manage the cash box."

As they finished their meeting with Hera, the sound of a bell indicated that the doors to the club would open in fifteen minutes. Frank hurried to his station in the little room that held the cash box, and Allan began his usual rounds of the building. He was in charge of ensuring that all the men who worked there were diligent, conscientious, and safe.

Tonight, he was particularly aware of Frank, who was closeted in one of the private rooms with the guest who had asked for him. No intimate services, Hera had said. But what could the lady wish to discuss that required such privacy?

There was not much he could do to help. Unless the building was burning down or a worker called for help, no one was permitted to enter the private rooms while they were occupied.

Still, he was relieved when the two of them emerged after nearly an hour alone. *Good lord. Frank is smiling.* Not only that, but he bent over the lady's hand when she held it out to him in farewell. What had got into their shy, awkward Frank?

Then the lady turned to walk away, almost bumped into Allan, blushed bright scarlet, and stammered as she made her apology. Frank hurried to her aid. "Do not be alarmed, Lady Andromeda. It is only my brother. Allan—Apollo, I mean—why were you just standing there? Come along, dear lady. I shall see you to the door."

Good heavens. Allan stared after the pair. Could it be that Frank was smitten? If so, from the lady's behavior, the feeling was mutual. What a pity that the brothers were about to flee. If anyone deserved a chance at happiness, it was Frank.

Allan could do nothing about that tonight, and it was time he reminded Isaac and Jerome, who were lost in their music making, to take it in turns to have a break and some supper. It was two o'clock in the morning but the club was just approaching its busiest time. They had hours of work still ahead of them.

MEL FOLLOWED THE brothers to the guarded back gate of a building. What were they there for? She had tried to engage the guard in conversation, but he just grumbled, "Clear out, or I'll biff you one."

Foiled, she retraced her steps along the mews lane and found her way to the front of the building. There, she soon found people who knew that the building was some sort of gathering place for women. "Ladies," said the crossing sweeper. "Masked, most of them," complained an indolent fellow who was propped against a wall, keeping company with a bottle. "Indecent, I call it. Hiding who they are and getting up to who knows what."

"All night long, they come and go," an eager flower seller added. "I sell out every night."

Up and down the street, the stories were the same. A mysterious club patronized by masked ladies. And, Mel guessed, by masked men like the Sheppard brothers who went in through the servants' entrance.

Two men came out of the front door, dressed in a livery of red and gold. They took station on each side of the door. Mel approached, but they ignored her except to wave her away with a frown when she came too close.

Could this be The Golden Adonis? Women spoke in whispers about a ladies' club, but its whereabouts was a closely guarded secret. Only members knew, and their identity was concealed even more carefully.

It was, so rumor said, a place where ladies could do whatever they pleased without social consequences. Take tea and converse. Listen to music. Dance with handsome young men. Read in a well-appointed library. Play table games such as cards, dice, chess, and backgammon. Conduct discreet liaisons. Yes, and indiscreet liaisons in the case of some of the racier widows who were rich enough and independent enough not to care about social censure.

As if to confirm Mel's conclusions, a carriage pulled up at the foot of the steps, and one such widow descended and marched up to the front door, holding out something for the doormen to see. One of them opened the door for her.

Some sort of token. Gold in color, but Mel was not able to see the shape.

After that, carriages continued to arrive, and ladies with tokens continued to be admitted. Without a token, Mel could do no more tonight. She was about to give up and go back to the tower prison of the young lords, when something about a new arrival caught her eye.

The cloak was a short one, displaying the wearer's skirts from the knee. Furthermore, the lady held the skirts up out of the mud, so her embroidered stockings and her footwear were also on display.

Mel knew those skirts and the stockings. She had, during one long month last year, worked as a seamstress in one of Mayfair's lesser houses, first embroidering the deep band of flowers around the hem of those skirts, and then creating matching flowers down the outer side of each stocking.

As for the platformed shoes that strapped on over the lady's slippers and kept her above the grime of the street, Mel had suggested them when the lady had come home with mud to her ankles and her slippers ruined after a thunderstorm turned the streets into a quagmire and a broken-down coach on the doorstep of a ball had forced all the guests to walk to their carriages.

During that month, Winifred had recognized Mel as an old acquaintance—they had once been neighbors. When she discovered that Mel was there to investigate her father for fraud, she had helped Mel to discover the true villain, her uncle, who had also defrauded his brother. In that short time, Mel had come to look on Winifred as a younger sister, and their relationship had only strengthened in the eighteen months since.

What on earth was Winifred Querrendale doing at the Golden Adonis? She was unmarried and a wallflower—and as innocent as a newborn lamb, if Mel was any judge. Even as Mel pondered the question, Winifred disappeared through the door into the club.

Winifred could help Mel get into the club, or at least tell her more about what went on in there. Would she be willing? There was only one way to find out. As a first step, she followed the lady's carriage, which was moving away.

It didn't go far, turning at the next corner and then again, through the arch of an inn. The coachman climbed down, left the horses to doze in the corner of the stable yard under the supervision of a sleepy stable boy, and went into the tavern next door.

Mel bought him three pints of ale and a half pint of gin before he became loquacious, and confirmed the identity of his passenger, who was the daughter of his employer, the classical scholar Dr. Querrendale. He then lowered his head onto his hands and went to sleep, so that when the errand boy from the club ran in to say Miss wanted her carriage, he was in no fit state to drive.

With the help of a couple of the other patrons in the tavern, Mel arranged to tuck him into the luggage net at the rear of the carriage. Thank goodness she had some experience driving a carriage, and that the horses were placid and well trained.

Trust Winifred to look up at the driver's perch and comment. "You are not my driver. Where is Tom Margate?"

"In the luggage net, Miss. Blind drunk," Mel explained, hoping that would be enough to convince the lady.

However, Winifred was not such a fool. "I am not getting into a carriage controlled by someone I do not know," she insisted, and turned back toward the club.

"Wait a minute, Miss," Mel said. "I can explain." She had already set the brake. Now she tied off the reins and clambered down.

Winifred put her hand into her reticule. "I have a pistol inside here," she warned.

"Good for you," said Mel, softly. "I remember when I first advised you on which one to purchase. And taught you how to load and fire it."

Winifred leaned forward to peer into her face. "Mel—" she began.

"Yes, it is I," Mel agreed. She glanced up at the doormen, who were craning to see what was going on. "Allow me to drive you home, Winifred, and I shall explain everything."

She would surely have enough time to take Winifred back to the Querrendale house in Mayfair, explain she was on an investigation and needed a guest invitation to the Golden Adonis, and get back to the riverbank to find the entrance to the tower and make her way back to her bed before the marquess's sons returned home.

Once the coachman had been delivered to the stables, along with the carriage and horses, Winifred led Mel into her house through a side door that led to Winifred's private parlor.

Mel gave a very brief explanation of her present disguise. "I am currently investigating a group of men, and being a man is safer in those circumstances. But now I need to enter the Golden Adonis. What can you tell me about the club? And can you get me a guest invitation?"

Winifred's response was enthusiastic. "Another investigation! Of course, I can try to get you a guest token. But Melody, surely I can do more than that? What are you trying to find out?"

"I cannot tell you what the investigation is about, Winifred," Mel said, "for I do not wish to put you in danger." If the marquess came after Mel, anyone associated with her might be caught up in the ensuing carnage.

Raised eyebrows hinted what Winifred thought of that. "I think you are making a mistake, for if you are looking for clues at the Golden Adonis, two sets of ears are better than one. But I shall not pester you over it, Melody."

Oh bother. Winifred was right. Mel bit her upper lip as she thought it over. "Get me in, dear friend, and then we shall see. If I am sure it will not put you in danger, I'll be glad to have your help. But tell me, how do you come to be a member? From what I have heard about it, it is not the place for a gently-born maiden who seeks marriage!"

"No, but just think, Melody. Father barely knows any older men, let alone young ones. Aunt Agnes is my sponsor, but she is hardly much better. She will not take me out more than twice a week, and when she does, she finds a corner in which to bury her head in a book. They may be happy to spend the rest of their lives alone in a library, but I should like to marry and have children. However, I shall wither and die an old maid if I do not learn to talk to men. And even before that, to attract them enough that they ask for an introduction!"

"I did not realize it was so bad, Winifred, dear. Look, when this job is over, I shall introduce you to some ladies who should be able to present young men to you. You certainly will not meet a husband at The Golden Adonis."

"No." Winifred shook her head, but her tone was regretful. "I know the men there are not marriage material and not of my class, though Faunus... Never mind. The point is, I wanted to learn to talk to men, and The Golden Adonis has men for hire. Just talk, Melody, masked and under an assumed name. I am not a fool."

"I beg your pardon. I did not mean to imply you were foolish. It is just that I worried for you when I recognized you there."

"You do not need to worry, my dear. I am being careful, and Hera does not permit any harm to come to her guests. Nor any of her employees, either. She is most strict about it. The man I was with tonight does not do... you know, *that*. A lot of them don't. Women go to the club for all sorts of reasons. Some to talk, like me. Some to dance. Some to meet other women. And some for what Hera calls 'intimate services,' which I do not require. Different men offer different services. The man I met is very gentlemanly."

She dropped her lashes and colored. "We spent most of our hour tonight talking about the stars. He, too, is interested in astronomy. He says that the secret of talking to a man is to ask him what interests him and then discuss that with him. He says that a man who wants to talk on and on about something that does not interest me will make a poor husband for life."

That sentiment set Mel chuckling. How right this mysterious gentleman was! Her own deceased husband could talk for hours and hours about the mysteries of horse racing and the joys of hunting, and little else. The subject ceased to entertain Mel after the first day. "He makes good sense," she said.

"He has not told me much about himself," Winifred admitted. "Only that he and his brothers work at the Golden Adonis to save money, because of a man who is their youngest brother's guardian, and who holds the brother hostage for their good behavior. As soon as the brother is of age, they mean to leave London with him, and meanwhile, they are earning as much as they can. I am sure he is a gentleman, though, even if he is poor."

So that was it. Suddenly, the behavior of the Sheppard brothers made sense. "Tell me about this Faunus," Mel said. "Perhaps, when he is free, he will want to marry you."

"He will not," Winifred answered. "He says he would like to, but he and his brothers must leave England. He says he is poor and lame, and cannot give me the life I deserve. I would not care about that, but I cannot go so far away from Papa, Melody. He would not leave his books, and he needs me."

Lame. Lord Francis or Lord Jerome, then. Lord Francis, almost certainly. He was the one with the telescope and the star charts. Apparently, in bringing the marquess to justice, she would also be helping the cause of true love!

"Perhaps something shall work out," she said to Winifred. "In the meantime, I shall continue to worry, if your only escort is a coachman that drinks too much. Admittedly, I bought him the drinks, but he needed no coaxing to consume them."

"He keeps his mouth shut, though, Melody. The more servants I let into my secret, the less likely it is I can keep it. Normally, I have my friend Parthena with me, and she brings a footman she trusts. She could not make it tonight. And I cannot go tomorrow night, for it is Christmas Eve and my father and aunt are taking me to a fancy dinner. I shall send a request to Hera, the proprietress, for a guest invitation, and you can come with me and Parthena on the evening of Boxing Day."

Excellent. Perhaps tomorrow, if the brothers went out into the night again, she could visit her own family! "I shall meet you outside the Golden Adonis at ten o'clock on the night of the twenty-sixth," Mel said. "If you have the guest token for me, I'll be dressed to come inside with you. Will you be using the same carriage and the same mask?"

"I shall," Winifred confirmed.

"I must go now. I need to return to the place where I'm staying before I am missed." Melody still had to get back to the riverbank, and she estimated it would take her at least three quarters of an hour, unless she could find a jarvey looking for a fare.

"I shall see you two nights from now," Winifred said, opening the door to the outside. "Merry Christmas, Melody."

"Merry Christmas, Winifred." Melody touched her friend's arm in farewell and slipped out into the night.

Chapter Five

THE NEXT DAY was Christmas Eve. Mel slept late, but not as late as most of the brothers. She spent some time writing in her notebook, but she also played a game of chess with Lord Francis, listened to Donald reading aloud to an audience of her, Gerard, Hudson, and Zero the cat—who slept throughout. She also praised Cornelius's painting, Ernest's poem, and Jerome's and Isaac's performance of a nocturne that turned out to be by Jerome. In other words, she did her best to seem a non-threatening but trustworthy companion.

She helped the brothers decorate the tower with greenery and ribbons that appeared as if by magic, and they sang some Christmas carols while they worked.

As the afternoon progressed, she moved from one brother or group of brothers to another—stopping to chat—doing her best to be always friendly, charming, companionable.

By now, they had become accustomed to her seemingly innocent questions and her intent interest. No doubt the brothers were suspicious—she was, after all, being paid by the marquess to ferret out their secrets. But nonetheless, most of them, especially the younger ones, confided in Mel.

Nothing that touched on the tower's secret hideaways and exits, or their work at the club. Nothing to trigger the intervention of the watchful Lord Kemble. But still, it was telling that they trusted her enough to tell her about their hopes, their dreams, and more.

For example, Lord Francis enthused about the beauty and intelligence of Lady Andromeda, though he did not say where he had met her. "I never expected to meet a lady who loved the stars as much as I do," he said. "If only I could go to balls and other Society events, and court her as a gentleman should."

Winifred's interest is returned. But what prevented Lord Francis from courting his lady?

"Does the marquess not let you out for Society events?" Mel asked.

"Not I," sighed Lord Francis. "Not Jerome either. Not since he lamed us."

Lord Kemble interrupted. "He finds physical deformity embarrassing. Even when he caused it himself."

"I suppose he thinks his sons are a reflection of himself," Mel suggested. "Nothing but perfection will do. And yet he does not see the goodness within you, Lord Francis, nor the corruption and infirmity of his own soul."

"I do not think the marquess believes in the existence of the soul," Lord Kemble declared.

At dinner time, she pulled the same trick of substituting the bowl and mug. She dressed in a simple round gown—it and a soft cloth bonnet were the only items of women's clothing she had with her—and lay down on the bed, the sheets pulled up over her in case one of the brothers came to check.

They didn't, but she heard some of them talking as they passed her room and went down the stairs. Cautiously, she crept out to watch. Then, after the brothers left the tower, she picked up her warm cloak and made her own way down the tunnel, diverting to explore the two side tunnels she'd noticed the previous night.

The barred gate at the end of the first led to a courtyard beyond which was a quiet residential square lined with tidy townhouses. She was viewing the courtyard from a different angle, but she was reasonably certain that it was part of the grounds of the marquess's mansion. All her skills at lock picking did not open the gate, and she did not want to be caught on the marquess's ground, in any case.

The second tunnel let out into a seedy-looking alley with warehouses and tenement buildings as far as she could see through the sleet-striped dark, and tiny dingy shops at street level. Another barred gate was as impenetrable as the first. She was not getting through it without the key.

She had a long night ahead of her, and could waste no more time on lost causes. With the brothers no doubt somewhere out on the Thames, she did not have to be as cautious as when they were ahead of her in the tunnel. She and her lamp soon made it to the riverbank, where she found the waiting boatman. She apologized for not needing him this time, and paid him for his lost time, and another sum to wait for her on the other side at four in the morning.

"Wait for half an hour," she instructed him. If she did not make it back to Southwark, she did not want him waiting all night.

With rising excitement, she hurried up the street from the riverbank to where the hackney that had taken her back to the tower last night waited as previously arranged. She had offered him the princely sum of ten shillings to be at her disposal from ten o'clock, with half paid up front, risking that he would not keep his promise, but hopeful that he'd turn out to get the other five shillings.

Or perhaps he was just an honest man. Either way, they were on their way to Marylebone, where Mel's sister had her home, and where the keeper of Mel's heart lived.

ON CHRISTMAS EVE, the club was packed, and all the employees were near running to keep up with demand. Allan had to press Frank into service again, this time to manage one of the gaming tables.

"Jerome can spell you when Lady Andromeda wants you," Allan told him.

Frank shook his head. "She will not be here tonight. She has a family thing. It's fine, Allan. I can manage the table."

Baldwin, Cornelius, and Donald were each engaged in a private session with a regular client for the night. Baldwin and Donald were single, but Allan was uncomfortable about Cornelius, who was a married man, even if he did not know where his wife was. When he raised the topic with Cornelius, though, he was firmly told to mind his own business. Which was fair enough. All three brothers were adults, and could make their own decisions.

Ernest and Gerard were also worrying Allan. They had both been available for private rooms when they first began working at the Golden Adonis, but recently they had asked to change duties.

Both had their eye on women employees of the club. Ernest and the club's official hostess, Thalia, were smelling of April and May. Perhaps it would pass. If it did not, and if she was still available and interested when they were finally free, it might be possible. She was clearly a gentlewoman by birth, and after all, Ernest was unlikely to ever be marquess.

Gerard, though, was enamored of a girl known at the Golden Adonis as Aedas. She worked in the ladies' retiring room, mending hems, pinning up curls, and otherwise repairing appearances. A lady's maid, and one whose employment history had such a disreputable entry as the club, was hardly a fit match for a marquess's son, even one eight steps from the title and without a penny to his name.

This was all on Allan's mind as he took his turn on the dance floor, resolved a dispute in the gaming room, packed a very drunk baroness off home in her carriage, helped the substitute cashier fix a discrepancy in the cash box, sent for another crate of wine and ten dozen more oysters, and otherwise kept things running as smoothly as was possible on such a busy night.

And continuously, under the surface concerns and the deeper stream of worries about his brothers was a vein of awareness that all was not as it seemed with their intruder. Something about Mr. Black was tapping against his consciousness, trying to get in.

But even the busiest of nights must end, and at last the brothers headed home, crossing the river in sleet and a bitter wind that cut through their warm coats as easily as a knife through butter.

It was a relief to reach the tunnel, and then the tower, where they could head for bed with a warming glass of brandy or port in one hand, and a few coals in a bed warmer in the other. Allan, in his own chamber, stripped off his wet clothes, vigorously toweled himself dry and warm, ran the bed warmer over the sheets, and plunged under the covers.

It was only then that he thought about checking on Black. No need, he convinced himself. The man was presumably sound asleep upstairs, and the drugs might be wearing off enough that Allan would disturb him. Besides, the floors were bitterly cold. Even bundled up with a banyan and slippers, all the good of the toweling would be dissipated, and he'd come back to bed chilled, and have trouble warming again.

He'd see Black in the morning, and perhaps then, he'd be able to work out what it was about the man that bothered him.

It was his last conscious thought, but he woke to the same sense of something just out of reach. He was, as usual, the first out of bed. One brother after another put in an appearance. No Mr. Black.

Still no Mr. Black an hour later. It was one in the afternoon. "Why is Black not up?" he asked Baldwin. "I asked you to lower the dose last night."

"I did," Baldwin said. "He should be awake by now. I'll go and check."

Moments later, brothers who were not in the central room

came out to their chamber doors when Baldwin shouted from Black's door, "The bastard is gone."

By the time Mel got to her sister's, the sleet had thickened, and the hackney driver refused to wait for her. "It's too 'ard on me old 'orse, Mister," he explained. "Ruby's not so young as she used ta be, and neither am I, to tell the troof. Fact is, we'd 'ave been 'ome with a warm mash inside 'er and a tot o' rum inside me this hour gone if ye 'adn't 'ad me promise ta bring ye 'ere. We're for 'ome now, even if we don't get our five shillings'."

"Of course," Mel agreed, feeling contrite. Poor horse, and poor man, too. They must both be chilled to the bone. She ought to have him take her back on his way home, so she could return to the tower. But she had come all this way, and she was within yards of her beloved daughter. Who would, in any case, be sound asleep.

What would be the harm if she stayed? Yes, Lord Kemble was likely to be upset by her absence—or not so much her absence as what it said about her knowledge of the tower's secrets.

But she had already decided to explain her true purpose and to offer an alliance. She could stay with her sister and daughter for Christmas Day and return tomorrow night, ready to go with the brothers to the club on Boxing Day, as she had promised Winifred.

Surely, with what she had learned about the marquess and what the brothers must know, they could figure out a way to defeat the wicked man?

"Go home," she said to the jarvey, giving him two silver crowns—the bonus being only fair for keeping his promise in the terrible weather. "Rest yourself and your horse. Happy Christmas to you."

She had a key, and she let herself inside. Almost immediately, she realized that someone was up. Light showed under the door that led to the kitchen. Harmony was sitting at the table, sipping from a cup. She leapt up when Mel entered the room and rushed to give Mel an embrace. "Mel! Darling! What are you doing here so late? Or is it early? It must be after midnight. Merry Christmas, dearest. Have you finished your investigation? Or… oh no! Have you been dismissed? Come and sit down. Would you like a chocolate? I think there is still some in the jug. Sit down and I shall pour one for you. Harriet will be so pleased to see you! You shall stay, of course, and we shall have such a lovely Christmas. What did happen with the investigation? And how did you get here on this dreadful night?"

Harmony tended to chatter when she was excited.

Mel laughed. "Sit down and sip your chocolate, Harmony, and I shall try to remember your questions and answer them. No, I have not finished the investigation or been dismissed. Yes, I should like a chocolate and shall pour my own."

She was suiting words to action even as she spoke, and she took the warm cup to the table and sat down. "I came in a hackney with a dear man who was anxious to get home to his family, and I'm here to spend Christmas with you, Harriet, and Benjie." Benjamin was Harmony's son, who was two years younger than Mel's daughter Harriet.

"Tell me, darling, how are you? How are the children?"

She relaxed as she sipped her hot chocolate and listened as her sister talked about the children's lessons—Benjamin was a great reader and Harriet was already reaching beyond Benjamin and even Harmony in mathematics.

"I am very grateful to the upstairs neighbor," Harmony said. "He has allowed Harriet to join his ward for lessons. The two girls are the same age, and Mr. Eastwood is very clever."

To house her sister and the children, Mel rented the downstairs of what had once been an elegant townhouse for a single family. This area on the western edges of Marylebone had been abandoned by the rich and fashionable, and was now home to families of the middle sort—office workers, comfortably placed tradesmen and shop owners, attorneys, and secretaries.

Like most of the other houses in the street, the house had been converted to two dwellings with a dividing wall through the front hall and two doors with locks, one opening to the ground floor and one to the stairs that led to the second dwelling.

Harmony rattled on about visits to the park, the price of eggs, the essay her son had written on the manners required of a gentleman, Harriet's insistence that the vicar was not a good Christian, because he was only interested in the souls of the wealthy, and other topics.

"Of course, she is quite right, but it is not proper for children to express such opinions, but at least she only told me, and Mr. Eastwood said that, rather than discipline her for saying something that is, after all, the truth, I should praise her for her discretion in not making the statement in front of the vicar or other people."

Mr. Eastwood seems to enter your conversation quite often, Harmony.

Her sister's interest in the man was confirmed a moment later when she blushed as she said, "You will meet Mr. Eastwood tomorrow, when he joins us for Christmas dinner. He and his ward, of course. But Mel, why are you letting me prattle at you like this? It is the middle of the night! I shall just go and put sheets on your bed while you help yourself to some hot water from the kettle and have a wash." Harmony yawned. "I need to go to bed myself after that. It will be a busy morning tomorrow, what with cooking Christmas dinner and going to church."

She continued talking while Melody washed her face and hands. Then they made the bed together—trying to be as quiet as possible, since Melody shared Harriet's bed chamber when she was in residence—hugged silently, and parted, each to their own bed.

As it transpired, church was impossible. The weather had only worsened in the night. Mel woke to Harriet's shriek of delight on seeing her mother, and the sound of the rain, wind and sleet driving against the window.

After collecting a jug of water, they washed and dressed while Harriet shared news about the month since they'd spent time together—Mel had visited only briefly between finishing her most recent case and beginning the investigation of the brothers and the marquess.

Lydia Eastwood featured frequently in Harriet's stories. She was, according to Harriet, the best, prettiest, cleverest, and most loyal friend. "But you shall see for yourself, Mama, for Aunt Harmony has invited her and her uncle to spend Christmas with us."

Sure enough, there was a knock on the door partway through the morning, and it proved to be the neighbors from upstairs. Mr. Eastwood was a tall, thin gentleman with a pleasant countenance. He carried a double armful of greenery—fir branches as well as hawthorn, rosemary, ivy, holly and hellebore. Lydia, his niece, did not look much like him. She had a familiar look about her, but Mel could not quite put her finger on whom she resembled.

"Mel, allow me to present Mr. Eastwood," said Harmony, "and his niece Lydia. Mr. Eastwood and Lydia? My sister, Mrs. Blackmore."

After greeting her politely, Mr. Eastwood spoke to Harmony. "Mrs. Little, since you are giving us Christmas, we have brought our greenery to add to your decorations. Lydia, show your friends the ribbons and charms in your basket."

The girl obliged with a merry smile, pulling back the cover on her basket to show ribbons of all shades and assorted shapes cut out of tin—bells, harps, angels, and more.

Soon, the three children were busily at work using the ribbons to tie the greenery into wreaths and swathes, adding the charms to dangle from the ties.

Mr. Eastwood had donned an apron and armed himself with a knife to scrape the carrots and parsnips, Mel was peeling potatoes, and Harmony was putting the finishing touches to a capon pie that was to join the goose already roasting in the oven.

"How festive," Mel said.

"How magnificent," said Mr. Eastwood, but he was looking at Harmony.

Lydia began singing, "The holly and the ivy," and they all joined in. One carol followed another, while the minutes flew by, they completed their respective tasks, and delicious smells filled the kitchen.

Yes, whatever Lord Kemble might think about it, Mel had made the right decision to stay.

Chapter Six

B LACK WAS GONE. They searched their entire section of the
tower, including the secret hiding places, but they found
neither hide nor hair of him. Yet his bag was still in his chamber,
with his spare clothes. His toothpowder and soap were on the
washstand, and a nightshirt was folded under the pillow.

And in the hiding place under his rug, they found a small
arsenal of weapons that certainly weren't there before Black was
assigned to the bed chamber.

Where had he gone, and why?

"He has betrayed us," said Baldwin. "He has found a way to
signal the footmen and has gone to report to the marquess."

"Or he has found the door to the stair and left the tower
through the tunnel," Ernest suggested. "He's a smart one."

"Or the marquess sent his men in somehow, and dragged him
out," Frank suggested. He waved at the evidence of the bed
chamber. "From the looks of it, he was either taken away or left
of his own accord but intended to come back."

It could not be the marquess's men. The bolts on the tower
side of the exit to the mansion hadn't been moved. Allan could
not see any way that men could have come from the house side
through this door, and nor could Black have gone out through it,
shut and locked it, and slid the bolts closed again from the other

side.

He must have left through the tunnel. And they could do nothing but wait to see whether he had betrayed them.

"It is Christmas Day," Allan said. "Let's have some Christmas carols, and play some games. And we shall make wassail to have with our dinner."

As they sang, Allan waited—no doubt they all waited—for the marquess's men to come storming the tower. Even the bolts would not stand up forever to a determined assault with a battering ram. At the first sign of an assault, they would flee out through the tunnel.

But the afternoon wore on with no such invasion, and Allan was feeling much more relaxed by the time they gathered in the dining room to toast Christmas itself, the Christ child, the king, and one another.

Perhaps Black had been telling the truth when he claimed to be on their side. But if so, why had he come? Why had he left without a word? And did he intend to return, or had he abandoned his possessions?

The cook at the Golden Adonis kept the Sheppard brothers well supplied with leftovers, and in the early hours of this morning, she had outdone herself. The club had gone all out for Christmas last night, including in its catering. "You might as well take all this," said the cook. "Most of us are going to family or friends for Christmas, so I shan't need it to feed the other employees."

She had loaded them down with slices of goose, beef and venison, roasted partridge, mincemeat pies, roasted and boiled vegetables, and other delicacies. Pears poached in brandy. Even a whole Christmas pudding that had somehow escaped consumption.

It made for a delightful feast, and if some of the brothers were wishing for other loved ones, Allan among them, they put on such a pretense of good cheer that perhaps, like Allan, they half convinced themselves.

After dinner, while Zero was gorging on meat scraps, they exchanged gifts—small things they had made themselves. Allan gave all his brothers a leather purse that could be worn around the waist, which would be a useful thing once they escaped the tower. He had learned leather work more than two decades ago, when the marquess had exiled him, Baldwin, and Cornelius during the marquess's third marriage.

They had spent two and a bit years on a remote family estate in County Durham, with no money for their keep or their clothes, so all three boys had gone out to work with local farmers and craftsmen. Baldwin had made himself useful to the local physician, Cornelius had worked with a neighborhood carpenter, and Allan had tried a little bit of everything, until the squire in the nearby manor offered him work as his secretary.

Ancient history, but Baldwin's interest in medicine was sparked then, and Cornelius was still a useful man with a saw and hammer, as shown in the little lap desks he'd made for each of them for this Christmas.

With no club tonight, they carried on with games after gift giving, then Ernest, who was the best reader of them all, continued the tradition begun by his mother, the marquess's second wife, and read the nativity passages from the Gospel of St Luke.

Threatened, hunted, beleaguered, yet the Holy Family had won through. Allan could only pray that the brothers' own escape into whatever Egypt they could find to shelter them would be as blessed.

His last thought as he composed himself to sleep was of Black. He found himself hoping that the man was true, that he was unharmed, and that he would return in the night.

The following morning, his first move on leaving his bedchamber was to see if Black was back. He wasn't.

It was unusual of them to have a day off, but none of them could relax. Every now and again, one of them would come up with yet another theory about why Black had left. Most of them involved more chicanery from the marquess.

But the day passed, and nothing happened beyond the bread and water rations arriving in the late afternoon, as usual.

They had leftovers from Christmas dinner to make something of a feast with the bread—slices piled with turkey and venison and slathered in sauce. On any other night, they would have found cause for cheer. But Black's disappearance cast a pall over them all.

It was a relief when the time came to head to the club.

THE BAD WEATHER persisted through Christmas day and overnight, and on into the next morning. Mel—who was loving the time with Harriet, Harmony, and Benjie—didn't worry about it over much. She would go to the club tonight and return to the tower after that. Time enough to face the problems that would arise when they occurred.

She spent a relaxed day with her family and their guests, for Lydia and her uncle joined them for much of the day. There was something between Eastwood and Harmony. For some reason, neither seemed willing to acknowledge it, but Mel saw the yearning glances that each gave the other when they were not aware.

The oddest of thoughts crossed her mind and became stuck there. Did she look at Lord Kemble like that? Ridiculous. She had never yearned after a man—indeed, she neither needed nor wanted a man in her life. Her father and her brother had both been disappointing in their own ways, and the lesson had been reinforced during her marriage and even more in her years as an investigator. Men could not be trusted, and were more trouble than they were worth.

Kemble was, of course, a magnificent physical specimen, and his loyalty to his brothers was genuine and admirable. But, by all accounts, he abandoned his wife when she was carrying their second child, and he somehow—nobody she had spoken to knew the circumstances—lost his first child shortly after his wife died.

Her heart wanted to believe there was another side to the story. But her logic and her investigation so far told her that more than bad luck was behind the disasters that happened to the wives of the Marquess of Teign and his sons.

The marquess was guilty. Meeting him had dissolved the last of her doubts. And the sons—or at least some of the sons—were also victims. The evidence pointed in that direction, and what Winifred confided added to her conviction. But Mel had seen enough of life to know that victims often preyed on weaker victims.

Falling in love with Lord Kemble would be stupid, and Mel had no intention of allowing free rein to such treacherous emotions.

Forget about Kemble. Rejoice in the fact that, for the second night in a row, she was able to put her daughter to bed. Or at least, since Harriet was ten years old, supervise the child's bathing, read her a story, and hear her prayers.

"Will you still be here in the morning?" Harriet asked, once she was tucked up in bed.

They had already had this conversation.

"No, darling. I must go back to work. I have loved being with you, but the money I earn is what pays for all of us to have a place to live, clothes to wear, and food to eat."

Harriet pouted. "I want you to stay with us. At least at night. Why do you have to go away?"

"I have explained this, Harriet. Living in a particular place is part of this job. Sometimes, I can come home each night and work only during the day, and sometimes I must live where I am told by my employers. This is one of those times."

She bent to kiss her daughter, who squirmed away and covered her face with her hands. "I do not want you to go, Mama," she said.

"I shall come back as soon as I can," Mel promised. "Sweetheart, is Aunt Harmony not good to you?"

That had the hands dropping. Harriet's eyes sparked with indignation. "I love Aunt Harmony. And Benjie. But I want you, too, Mama."

"And I want you, but I also want you to have a roof over your head and enough food. Harriet, I shall see you as soon as I can. Go to sleep now, there's a good girl."

Harriet turned over in the bed and buried her face in her pillow. Mel backed out of the room. These painful farewells tore at her heart, but what else could she do?

Two widows left penniless by a spendthrift father and brother, and careless husbands. Two children who deserved to be raised as the young lady and young gentleman they were by birth, and given a chance at a decent life as adults.

Someone had to earn the money—not just for the house, food, and clothes Mel had mentioned, but for lessons, too. Benjie was already outstripping Harmony's knowledge of Greek and science, and Harriet would also soon need more from her education than Harmony could provide.

Above all, for savings, since illnesses or accidents could strike without warning, and one day both children would be young adults, needing money for whatever path they chose in life.

Perhaps it would be easier if Mel had not returned until the job was over and she could stay longer. But no. One day, Harriet would look back and realize that Mel came home as often as she could, because Harriet was the most important person in Mel's world.

She retreated to her own room to dress for the night at the club, selecting a deep red gown that she normally wore with a fichu to make the plunging neckline more modest. Not tonight. Her aim was to make sure that none of the brothers recognized her, and if they were studying her decolletage, it was unlikely to occur to them that this was the unwanted male guest their father had foisted on them.

To further confuse the issue, she chose a wig of white-blonde hair, with ringlets cascading from a high pile of artfully pinned curls. Yes, even Lord Kemble's sharp eyes would not see Mel Black in this guise.

But throughout her preparations, her mind went over the conversation, wondering what she could have said to have made her daughter happier about her absence. But when she went out to the parlor to wait for the hackney she'd sent for, Harmony assured her that Harriet's feelings were natural and so were Mel's.

"She wants an ideal life, of course," said Harmony. "She is not yet old enough to know that ideal lives belong in story books. You are doing the best you can for all of us, Melody, darling. I, for one, am so grateful to you for earning the income we need to live."

"And I am grateful to you for caring for my Harriet so that I can earn." Mel hugged her sister, who hugged her back, just as the knocker on the door sounded. A moment later, the little maid of all work announced that Mrs. Blackmore's hackney was here.

"I shall be home as soon as I can, and I shall write if I cannot be here in seven days at the most," Mel told her sister. She was soon in the hackney, and wrenching her mind away from what she had left to think about what was waiting for her.

Tonight, she would get some more answers, she hoped. At the very least, she could find out what the Sheppard brothers actually did at the Golden Adonis.

MANY OF THE ladies who patronized the Golden Adonis must be out of town or tied up with family, for the club was quiet this evening, and Allan had little to do and a surplus of time to keep an eye on his brothers and worry away at the problem whose name was Mel Black.

Baldwin's regular lady was an early arrival, and they had

disappeared into a private room. If other nights were an indication, they would not appear again until the club was nearly ready to close.

Donald was also with his regular lady—on the dance floor, rather than in the private room that Lady Hestia had undoubtedly hired for the night. Isaac and Jerome were at their instruments.

The other brothers, even those who had regulars, were also on the dance floor. It was a Golden Adonis rule. Any escort who was not otherwise engaged had to offer to partner any of the lady clients of the club who wanted to dance.

Thalia, the club manager, was watching Ernest. Her expression was hidden by the mask she wore, but her stance signaled yearning. Allan, half out of sympathy and half for something to do, approached her.

"Good evening, Mistress Thalia," he said.

She put on her practiced professional smile, all false warmth and watchful eyes. "Lord Apollo. How are you this evening?"

"Well enough, thank you. Did you have a pleasant day off yesterday?"

That prompted a genuine smile. "I did, thank you. I spent it quietly with my mother. Such a gift of a day. She insisted on getting up for dinner—she was even able to eat some of the goose that the cook gave me!"

"It is just you and your mother?" Allan asked, more for something to say than because he was genuinely interested.

"I am the only child of parents who were both only children," Thalia explained. "My grandparents are gone, so I cannot even ask if they had cousins—or, perhaps, brothers and sisters. As far as I know, Mama and I are all there is." Her wistful look transformed into another warm smile. "But rare things are all the more special, Lord Apollo."

"I cannot imagine being without my brothers," Allan confided.

Thalia laughed. "And I cannot imagine having so many brothers," she retorted, and then, more wistfully, "or any at all, really." Her gaze turned back to the dance floor, as if thoughts of brothers had naturally led her to watching Ernest.

She would have nine brothers if she married Ernest. Allan dismissed the thought as soon as it occurred. They could not start adding wives to their escape plan, and Ernest could not stay within reach of the marquess.

Nonetheless, he said, "My brother Eros likes you." Eros was Ernest's use name at the club, and "like" was a pale word. The pair cooed like turtledoves whenever they were together.

Her gaze returned to him. "Your brother Ernest loves me, and I love him. But do not worry, Lord Apollo. We know it is impossible. Even if I did not have a sick mother to support, even if Ernest was free to pursue me, I am not of his world."

"I wish…" Allan began, but trailed off. If he said that he wished they could marry and be happy together, she would hear it as a meaningless platitude, even though he meant every word.

"So do I," said Thalia, sighing. Then a maid tapped her on the arm. "Mistress Thalia, we have new arrivals. Two members and a guest."

"Thank you, Galanae. Duty calls, Apollo."

Allan bowed, and she walked off toward the west parlor, where the club members would be waiting with their guest. She would be back soon. Depending on what the three new arrivals wanted, Allan might be needed. He waited and watched.

After several minutes, Thalia entered with three ladies, all masked. He recognized Lady Andromeda's owl mask, and her identity was confirmed a moment later when Frank approached her, bowed to the other ladies, and went off with Lady Andromeda to the private room she had reserved.

One of the other ladies also had a mask Allan remembered— it represented the face of a lioness. Lady Thisbe, then. She had spent time with Hudson last time she was at the club, and sure enough, Hudson was bowing to her now, and leading her away to join the dancing.

Since those two ladies were members, the other, with her

deep blue flower mask, must be the guest. Thalia nodded at Allan, said something to the flower-masked-lady, and led her across the room.

That he was their destination became obvious when Thalia turned away all those who tried to stop her with a raised hand and a shake of the head. In moments, the pair of them were before him.

"Lady Mnema," said Thalia, "Allow me to present Lord Apollo. He is in charge of the gentlemen who work here."

"A supervisor, of sorts," said Lady Mnema, offering her hand. Hers was a full-face mask, so he couldn't see her smile, but he could hear the amusement in her voice. "Or an older brother, perhaps."

Allan bowed and kissed the air above the lady's hand. "Older brother, by all means, my lady."

"Lady Mnema would like you to give her a tour of our club, Lord Apollo," said Thalia. "I will leave you in Lord Apollo's hands, my lady."

She walked away. Unusual. Most guests were given their initial tour by Thalia or by Madam Hera herself. However, he had no objection to showing the lady around. "You have seen the visitor's parlor, my lady. This is the members' parlor. If you would allow me to escort you, I shall show you the other rooms."

He offered his elbow, and she tucked her hand around it. "Thank you," she said.

Something about her voice was familiar, but he could not match it with a person. Perhaps she was a relative of one of the women he'd pretended to court at his father's insistence. Yes. That was probably it.

Of course, she was here incognito, like most of the guests. Could she be a mother of one of the prospective brides he'd met and managed to discourage? Her hands were timeless, the shape of her body nothing less than delectable, and the neck below the mask did not show the ravages of time. A fair ringlet fell across the expanse of unmarred porcelain skin that showed below her throat, all the way to the upper swells of her delectable breasts.

A gentleman would not stare at them, even if the hair appeared to have been artfully placed to point in that direction.

"On this floor, my lady, we have the two parlors you have seen, and if we pass through the doorway," he suited word to action, the folding doors being open, "the dancing floor." The open doorway was usually sufficient separation between ballroom and parlor, but the doors could be closed if necessary.

Hudson and Lady Thisbe turned, bowed, and turned again on the floor, absorbed in one another. Trouble was brewing there. Allan needed to remind Hudson of what was at stake if he refused to hide with them, or if he insisted on bringing the woman. One more victim for the old man. One more mouth to feed. One more person to leave clues to destroy them all.

"Shall we look at the next room?" Lady Mnema asked. Despite the prompt, she stood relaxed, her hand still resting lightly on his arm, as if she could wait all night for him to move.

"Of course," he said, and led her to a door in another wall. "Through here, my lady, is the gaming room, and beyond that, the billiard room. Both rooms, and the parlor, open into the dining room." He took her from room to room. The cashier's desk was in the corner of the gaming room, currently operated by Ernest, who must have taken over to allow Frank his time with Andromeda.

In the billiard room, a group of ladies were playing a friendly game while one of the club escorts looked on. Allan explained that both escorts and servants were dressed in evening suits with a mask, but the servants wore simple half masks and a black stock rather than a white cravat.

The dining room was set up with buffet tables full of all kinds of delicacies. Supper would be served all night, and the tables would be constantly refreshed.

All this and more, Allan elucidated as they walked around.

"And upstairs?" Lady Mnema asked.

"Madam Hera's office and parlor, and the library," Allan said.

"Also, several private rooms which ladies can hire by the hour or for a night. Or longer, if they have the money and the will."

"What happens in those private rooms?" Lady Mnema enquired.

"That depends on the lady and those she invites." The Golden Adonis was not a brothel. Madam Hera made that clear to all who needed to know: guests, members, employees, and escorts. "The Golden Adonis takes a fee for rental of the room. It is not concerned with, and nor does it profit from, whatever happens between those inside a room, provided that all parties give their free consent."

"I have heard," said Lady Mnema, walking her fingers up his arm, "that some of the male escorts offered intimate services. Would you do so, Lord Apollo, were I to hire a private room?"

Chapter Seven

MEL FELT A shiver run through the upper arm under her fingertips. Lord Kemble was not unaffected by her. Come to that, she was far from unaffected by him.

Nonetheless, the invitation to share a private room with her was not about bedding the man, as much as her mind might linger on the thought. If they could get away from everyone else, she planned to take her mask off and introduce herself properly.

If she was here in the club when she told him that she was Mel Black, and if he reacted badly, she could call on reinforcements to defend herself. In the tower, she would be locked in with him and his brothers.

However, he said, "I must regretfully decline, Lady Mnema. I am not available for those duties. I can introduce you to several other men who would be willing."

Bother. Mnema shook her head. "I want you in particular, Lord Apollo."

"I oversee all the men, my lady, and must be available to sort out any problems. It is our rule that no one is allowed to enter a private room during the time it is hired. I cannot be away from the public rooms. Besides, with all due respect, there are some activities I cannot perform for hire. Call it a personal quirk, if you will. But the answer is no, my lady."

Their conversation was attracting attention. Two of the escorts had approached and were smiling hopefully at her. "May I present Kairos and Matton?" Lord Kemble asked. "Either gentleman is bound to give satisfaction in the bed chamber."

Mel waved them off. "Not tonight, gentlemen, but thank you for your interest. Lord Apollo, perhaps you could show me the library?"

It did not suit her purpose, since several other ladies were already enjoying its wide array of books, its comfortable sofas and chairs, and its commodious desks. Lord Kemble showed her an unoccupied private room, but stayed in the corridor, where anyone passing by could hear their conversation.

Back to plan A, Mel decided. She would make her way back to the tower. Kemble was usually the first man to rise. She would set her mental clock to wake her early, and speak to him before the others were up.

"Thank you for the tour, Lord Apollo," she said. "I shall remain in the library for a while. Please feel free to return to your usual routine."

The man bowed and quit the scene. His eagerness to escape her company was discouraging, but she supposed he now saw her as a predatory female who had difficulty accepting "no" as an answer.

Her head was hot under the wig that gave her the full head of hair required by fashion. In fact, she hadn't been feeling at all well all evening. Harriet had had a sniffle, and perhaps Mel had caught it. A glass of brandy might help her sore throat. Just one. She had never had a head for liquor.

She had hoped to confront Lord Kemble, make an alliance with him—or fail to do so—and then leave. But there was more she could learn just by walking around and observing. Were the other brothers as fastidious about selling their bodies as Lord Kemble? Did they have any favorites among the women? What, in fact, were they up to here at the Golden Adonis?

ALLAN WASN'T QUITE sure why he checked Black's bedchamber when the brothers got home. He had an uneasy feeling about the whole evening, but he did not really expect their intrusive investigator to have returned.

However, Black was there, in bed, apparently asleep. Allan put a hand on the back of his neck. Black didn't react, but the touch was enough to make Allan concerned. After checking Black's pulse and his forehead, he went looking for Baldwin. "Black is back. He is unconscious. His skin is chilled, and his pulse is fast. Will you take a look?"

Baldwin nodded and took the stairs two at a time, and while the other brothers crowded in behind him, he pulled back the blankets. Black didn't move. Baldwin placed a hand on his back and then on his calves. "Hmm," he said, then bent over the man and sniffed.

"He's been drinking," he reported. "His temperature suggests he has been out in the cold. I suspect he arrived home shortly before we did and passed out from a combination of the cold and the drink. He shall probably wake with a sore head, but just in case, I'm going to sleep with him for a while, and make sure he lives long enough to wake up."

Allan felt a revulsion of feeling that he could not explain. Watching over Black was his job. He found a reasonable explanation and gave it to Baldwin. "You've been with a client all night. Have a wash and a sleep. I'll watch Black and call you if his condition changes for the worst."

His brother grimaced but agreed, and told Allan what to look for. "Call me if he gets colder still or begins to feel clammy. If he has trouble breathing. If his pulse beat speeds above 100 beats a minute or slows below 40. It is at about 70 at the moment, which is too fast for a man who is sleeping. Don't let him roll onto his back. If he vomits while on his back, he might choke to death.

Other than that, let him sleep it off."

Baldwin and the other brothers wandered off to bed. Allan took his book and a candle upstairs to sit with the investigator. Baldwin was right. The man's cheek felt as if it had been chilled by the bitter wind outside, and when Allan fumbled under the covers, he found hands that were almost as cold.

Perhaps he was not asleep. Perhaps he had only just arrived home and was feigning slumber. He continued to breathe deeply and slowly, and his pulse, when Allan counted the beats, had dropped to a little faster than a beat a second. Allan pulled the chair so that he could look up from his book and see Black's face, then set the candle in its holder where the light would fall on the page.

He read for a while and then checked again. Black's face was no longer icy and his hands were warm. His pulse had slowed, too, and was within what Baldwin said was normal for sleep.

No point in waking Baldwin. Allan could stay awake, and doing without sleep for one night would do him no harm. But at some point in the next hour, his good intentions succumbed to his exhaustion, and he fell asleep in the chair, for the next thing he knew, he was woken by a shriek from the bed, almost instantly muffled.

"Lord Kemble," said Mr. Black's voice, in a far lower register than his shriek, "to what do I owe the honor of your company?"

Allan's eyes did not want to open but he forced his lids far enough apart to focus on Black, who was sitting upright, the covers held primly up around his chin. The candle had burnt out at some point, and the room was gloomy, but there was light enough to see the man's face and the bundled bedding below it.

"Mr. Black." The unlikely thoughts that were teeming around Allan's brain needed to be put aside for the moment while he dealt with this. "You alarmed my brother Baldwin last night. We thought you might be sickening for something, because you were so cold. I sat with you so that I could monitor your wellbeing."

"Then I thank you," said Black. "Perhaps it was something I

ate, for I feel well now, if a little sluggish."

Sluggish was normal. The illness in the night was nothing serious, then. If it was an illness. Black had been out, and who knew where and with whom. He had been drinking. No man had ever found out the tower's secrets without being shown them. If Black was a man. No. Allan's thoughts were too outlandish to be true.

"Something you drank, I gather. If you are well, then I shall leave you. We mean you no harm, Mr. Black, but we shall have an explanation from you of your little expedition these last two nights."

"And I mean you and your brothers no harm," Black insisted. "Indeed, the reverse is true."

That remains to be seen. No one was around when Allan walked downstairs, and his pocket watch confirmed it was still before noon. He would have to catch a few winks later in the day, but for now, he would make do with coffee.

The smell of the beverage must have drawn his brothers, for one by one they appeared in the living area, yawning and stretching. Each claimed a mug and poured the morning drink of their choice—Allan had also made a large pot of tea and one of chocolate.

Mr. Black came too, strolling down the stairs in his shirt-sleeves and breeches with his hair mussed and his eyes sleepy. Allan's new suspicions were strengthened by a close look in the better light of the living area—luxurious lashes, fine bones, no Adam's apple, and a morning shadow that had not been present on Black's cheeks less than an hour ago.

His body already believed those suspicions to be true. It was responding to Black's disheveled appearance as if it was personally responsible. Allan moved to put the table between him and everyone else while he tied an apron around his waist as further concealment. "I shall chop the meat for the stew," he said, to explain the apron.

"Is there hot water for a shave?" Black asked, his tone deceptively innocent. *Her tone. Tell it like it is.* Either Black was a woman or the marquess had finally succeeded in driving Allan mad.

"In the kettle on the back of the stove," he replied. "Jugs in that upper cupboard," he pointed, "on the left of the dresser."

"Thank you."

Black poured her water and wandered off back up the stairs. Even though she strutted like a man and she'd left her shirt untucked at the back so it hid the flare of her hips, Allan could see the difference now he was watching for it—the slight tilt of her pelvis at each step, necessitated by the wider set of the bones.

She must be wearing padding around her waist and binding at her breasts to disguise the rest of her womanly shape. Allan had no doubt that she had one.

"Are we not going to question Black?" Donald asked.

"You didn't wake me," Baldwin commented.

"He…" Allan choked on the implied lie. "I checked the temperature and the pulse regularly, and they both improved quite quickly. Black continued sleeping on one side. I saw no danger, so I let you sleep."

Both Baldwin and Cornelius, the brothers who knew Allan best, studied him with narrowed eyes. Or perhaps it was just Allan's conscience that assumed suspicion where none existed.

Why did he not simply announce Black's deception? Then, if Black denied it, they could strip his shirt off and settle the issue once and for all.

But something in him baulked at that solution, and he kept Black's secret then, and when she—he—came back downstairs now fully dressed.

Oh bother. He decided he would just refer to her as a she, instead of a he, for what was the use—at least in his private musings—of pretending she was a man when he, at least, knew she was not?

Baldwin glared at Allan. "Are you going to question this interloper? Or shall I?"

Allan waved a hand, inviting him to take the lead, and Baldwin began the questioning.

"Explain yourself, Black. Where have you been and how did you get out?"

"I spent Christmas with my sister, my nephew, and my daughter," said Black. Not a response that Allan expected, and Baldwin, too, appeared nonplussed.

"I swapped the bowls," Black added. "You drugged me the first night, and the bowls were the only way it could have been done. Just to be certain, I switched the mug set out for me for a clean one, as well. On the second night, I followed you to the Golden Adonis, but on Christmas Eve, I went home, to see my family."

"Or to collude with our enemy," Cornelius growled.

Black ignored the hostility in that remark. "Your enemy is my enemy," she said, calmly. "I have been trying to find evidence to convict the Marquess of Teign of at least some of his crimes. When he advertised for an investigator, I thought it a chance to enter his home with a license to poke around." She shrugged. "I did not expect to be shut in a tower with his sons."

She sounded sincere, but then, she was a practiced liar. Allan didn't know what to believe. "Having discovered you would not have the freedom of the house, you came back," he pointed out. "Why?

"To make common cause with you, if I can, and to help with your escape," Black said. "Escape is the plan, is it not?"

The brothers exchanged glances, and Baldwin swore, and lunged toward Black, reaching for him—whether to shake him or strangle him, Allan didn't know. He put out a hand to stop his brother and addressed Black. "Explain how you came to that conclusion."

"Some of it, various ones of you have told me, some I have overheard, some I have deduced. You have been trapped in this tower by your love for one another. The marquess never lets you all out at the same time. If any of you disobey his orders, the others are hostages to be beaten or otherwise abused at his command." Black raised her brows. "Am I correct so far?"

Allan nodded, while others murmured affirmatives.

Black continued. "You are all working at the Golden Adonis. I deduce you are saving your wages, for you eat leftovers from the club and have few luxuries here in the tower. Saving for what? The rest is largely deduction. The first duty of a prisoner of war is to escape. In your case, the escape of one is a risk to the others, so you must all escape at the same time. It follows that you are saving to escape."

"We should kill him now," Baldwin said. "Who knows what he has told the marquess?"

Black didn't flinch. She calmly said, "That would be a mistake, Lord Baldwin. I propose an alliance. You want an escape. I want the marquess's complete defeat, and with it, your freedom."

At that moment, the bell rang to announce a visitor in the antechamber. It proved to be Farnham the steward, one of the marquess's worst henchmen, come for Black. Allan felt so strong an urge to protect her that he nearly punched the man, and damn the consequences.

Black, however, seemed unafraid as she said to Farnham, "I have nothing to report yet, and the two weeks of the contract are not up. I am happy to come and tell the marquess that I know nothing, if you are more concerned about giving him that message than about wasting his time."

Farnham gaped at her while he considered the marquess's likely reactions, and then came down on the side of caution. "Stop gabbing and come along," he growled, grabbing her arm.

"I am coming, Mr. Farnham," she told him, with an amused smile. "No need to rumple my coat." She shook him off, and strode toward the door. The brute was so surprised he allowed it.

Gritting his teeth and clenching his fists helped Allan not to make a futile effort to stop the steward. Futile, because all it would get him was the invasion of an armed force of bully boys, ready to beat all his brothers for Allan's transgression. But it was hard to see her blithely strolling away into the lion's mouth.

She is the enemy, he told himself. But his heart didn't believe it.

He paced the floor until Baldwin asked him what on earth was wrong. "If Black is beaten by his lordship, what is that to us?" he asked.

"Hardly fair, Baldwin," Frank objected. "Black has been as honest with us as he can. We're the ones who have been lying. He says he wants to help us, and I believe him."

"That's because you don't have a false bone in your body, Frank," said Cornelius. "Black certainly has charm. I'll give him that. But charm is not to be trusted. Allan's wife was charming. His lordship can be charming."

"Yes, yes," said Allan. "And your wife was charming. And true to the core. And so duplicitous that she was able to escape even his lordship without leaving a clue to her whereabouts."

Cornelius snorted. "That was the plan," he pointed out.

"Precisely." *Couldn't Cornelius see the point? One should never underestimate a woman.* Of course, Cornelius didn't know that Black was a woman, so Allan couldn't blame him for not understanding what Allan meant.

He realized he had begun to pace again. Throwing himself down into his chair, he picked up the book that happened to be on the table next to him and opened it at random. He could feel his brothers' stares, and waited for them to go about their own activities. It didn't happen. After several minutes he looked up and found them all staring at him.

"What?" he demanded.

"That is my copy of *Chess Analyzed*," Frank said. "Since when do you read chess books?"

"You keep beating me," Allan said. "I need to improve my game."

"You will learn more if you turn the book right side up," commented Baldwin.

Damn it.

At that moment, the bell rang from the antechamber. Isaac

was nearest the stairs, and was bounding up them two at a time to check the peephole before the sound had died. "It's Black," he called down after a moment. "He's on his own."

Allan wasn't closest to the door, but he reached it before Donald drew back the bolts, turned the key, and opened it. Black swaggered in, all in one piece. The relief made Allan furious, and when he left Donald resecuring the door and caught up with Black, his fury surged and found a focus.

One side of her face was swollen and bruised, and her lip was cut, obviously from a blow. The marquess would pay for this. One day. It was not the worst thing he had done by any means, but it was going on the list.

As for Black… "Baldwin, Cornelius, we're taking Black out with us tonight. Black, it's time for you to go home."

"What?" Black glared at him, her eyes sparking fire. "I'm not leaving. I have not finished what I came here to do."

"Woman, you are already hurt. Who knows what he'll do to you next? What if he orders you stripped for a beating? He'll discover your secret." He stamped a foot for emphasis, forcing the desperate words out through gritted teeth. "I cannot lose another person under my protection. I will not, Black." He growled. "Aaargh. What is it? Miss Black? Mrs. Black?" An alarming thought occurred to him. "Is there a Mr. Black?

Chapter Eight

M EL COULDN'T UNDERSTAND this man at all. He was angry, yes, but not—or so it seemed—at her deception, but at the risk she had taken. She found herself explaining, which she never did. After all, her choices—and her risks—were her own. It was one of the many benefits of being a widow.

Even so, the words were on her tongue before her mind caught up. "There was a Mr. Blackmore." She put a slight emphasis on the second syllable in the name. "He died seven years ago. I am a widow. Your father's steward hit me, yes. I heard the marquess tell him to beat me up, since I had told him nothing and insisted on the full fourteen nights written into the contract we both signed. Farnham managed one blow before I punched him where men are most vulnerable."

She shrugged. "He should not have waited until we were away from his accomplices before attacking me. I can tell you that I did not let your father know about your many hiding places and your excellent cuisine, let alone about your tunnels. Nor do I intend to do so."

"Then escape tonight, Mrs. Blackmore. I'm not allowing you to stay here to be killed by his lordship."

Perhaps a compromise was in order. "I told the marquess I had discovered nothing so far. I pointed out to him that calling me to his presence all the time will make you suspicious, and that I have the remainder of the two weeks to uncover your secrets. The marquess has agreed to leave me alone at least until the maids come again, at which time I am meant to send a message to let him know the progress of the investigation."

A thought occurred to her and she grinned up at Lord Kemble. "You could help me write the message."

"What is going on here?" Lord Baldwin demanded. "Allan, for how long have you known that Black—Blackmore, I should say—is a woman? Why did you not tell us? And Blackmore, what is your real purpose?"

"Melody Blackmore!" The name burst from Lord Cornelius as if it was a discovery. "Thomasina's cousin?"

The other brothers turned their attention to Lord Cornelius, and Lord Francis said, "Thomasina, as in your wife?"

"Yes," said Mel. "In fact, that is one of the major reasons I accepted the position—to find out what happened to Thomasina, and who was responsible."

Baldwin grabbed Kemble's arm and repeated his question. "How long have you known that Black is a woman?"

"I only figured it out this morning," Kemble told him. "It's in the way she walks. Also, when she woke this morning, she had no beard, then she came out of her room with a shadow asking for water for a shave, and now she is smooth-cheeked again. A lot of little things."

He narrowed his eyes at Mel, another piece falling into place. "Lady Mnema," he said.

She hadn't expected him to make the connection, but she wasn't going to deny it. "Yes. A friend of mine—you know her as Lady Andromeda—arranged a guest pass for me. I thought going to the club would help me confirm some of my assumptions about you."

"And did it?" Cornelius asked.

It did, and it also raised new questions. Cornelius, for example. The gossip at the club had him spending every night with the same woman—someone known as Lady Opora. Mel had hoped to meet the lady, but she left her assignation with Cornelius and went straight to her carriage.

In fact, except for Lord Kemble—or Lord Apollo, as he was known at the club—and the two youngest brothers, all the brothers had a "regular" romantic connection with a member of the club or an employee.

"What I have observed is that most of you have a reason to defeat your father once and for all, so you can be free to love and to live. And wouldn't that be better than merely escaping him?"

"How can you trust her?" Baldwin demanded. "She has probably betrayed us. Any moment, the marquess's men will burst in, or they will be waiting at the mouth of the tunnel, or at the club."

"I have not betrayed you," Mel told him. "I am on your side."

"That is what you say," said Ernest. "Why should we believe you?"

"There is a way to test it," Cornelius said. "I haven't told you, brothers, but Lady Opora, the lady I have been meeting at the club—she is my wife."

There was silence for a moment, and then Baldwin said, "But you already have a wife."

Cornelius rolled his eyes and Mel realized what he meant. "You mean, Lady Opora is actually Thomasina, my cousin."

Cornelius nodded, and Mel sagged with relief. "Thank God. She *is* alive. I have been so afraid for her. I heard one of you tell another that you had helped her escape, but I never expected her to be in London."

"That makes two of us," said Cornelius, with a touch of humor. "Imagine my surprise when Hera insisted I meet with Lady Opora privately, and she removed her mask."

Baldwin shook his head, in disgust, apparently, rather than denial, for he said, "You did not tell us. You did not even tell me."

Cornelius put an apologetic hand on his brother's shoulder. "It didn't seem real. It still doesn't. But it is time to let you all know, for when we leave, I am going with Thommie."

Baldwin's glare faded. In an abrupt move, he hugged his twin. "I am glad for you, brother," he said. "If we safely can, I should like to see my sister Thommie before we all part."

"Or," Mel insisted, "we can defeat your father and you can all stay. Lord Cornelius, if you and I meet with your wife tonight, she will know me, and will be able to tell you I can be trusted. Is that what you meant by 'test'?"

Cornelius nodded.

"And Lady Andromeda, too," Frank said. "You know her, you said, Mrs. Blackmore."

"She is a friend of mine," Mel confirmed. "She will vouch for me, and so will Lady Thisbe."

"Good," said Lord Kemble. "Tonight, at the club, we shall confirm your identity and your character."

"Don't discuss my wife's identity or presence in London," Cornelius warned. "Even among yourselves."

At that point, the bell rang. The growing amity in the room vanished as Ernest hurried upstairs to use the peephole.

"It is Farnham," he reported. "On his own."

Most of the brothers paused in their hurried tidying to glare at Mel. "Sent by the marquess or here of his own accord?" she wondered. "I didn't think he would report his failure to beat me to the marquess, nor how—and where—I wounded him."

"He probably didn't," Lord Kemble theorized. "If the marquess sent him, I'd expect him to have reinforcements. But he has come on his own. Rather daring of him."

"He thinks you are cowed and without power," Mel suggested. "My guess is that he'll demand you turn me over." Botheration. Leaving her pistol upstairs had been an act of good faith, but she regretted it now.

"Open the door," Lord Kemble said to Baldwin.

The second brother shook his head and scowled, but followed the instruction.

Farnham stormed through the door, brushing Baldwin to one side, heading straight for Mel. Lord Kemble stepped in his way, and when the steward tried to dodge around him, moved to prevent him.

"Out of my way," Farnham snarled.

"My lord," Lord Francis suggested. "That should be, out of my way, my lord."

Farnham aimed a punch at Lord Kemble, who dodged and punched him back, knocking Farnham off his feet.

Mel decided it was time to take a hand. She skirted Kemble, who was standing over a groggy Farnham, waiting for him to recover enough to get up. "Farnham, I take it you were not satisfied with the outcome of our last meeting," she said.

"You bastard," Farnham complained. "I'm going to beat you to a pulp. You, too, Kemble."

With a flick of her wrist, Mel activated the catch on the sheath of the knife she wore strapped to her right forearm. The knife dropped into her hand. "Or," she said, holding it up so he could see it, "I could skin you. You'd be more use as a lampshade."

She shook the knife from her other arm down into her left hand.

"My lords, if any of you are sensitive around blood, you might wish to look the other way."

"I'd be happy to hold him for you," Kemble said.

"I'll help," said Baldwin. "Do you happen to have a spare knife, Mr. Black?"

Farnham was scooting backwards towards the door, with his rump on the floor and both legs working furiously. "I'll tell the marquess," he threatened.

"What? That you were fool enough to come here alone, unarmed and without his orders, after I had already beaten you once?" Mel chuckled. "From what I observed, the marquess is not one to tolerate stupidity, but try it, by all means. I shall watch with interest."

Farnham kept going until he was in the anteroom. Baldwin shut the door and locked it.

"That," he said, "was very satisfying."

WHEN MRS. BLACKMORE came downstairs dressed in her red gown, her mask in her hand, Allan had to wonder how any of them had mistaken her for a man.

Tonight, she had foregone the wig she must have been wearing last night. Her short-cropped brown hair was fetchingly adorned with a confection of lace, ribbons, and flowers in colors that matched her gown.

The bodice of the gown was even lower than the one she wore last night, when he'd spent all the time in her company disciplining his eyes not to stay riveted on her breasts. She wore a locket on a chain that made things worse, dropping to nestle between the soft mounds.

Allan was grateful when she covered herself in a warm cloak. He offered his arm as if they were going for a walk, and insisted on going ahead of her on the steps down to the tunnel.

Baldwin had spent part of the afternoon reiterating the likely places for an ambush, if Mrs. Blackmore had betrayed them and the marquess's men were waiting. At the foot of the steps. Where each side tunnel met the main tunnel. On the riverbank after they emerged. At the docks on the other side of the river. Outside the club.

They saw nothing but the usual traffic along the river and the streets beyond; heard nothing but the sounds of London, the Thames, and then Southwark at night.

Inside the club was another possibility. Madam Hera was powerful, but the marquess's reach might stretch even here. However, they entered by the kitchen door, as usual, and went together up to the parlor, as usual.

"I shall speak to Madam Hera about using her private parlor for our meeting with Lady Opora," Allan said, and went to find the club's proprietor.

Baldwin continued to hover. He was the brother most suspicious of Mrs. Blackmore's motives and loyalties, and refused to leave her unescorted except by Allan. "You are half in love with her," he accused. "You want to see the good in her. I won't trust her until she proves herself."

"Which is fair enough," said Mrs. Blackmore. "I would be the same in your shoes."

Even after the arrival of Lady Melissae, Baldwin's usual client, he wouldn't leave, and they stood in an uncomfortable foursome, making awkward conversation, until Mrs. Blackmore happened to mention she was a widow, and then the two ladies were comparing notes on widowhood and difficult marriages, leaving the brothers with nothing to say.

One by one, the other ladies arrived. Lady Andromeda and Lady Thisbe first. They came straight to greet Mrs. Blackmore, who introduced them to Lady Melissae.

"Have you known this lady long?" Allan asked Lady Andromeda, just as Frank and Hudson joined the group.

"Since we were girls," said the lady. "We grew up in the same neighborhood. Of course, the pair of us were only children when Mrs. Bl... I mean, when Lady Mnema married our neighbor, but she was always very kind to us. And recently, we have become reacquainted, have we not, Mel? May I tell them about how we met again?"

"Go ahead," said Mrs. Blackmore.

"Someone in my father's family was embezzling. Mel came to work for us, to find out who it was. She pretended to be a seamstress—she is very good with her needle. When I recognized her, she took me into her confidence, and I helped her discover the villain, and we saved my father and my family name. Since then, she has been the big sister I never had. Par... that is, Lady Thisbe and I look up to her so much."

"She taught us how to shoot so we could defend ourselves," said Lady Thisbe. "And where to hit if we are assaulted, so we can lay them low and get away." Lady Thisbe's soft voice was nonetheless infused with relish as she conveyed the bloodthirsty sentiments.

Allan raised an eyebrow in Baldwin's direction, even as Lady Melissae expressed awe and envy. "I wish I might learn," she said. "A widow, especially one with money, is always a target."

Baldwin patted the lady's hand, which was tucked in his arm. "You need a man to protect you."

"Unfortunately, it is often the men in our families, those who should protect us, who are the ones doing us harm," Mrs. Blackmore said, and all the ladies nodded.

Given what the marquess had done to his wives and others, Allan could only agree.

Ah! Here was Cornelius, beckoning him and Mrs. Blackmore. "Lady Mnema," he said to her. "We have a meeting. Ladies, brothers, if you would excuse us."

Any lingering doubts disappeared when they entered Madam Hera's private parlor, and Thomasina said, "Melody!" and cast herself into Mrs. Blackmore's arms.

"Thommie, I have been so worried about you!" said Mrs. Blackmore. "You just disappeared. At first, I wondered if your husband had killed you, but apparently you still like him, so that wasn't it."

"It was the marquess, Mel," Thomasina explained. "He tried to have his way with me. He has no shame, the horrid man. Cornelius helped me to get away, and said he would come for me when Jerome reached twenty-one. I have been in hiding ever since, but Jerome will reach his majority soon, so I came to London to be ready when Cornelius was free."

She reached a hand to Cornelius without looking at him, and his was there to clasp it against his heart.

"But where have you been?" Mrs. Blackmore asked. "I could find no trace of you."

"In France," said Thomasina. "We have a home there, Cornelius and I."

Mrs. Blackmore beamed. "On the vineyards of your mother's family! I wondered. But nobody with whom I spoke had any idea where in France I could find your family estates! They still belong to your family?"

"To my three French aunts. My only remaining relatives. They are widows, all three, and lost brothers, husbands, and sons to the war, but they welcomed me, although I was half-English." She leaned back against Cornelius, and smiled up at him. "And they shall welcome Cornelius, too. The estate shall be ours, in time. And our son's after us."

"Thommie!" Mrs. Blackmore exclaimed. "You have a son?"

Thomasina smiled and Cornelius grinned broadly. "Elias. He shall be six on his next birthday," Thomasina confided. "He is so looking forward to meeting his father."

"And I him," Cornelius added.

A son. Allan was thrilled, astounded, worried, a little hurt that he'd been kept in the dark—such a maelstrom of feelings that all he could say was, "Belated congratulations, both of you."

"I am also looking forward to meeting my wife's aunts, who have been mother hens to her since the day she arrived on their doorstep. I cannot wait to tell them how grateful I am. They came to England with Thomasina, Allan. The aunts and our son. They have a house in Spitalfields. As soon as we leave the tower, I shall join them, and then we'll be off for France."

"Can you not leave now?" Mrs. Blackmore asked. "Why do you have to wait for your brothers?"

Allan exchanged a glance with Cornelius, who waved a hand to indicate that Allan should explain. "You are aware that the marquess will punish the rest of us if any one of us goes missing," he said.

"How will he know one of you is gone?" Mrs. Blackmore asked. "The only people who go into every room—or at least the only ones I've seen since I have been with you—are the maids, and surely you could think of a reason why they cannot go into Lord Cornelius's room? After all, it will only be a few days, and you will all be gone."

"A few days?" *What brought her to that conclusion?*

She sounded apologetic when she said, "I have good hearing. You told your brothers that your father plans a joint wedding for you, Lord Baldwin, and Lord Ernest, and that all the brothers would need to make their escape before you three were forced to go through with it. And one of the ladies here yesterday evening was boasting that her daughter is going to marry Lord Kemble a couple of days after Twelfth Night. So, I assume you are leaving within the next nine or ten days, unless we can find a way to stop the marquess for once and for all."

"Stopping the marquess would be a good idea," said Thomasina, with a firm nod.

As he absorbed what Mrs. Blackmore had said and readjusted his own thinking, Allan felt rather as if he had had several blows to the head. The wedding, so soon. The idea that they could hide Cornelius's absence and let him reunite with his family. The concept, which he had initially dismissed, that they might defeat the marquess.

"Can we really fight the marquess and win?" Cornelius asked, in a tone that suggested hope.

"Whenever we have tried, someone we love has ended up hurt," Allan reminded him.

"He has weak spots," Mrs. Blackmore insisted. "We need to find and exploit them. He has too inflated a sense of his own invulnerability, for a start. His men obey him out of fear, not conviction, and Lord Kemble, you saw for yourself that his steward is prepared to lie to him, because confessing failure would mean punishment. That is a weakness, that he surrounds himself with people who are afraid to tell the truth."

"We only have to keep Jerome out of his hands," Cornelius said, thoughtfully. "He has no legal right to tangle with any of the rest of us, and if he tries, the law will be on our side."

Allan snorted in disbelief. "The law is always on the side of those with the most status and power."

"You are the Earl of Kemble," Mrs. Blackmore said. "You have status and power, if you care to use them. You shall need allies, of course. You have all been kept separate from the rest of the ton, presumably so you cannot build alliances to protect yourselves. But that can be amended."

"Who would stand with us against the Marquess of Teign?" Allan said. He meant to scoff, but the question became sincere on his tongue. The marquess had been the ogre of his childhood—of his life, really. But Mrs. Blackmore was correct. The man was not all-powerful.

"Anyone he has offended, for a start," said Thomasina. "Including me and my family. And what of the families of his wives?"

Mrs. Blackmore nodded. "Disgruntled business contacts. Husbands whose wives he has seduced. Women who have been mistreated by him. Anyone at all who values justice and ethical behavior. I know of several high-ranking peers who might take an interest if we can produce evidence of wrongdoing."

"Can we?" Cornelius wondered. "Beating one's children is not, unfortunately, illegal. Attempting to force one's daughter-in-law to engage in an illicit act may be highly immoral, but is it illegal?"

"I should like to know how his wives died," Mrs. Blackmore said. "Also, it is not only his family he has terrorized. Servants. Political rivals. Other innocent women of all walks of life. I have been making notes and finding patterns. He believes he is above the law. So far, he has been right. I'd like to see that change."

Was it possible? Looking at Mrs. Blackmore's determined face, Allan couldn't help but hope.

"We need to talk to our other brothers," he cautioned.

"Thommie, I can't risk my brothers without asking them first," Cornelius said to his wife, "but if they agree, I should like to be with you and Elias."

As it should be, Allan reflected, ignoring the sinking sensation that was his reaction to the knowledge that soon their close-knit circle of brothers would be split apart, as they went their separate ways.

Chapter Nine

MEL SPENT THE night moving from room to room around the club, joining conversations with groups and initiating chats with individual ladies. Her presence as a guest acted as a guarantee of wealth and status, and the masks most of them wore relieved them of social obligations such as introductions.

She found it easy to be accepted as one of them—married women and widows with money to spend and the freedom to please themselves.

Guiding the discourse in the direction she wanted it to go was also easy. A mention of the Marquess of Teign prompted all the gossip she had already heard, and much more. He was ruthless, amoral, resented, and feared.

The club member who was boasting of a wedding the previous night—she was the mother of one of the brides—was occupied in a private room, but two of her friends—or *rivals* might be an apter term—were happy to share the news of the marriage agreement.

"Lord Ernest Sheppard is reluctant, I've heard," said one of them. "He tried to frighten my friend's daughter by telling her that Teign expects to sleep with his daughters-in-law. Do you think it is true?"

"I should not be surprised," said another of the women. "I

take it our dear friend does not believe it."

"She says not. She told her daughter it was all nonsense. I do not think she cares one way or another, as long as she can boast of marrying her daughter to one of Teign's sons."

"Those Sheppard brothers all tell such stories," scoffed one of the listeners. "I've heard similar tales from several mothers who backed out of a marriage agreement with Teign. I daresay the brothers are just marriage shy, and make the stories up to scare off their brides."

A woman in a cat mask did not agree. "But what about Lady Kemble? Do you not remember the rumors? That she and Kemble were estranged and her second child was Teign's?"

They gossiped on, but Mel learned nothing she did not already know.

In another group, she heard from women whose husbands had been cheated by Teign, whether in politics, in racing, or in a business deal (though these *ton* ladies concealed the nature of the deal to remove any implication that their husbands dabbled in trade).

Several ladies whispered of more intimate problems with Teign—seductions and outright assaults—though even in this secretive environment they spoke of "a friend of mine" or "the daughter of a friend" or "someone my cousin knows."

Most conversations gave her the same result—verification that Teign was widely mistrusted and disliked, but also that his very reputation protected him, since no one dared go against him without iron-clad facts that would stand up in a trial by his peers—for he was a marquess. Getting a case to trial would be hard enough. Convincing the House of Lords to convict one of their own would be near to impossible.

Still, she did confirm that his fall would be applauded within the ton, at least by most of those families represented here tonight.

Again, this was nothing new. To stop him, she needed evidence he had broken the law in ways that the House of Lords would take seriously. Rape and assault wouldn't do it, unless the victim had a rank equal to Teign's. The man could probably be acquitted even of murder, if the corpse was from the lower sort.

But did she need him to be tried and convicted? When she had believed him guilty of Thomasina's murder, that had been her goal, but Thommie was alive and well. Perhaps she should be rethinking her objective.

The thought surfaced in her mind. *Help the Sheppard brothers to break free of the marquess, and to stay free.* Yes. That was it. That was her objective. It would mean finding a way to neutralize the marquess, but she was confident that, if she marshalled his enemies, starting with his sons, they could get the job done.

By the first light of dawn, she and the brothers made their way back to the tower. Most of the brothers. "Cornelius has somewhere else to go today," Kemble told his brothers, when they were gathered on the wharf waiting for the boats to take them across the river. "I shall tell you all about it once we are home."

Hidden by her mask and the hood of her cloak, Mel allowed herself a smile that she didn't want to have to explain. Not yet. Not until they had heard her out. But even without their consent, the change had begun. The first of the Sheppard brothers was out of his cage.

THE BROTHERS WERE tired after working all night. Mel would get a better hearing from them once they had slept. She listened while Kemble gave a brief outline of what had happened when he, Cornelius, and Mel met with Thomasina. "Our brother's wife vouches for Mrs. Blackmore," he said. "Furthermore, Mrs. Blackmore pointed out that we can hide Cornelius's absence for the few days left until we all must disappear. He has gone with his wife to meet his son. He'll return to fetch his belongings, but he is the first of us to escape. I rejoice for him."

"Cornelius is truly blessed," said Lord Baldwin. "Brothers, we must make certain that he remains free to enjoy his family life. Mrs. Blackmore, you say that you came here to find a way to find out Thomasina's fate, and to punish whoever harmed her. Why are you still here? Are you not satisfied to know that she lives?"

So much for her intentions. "The man who stole years of her marriage still walks free, and will hurt her again, if he can. I shall not be satisfied until the marquess can do no further harm to my cousin, her husband, or anyone else, for that matter." She fought back a yawn. She really needed to get some sleep.

"Bold words," said Kemble. "But who can touch him? Those who have gone up against him in the past have all failed and suffered for it."

"Are you so certain?" Mel asked. "Separately, we are no match for the man. That is true. But together, have you not deceived him and resisted him for years? For nearly long enough to break free of him altogether? What if we build an alliance of all those who have reason to oppose him? Can we not bring him down?"

"Perhaps," said Baldwin, "this is one of the reasons he keeps us isolated. To prevent us from seeking allies. Allan, she makes good sense."

Mel couldn't resist the yawn any longer, and hers set off Frank's. She shared a sheepish grin with him, and then laughed when Donald and Ernest yawned too.

"That's it," Allan said. "Let's pick this up after a good sleep."

"Good," said Mel. "Together, we are strong." *Or at least they would be after they slept.*

IT WAS A full council of war when they met again after noon. Even Cornelius and Thomasina were there, having entered through the tunnel. All the brothers were keen to fight back, but for some time, the discussion centered on the marquess's wrongs.

Allan didn't particularly want to discuss his marriage. "Ancient history," he said. "My wife's second child was a stillborn son. Not mine. I had not shared her bed for over eighteen months, ever since she and the marquess taunted me with their affair. She died of childbirth fever a few days after the little boy. No need to revisit any of it."

Mel left the subject alone and forbore to add those sad details to her notebook. Allan clearly still carried considerable pain over the matter. At some point, though, she needed to know what had happened to his first child. *And was the marquess responsible?*

Cornelius was brutally frank about his marriage. He had seen what happened to Allan and had not wanted to marry, especially to someone chosen by the marquess. However, he and Thomasina had been attracted to one another from their first meeting. Their happiness was fleeting, though. The marquess soon attempted a seduction, and when Thomasina rejected him, he had both her and Cornelius beaten. With the help of Allan and Baldwin, Cornelius and Thomasina arranged her disappearance, leaving evidence behind to suggest that she had committed suicide.

The other brothers had tried various methods to discourage the matrons of the ton from considering them as prospective husbands.

They pretended to be fools, or rakes, or profligate gamblers. They talked about the marquess's predilection for raping anyone in skirts, including his daughters-in-law. They hinted at something shady about the deaths of his three wives and Allan's wife.

Indeed, it had been the antics of some of the brothers—and Allan's open support of those antics—that had resulted in them joining Jerome and Frank in the tower.

"Jerome had been here since he was ten, and Frank since he joined the army and was forcibly retrieved," Baldwin explained. "They had been exploring and had discovered many of the hiding places. And in one of them, they found a previous Teign's journal."

The man had been the predecessor to the current marquess, but back when he was merely the heir, he had lived in the tower. In his journal, he wrote about its secrets. "My ancestors secretly continued to follow the old religion," he had written. "When the Roman Catholic mass was forbidden, they converted the lower tower to be a chapel and a hiding place for visiting priests, while the upper tower was traditionally the home of the heir."

"So why was the knowledge of the secret ways lost?" Mel wondered.

"Ah," said Cornelius. "That was because the current marquess was a distant cousin to his predecessor. But when the man and his three sons were all killed in a carriage accident, Teign inherited, having—as far as we know—never met his predecessor nor set foot in the house before it became his own."

"We discovered some of the secrets, though, when Allan, Baldwin and I were shut up here the first time," Cornelius explained. "That was when the marquess married his third wife, Isaac's and Jerome's mother. He thought we—and Allan in particular—were too friendly with his bride."

"Too handsome and too close to her own age for him to compete, I imagine," was Thomasina's dry comment.

"It was all in his own mind," said Allan. Irene had made a confidant of him because she feared her husband and was miserable. Allan, who was the same age as his stepmother, felt sorry for the timid lady, and had tried to be kind. It had got him and his full brothers imprisoned in the tower and then exiled to a remote estate in the north of England.

Mrs. Blackmore nodded. "We see in others a reflection of ourselves, my nanny used to say." She went on to ask, "What happened to his third wife? In fact, tell me about all three wives."

"My mother died when I was five, and the twins were three," said Allan. "I have a vague memory of a pretty, sweet-smelling lady with soft skin and a gentle voice."

"I don't remember her at all," Baldwin offered.

Cornelius agreed, adding, "As to how she died, she had a fall on the stairs at the marquess's country seat. Ever since I found that out, I have wondered whether the marquess killed her, but no one has ever suggested that in my hearing, and it is more than thirty years ago, so it is unlikely we shall ever know."

"She was the only child of an earl," said Allan. "The Earl of Arlesley. He died without an heir not long after Cornelius was born. She inherited everything that wasn't entailed, and the title became extinct."

"The marquess married his second wife shortly after our mother's funeral," Allan said. "The lady was kind enough to the three of us, even after her own sons began to arrive. If she was at home with us in the country, we were all taken to see her most evenings, while she was dressing for dinner."

Given how quickly the marquess married his second wife, Mel wondered if the evil man had murdered his first wife to make room. Yes, and perhaps his father-in-law as well, but—as Cornelius had pointed out—more than thirty years had passed. They would probably never know.

"Our second mother always smelt wonderful, and she asked each of us to say what had been the best thing about our day." Cornelius's voice was soft with memory.

"My mother gave birth to a son every two years," said Donald. "I was six when she died of childbirth fever not long after the twins were born. I remember her, but only just. As Allan said, we saw her every evening when she was at home, but if one of the babies cried, we were all sent back to the nursery, even if we had not had our turn to talk to Mama."

"Isaac and I don't remember our mother at all," said Jerome. "Don, you knew her the best."

"Yes, I was ten when she arrived. At first, I was inclined to resent her, because the marquess said he had to send Allan away, since our new mother was only a little bit older, and Allan might bother her. I didn't understand it, then. I only knew that I missed him, for Allan was both father and mother to us, and I missed Baldwin and Cornelius, too, for they were sent away with him."

"But she won you over," Allan commented. "You were heartbroken after she died. You all were." The marquess had sent for his three eldest sons after his third wife died, leaving two sons, one just turned three and one eleven months younger. They had arrived back at the marquess's country estate to find the nursery party in deep mourning.

His five sons by his second wife had had her as their mother for only four years, but she had spent more time with them during those years than any other person had done in their lives.

Of course, the servants hired to care for the children were with them for every hour of the day, but their tenure tended to be short. Allan could not think of a single nanny or nursemaid who'd lasted in the marquess's employ for more than six months.

That would be, in part, because servants were also victims of the marquess's volatile temper and his lusts, and in part because they were neither well paid nor well housed. The marquess persisted in thinking that working for him was reward enough. Given that they mostly went on to better positions on the strength of their time in a marquess's house, he had no problem replacing one hapless skivvy with another.

"How did the third marchioness meet her end?" asked Mrs. Blackmore.

"According to gossip at the time," said Allan, with a glance at Isaac and Jerome, "she died in a carriage accident while running away with a lover."

"It's a lie. She would not have run away without her sons," Donald insisted.

Mrs. Blackmore continued asking questions and making notes in her little book. Allan didn't see how any of this sordid and miserable history would help.

Baldwin said so.

"It will help us to find his enemies," said Mrs. Blackmore, calmly. "It may take time, though, to marshal the resources to stand against him. In the meantime, you need a solution before Lord Kemble, Lord Baldwin, and Lord Ernest are forced into an unwanted marriage."

"We shall refuse all the way to the altar," said Allan, firmly. "Even if the three prospective brides are harpies-in-training, I'll not bring them into the mess that is our family."

"A pity you don't have time to find wives of your own choosing," said Thomasina. "Cornelius cannot be forced to marry by any power under Heaven."

"True," said Baldwin, thoughtfully. "If I were already wed, I could laugh in the marquess's face."

"What gives your father power over you?" asked Mrs. Blackmore. "Money, is it not? And Jerome's age?"

Cornelius spoke up again. "And Isaac's, initially. And the marquess's willingness to interfere when we try to strike out on our own. Mrs. Blackmore, we have all tried to find work that would make us independent of the marquess, but he has stopped us at every turn. Then, when we were imprisoned and found a way out, we had to be careful. We couldn't risk coming to the marquess's attention. Then Ernest told us about the Golden Adonis. What the marquess does not know about, he cannot stop."

"I heard about it from a friend at one of the events his lordship commanded me to attend," Ernest offered.

"We have been able to save a small nest egg," Allan said. "Enough to get Jerome and Isaac out of the country for a while, and to give each of us money to start us somewhere new. The problem is that his lordship won't accept our escape."

Thomasina emitted a huff of contempt. "What can he do?" she demanded. "You are all of age. He cannot demand you return home."

"What he has done before," Mrs. Blackmore explained. "He can make it impossible for them to find employment. Bribery, threats, coercion. Whatever is required to convince an employer to let them go. He will assume that, when they are hungry enough, they will come home."

"Cornelius is coming to France with me to be a vintner," said Thomasina, firmly. "It is a family business in another country, and the marquess can do nothing about it."

"Except discourage your customers," Baldwin grumbled.

Thomasina glared. "Let him dare, and he shall see what Frenchwomen are made of."

"Best to stop him before things go that far," said Mrs. Blackmore.

But in years of thinking about it, his sons had not been able to discover a way to stop him. Allan summarized the situation as it currently stood. "If he can find us, he will make sure our lives are ruined, and the lives of those we care about. So, we shall split our savings and scatter and run, change our identities, hide ourselves away. Some of us will make it."

"Jerome must go," said Mrs. Blackmore. "I quite agree. But what if the rest of you stay? Make targets of yourselves? And put watchers on your father to catch him in illegal acts? For you can be certain he is arrogant enough, entitled enough, to do whatever he pleases, thinking no one will hold him to account. With reason, for nasty things happen to those who stand in his way. Let him try to bully you in full view of Society and, if he is overconfident enough, the law. If it works, you might all be able to live in the open and in peace."

There was silence for a moment, as Allan and his brothers and sister-in-law absorbed what she had said.

Baldwin was the first to speak.

"By Jove's purple stockings, Mrs. Blackmore. That might actually work."

Chapter Ten

F OUR PREACHERS IN black clerical garb were holding some kind of meeting outside the front door of the Golden Adonis. One was preaching in a loud voice, talking about male whores, Sodom and Gomorrah, and the sins of Eve.

The other three were stopping ladies as they arrived, trying to convince them to turn around, to return to their hearths and homes, and their duties to their husbands.

When Mel arrived, she was in time to see the lady in an extravagant nymph mask hit one of the men with her umbrella, and when the other two turned to harangue her, she gave as good as she got. "Worms," she called them. "How dare you attempt to stop me. I shall have you up for disturbing the peace! Can a lady not go out for a quiet evening with a few lady friends without you morbid crows maligning her good name? Appalling!"

Right through her speech, she kept hitting them with her umbrella, even when the preacher approached her with his hand out, saying, "Sister, we mean only to save you."

"Save yourselves," she demanded, fetching him a good whack. "And address me as 'my lady.' I do not have brothers such as you."

Several of the other ladies cheered, and the usual loiterers jeered. Other ladies took up their own umbrellas or fans or, in one case, a shoe, to chase the poor men off.

Mel's sympathies changed sides. She had initially seen the ladies as the victims of a group of judgmental men who wanted to tell women what they could and could not do, and that was part of the truth, though only part. After all, she had read about such displays outside of gambling dens and brothels that served a male clientele.

No doubt there, too, wealth and status won the day. The preachers, unable to fight back, could only flee. Would they be back tomorrow? Or would they stay away and tell their congregations about the wicked women so lost to sin that they even attacked those trying to save their souls?

Hmmm, that's a thought. Was there a way she could harness religious sentiment? Twenty-six bishops sat in the House of Lords. If it came to a trial, they would be a powerful influence on the outcome. Meanwhile, it would not be at all difficult to paint the marquess's deeds in the darkest tones in the eyes of churchgoers and clerics.

Mel had an errand inside the Golden Adonis, and then other plans for the evening. One of the ladies who came maskless to the club was known to have been Teign's mistress several years ago. If the lady would talk to her, she might gain further insight to inform the campaign against the evil marquess.

Later, as she entered the hackney that Lord Kemble had called for her, Mel was thoughtful. She had spent more than an hour with the ex-mistress, who had been reluctant to talk at first. But a promise of complete discretion and the temptation to unburden herself proved a winning combination. The fact that she had arrived at the club already tipsy and had been steadily drinking since she'd arrived undoubtedly helped.

Whether the information that spewed forth in a rambling monologue would prove useful remained to be seen. If nothing else, Mel had the names of the mistress before and the mistress after her informant.

Mel took a deep breath and released it slowly. *Let the infor-*

mation go. See if it makes sense when you write up your notes. The hackney was taking the road to London Bridge, and was heading for the edges of Mayfair, to a townhouse in Primrose Square. She had penned a message to her friend Clementine Satterthwaite before leaving the club early this morning, and a reply had been waiting for her.

Dear friend, I am at home this evening, and would be glad of a visit from you.

The first and most urgent activity once Mel arrived was a trip to the nursery to admire the sleeping children. Clemmie and her husband Chris were blessed with twins who had just turned three years of age, and Clemmie was expecting another blessed event early in the Spring.

The two women then descended to the family parlor. "The children have grown so much since I stayed with you in the summer," Mel commented. She grinned and winked. "As have you, Clemmie. Are you all keeping well?"

Clemmie patted her burgeoning belly. "Very well. And you, Mel? How are you? How is Harriet?"

They talked children for a few minutes, not only Clemmie's twins and Mel's daughter, but also the children that Clem and her husband supported in the school they sponsored.

The two women had first met three years ago, when Mel, in the course of an investigation, joined a discussion group for ladies that met in members' homes once a week. Clemmie was also a new member, and the two of them were drawn together.

Even though Clemmie was wealthy and a young wife in a happy marriage, and Mel was impoverished and a widow, they had a similar outlook on life and many of the same interests. Mel counted Clemmie as one of her closest friends.

"I did not expect you to be in town at this time of year," Mel commented. "I heard someone mention your presence in passing, so I sent my note in the hope that it was true."

"Chris has some business dealings that need his attention," Clemmie explained. "We decided to spend the Christmas season in town so we could all be together. Poor Chris has to face the fog and the slush, but the rest of us can stay at home in the warmth. He is out this evening to meet with potential investors at a ball, so I was particularly pleased to receive your note."

She placed a hand on her belly. "I'm sure you know how London Society expects women in my condition to remain at home. The country is much more accepting of nature and all its ways. Poor Chris. He will be home as soon as he can be, for he doesn't enjoy these events unless I am with him."

"I shall wait with you, if I may," Mel said. "I would like to ask for Chris's help. I have two friends who need to leave the country secretly, without their names appearing on any passenger list, and without any publicity. They can pay for their cabin and passage. I want to know if Chris has an interest in any ships in port that are going to Italy or Greece or somewhere else close enough to return to England with relative ease."

"If he doesn't have such a ship docked in the London Pool or close by, he will know who does, Mel. What is their story? Have they committed a crime? Are they falsely accused?"

Mel had just come here to find out if her idea for removing Isaac and Jerome from danger was realistic. Without their knowledge or permission, she did not want to tell her friends the full story.

"They are being used to coerce some other people I know into acts those people don't want to perform," she replied, vaguely. "If the other people do not comply, these two are beaten unmercifully. One has already been permanently lamed. Since the persecutor is guardian of the younger of the two—though only for another few months until the young man reaches his majority—any attempts to reach out to the law have only resulted in further beatings."

Clemmie accepted the explanation. "How dreadful! My father was just such a man. Determined to have his own way, no matter who was hurt. I am certain Chris can and will help."

And sure enough, when he arrived an hour later, Chris Satterthwaite suggested two ships that might serve the purpose, both due to leave within the week, one from London, and one from Southampton.

"I shall need to speak with my two friends to confirm," Mel told him. "I shall return tomorrow night, if that is acceptable." And tomorrow, she would ask the brothers if she could tell Clemmie and Chris a little bit about the marquess, for the couple had contacts from the highest of high Society to the lowest of the slums, and at every level in between. *Surely, they will have information of use to us?*

"I must say goodnight to the pair of you. Would you be able to send a footman to call me a hackney?" she asked.

"I'll do better," said Chris. "One of our carriages can take you. What is your destination, Mrs. Blackmore?"

"The Golden Adonis in Southwark," Mel told him, watching closely to see how he reacted. Had he heard of the club? Did he know of its reputation?

From their previous interactions, she did not expect him to come over all moralistic and protective, and ban her from the house to keep her from contaminating his wife. His reaction did surprise her, however.

"The Adonis? Say hello to Madam Hera for me. She is one of the ladies who raised me."

What a lucky chance! Though Chris Satterthwaite was closely related to two earls, he had been raised in the slums—by prostitutes at the behest of a gambling den owner, or so rumor said. She had not thought he might know Madam Hera, though.

"Mr. Satterthwaite," Mel said, "what if I wanted Madam Hera to help me find incriminating evidence about a wicked man who is using his power and wealth to terrorize and imprison his own family? Do you think she would be open to that?"

"You would have to ask her," Chris replied. "I cannot speak for her. I can tell you that she values honesty and loyalty. Ladies in her profession see so little of it. You can trust her, Mel. She appreciates strong independent women, and has a very low opinion of men, with few exceptions. Indeed, that is why, when Ramping Billy retired and gave her ownership of her own house, she sold it and started The Golden Adonis."

Ramping Billy had been the power in the slums who had rescued Chris as a child. He had disappeared eighteen months ago. Dead, said some, but if Chris said retired, he probably knew.

"Thank you," she said. "I shall keep that in mind."

⟫⟩✕⟨⟪

THEY HAD THEIR argument in the antechamber of the Golden Adonis after all the guests had left, except for those few who were most closely involved.

It was Allan against his brothers.

"It makes sense," Cornelius insisted. "You said yourself that my marriage means the marquess cannot force me into a match that suits him. If it applies to me, it applies to Baldwin, Donald, Ernest, Frank and Hudson. Gerard is well on the way to finding a bride, and you should, too."

"I'm marrying Clara," Baldwin said. "You have no say in it, Allan."

Allan couldn't believe his ears. "Marriage is a lifetime commitment, and you're talking about using it just to stop our father? With some lady who frequents a place like the Golden Adonis? Who has been using you for a cheap thrill?"

"Watch your tongue or I'll shut your mouth for you," Baldwin snapped. "Clara and I love each other. Yes, and the same goes for the rest of us."

"Our ladies might be unconventional," said Frank, "but that is the very reason they suit us. Allan, we might be rushing things to take away one of the threats against us, but we have all been courting our ladies. This is where we were heading anyway, but we believed it to be hopeless, since we were leaving."

"That's right," Donald agreed. "Then yesterday, Mrs. Blackmore started talking about marriage protecting Cornelius, and about staying in London. Verity and I have been seeing one another for nearly a year, and she has stood by me even though I told her about the marquess, and about having to leave. Then, tonight, when she heard we might stay, she said she would marry me right away. Today, if possible. I am going to the Bishop of London to ask for a license whether the others do or not."

"It is the same for me and Rosina," said Ernest. Rosina was Thalia, but apparently, she was also the daughter of a country gentleman who had been working to look after her sick mother. There was no mismatch between her and Ernest. Allan couldn't use that as an excuse.

"And for me and Parthena," Hudson insisted. "Be happy for us, Allan. We have grown to know our ladies over the last few months. We have chosen them, and they have chosen us."

Allan clenched his fist, and Mrs. Blackmore slid a hand into his elbow and gave it a gentle squeeze. "I imagine your brothers have spent more time with their chosen brides than I did with my louse of a husband," she said to him, thoughtfully.

Whether it was her touch or her words, the black edges of his temper receded and he began to think clearly again. And she wasn't wrong. He had danced with Alberta three times and sat beside her at dinner once—the sum total of their interactions until they met in front of the altar.

In recent months, his brothers had been spending hours seven nights of most weeks with the women they wanted to wed. "You are determined on this?" he asked, addressing the question to the five of them.

They chorused various versions of "yes" and "I am", and Allan nodded.

"Then go and see the bishop. I wish you all well. Please let me know the times of the weddings, so I can come to witness."

They lined up to shake his hand, and Ernest even gave him a hug.

The ladies his brothers wanted to wed were all waiting on the other side of the room. Three of them had carriages here, which between them would convey the party to the residence of the Bishop of London to purchase a common license per couple.

As they filed out of the club, Madam Hera emerged from the parlor. "Apollo, a word, please." She had removed her mask, but her expression was another concealment—an implacable facade that gave nothing away.

It suddenly crossed Allan's mind that he'd been concerned about the wrong thing. His brothers were old enough to make their own choices, but they'd just removed five escorts, two female staff members and three clients from the Golden Adonis in one swoop. Six escorts and four clients, in fact, with Cornelius. And the other four brothers would be leaving soon anyway.

Madam Hera had every right to be annoyed.

Mrs. Blackmore had not released his arm, and now she spoke up. "Madam Hera, I visited this evening with my friend Mrs. Christopher Satterthwaite. Her husband asked me to give you his regards. He said you are a woman who values honesty and integrity, and that I and my friends can trust you."

The woman's implacable face softened. "How are the dear children?" she asked.

"Clemmie says they are well. They were asleep when I saw them. She says the next one is due in the Spring."

With a wistful smile, Madam Hera said, "Dear little ones. I helped to raise Chris. I suppose he told you that? Foolish boy. Do you think less of him, Lady Mnema?"

"I'm Melody Blackmore, since we are here unmasked," said Mrs. Blackmore. "Allan, trust her. If she knows what you and your brothers are up against, she might be able to help. She has sources of information of which you and I can only dream."

"Melody Blackmore, the lady snoop," said Madam Hera, with narrowed eyes.

"I prefer the term *investigator*," Mrs. Blackmore replied calmly, her own eyes amused.

"Hmm." Madam Hera looked from one of them to the other

then gave a decisive nod. "Come through to my office."

With an inclination of his head, Allan gestured for the four brothers who remained to come along, and he and Mrs. Blackmore followed Madam Hera. He would trust Mrs. Blackmore again. Indeed, Madam Hera had been more than fair to him and his brothers since they first came to her back door, looking for work. It was time to let her know who her employees were, and what risks she might be taking if she continued to support them.

Madam Hera's refined accent did not survive the brothers' revelations. "You mean to tell me the Marquess of Bleeding Teign is your Pa!" she demanded. "That bastard. Crippled one of my girls, 'e did. I banned 'im, and 'e came back the next day wiv a band of bullies and broke up my place. Billy taught 'im what for, though."

Her reminiscent smile gave Allan a shiver down his spine. Just so, he imagined, the knitting women who witnessed the deaths of French aristocrats smiled as they remembered the guillotine.

"He has been no kind of father to us," Allan told her. "We have been his victims, as have our mothers, our nannies, and our wives. He crippled two of my brothers, too."

"Lord Kemble and his brothers want to stop him, once and for all," said Mrs. Blackmore. "Not just for their own sakes, so they can live in freedom, but for all of his past victims, and especially for those who will be hurt by him in the future if we do not clip his wings and shackle his ankles."

"I see," said Madam Hera, her aristocratic tones firmly back in place. "I agree. He's a vile man. But why should I help you? You are about to decimate my business, removing my best workers and at least half a dozen of my clients."

"Because you hate men who bully others," said Mrs. Blackmore, "and because those of your employees and clients who marry into the Sheppard family will praise the Golden Adonis to their friends."

Allan put his hand up to his mouth to hide his smile. Once again, Mrs. Blackmore proved she had a nimble mind and a clever tongue. It worked, too, even though Madam Hera grumbled, "You think you are smart, Mrs. Blackmore. Away with your cozening. Very well, Lord Kemble. I shall trade a favor for a favor."

Chapter Eleven

MEL ARRIVED BACK at the tower long after their usual time and with a diminished group of brothers. Not only had the five would-be grooms not returned, Cornelius had returned to Spitalfields and his wife and child.

"We shall sleep, and then talk," Lord Kemble decreed. Since Mel could barely keep her eyes open, she didn't argue.

She only had a couple of hours sleep before Kemble was there, shaking her awake.

"You just missed a visit from Baldwin," he said. "He called to say they have the licenses from the Bishop of London and the weddings are to be all together, at St Margaret's. I woke you because I thought you might wish to attend, Mrs. Blackmore."

Mel sat up, clutching the sheet to her chest with one hand. "Yes. I'd like to."

"Get ready then," he said, and handed her a cup of coffee, made just the way she liked it. She sipped it as she set out a clean petticoat, other underthings, and her walking dress, and finished it as she fetched the jug of hot water someone—Kemble, she would lay odds—had set at her door.

He is far too fond of being in charge, but gestures like this are second nature to him. Even his habit of barking commands, annoying though it might be, was an aspect of his urge to look after those he perceived to be under his care.

Everything she put out to wear was designed to lace, hook or button at the side or the front, and she was soon washed and dressed. With her shoes on, and her bonnet and gloves in her hand, she was downstairs within twenty minutes of waking.

"A piece of toast to keep you going until the wedding breakfast?" asked Isaac. Looking smart in formal day dress, with an immaculately tied cravat, he was juggling a couple of toasting forks before the fire. "Jerome will be out in a minute, Allan is fetching something, and Gerard has gone ahead to procure a hackney."

Mel had only had time for a few bites when Jerome emerged, already wearing an outer coat and a muffler, and carrying his hat.

"Ready, Mrs. Blackmore?" he asked, accepting one of Isaac's slices of toast on his way to the hidden door. "Let's go."

Isaac was pulling on his own coat, and Mel dusted the crumbs of her fingers to do likewise. She tied on her bonnet even as she made for the door.

They had made it down a full circle of the spiral staircase to the first landing when a wall swung open, and someone stepped out. Mel, her eyes adjusting to the sudden light from behind the newcomer, managed to keep her startled reaction from showing. It was Kemble, of course, coming in from one of the lower rooms on the tower. So, they were still accessible, after all. Of course. This staircase was probably once the main way up and down the tower, before the top of it was hidden in the corner of the dining alcove, and probably those priests Kemble had mentioned yesterday had used the tunnels to come and go from the lower tower.

"I've selected five rings from the family jewelry stored in the lower tower," Kemble said. "Come." And he hurried down the steps ahead of them all. Just as well, for if he hadn't been ahead of them, Mel would have walked right past the side tunnel into which he turned. Did he have a key to the gate?

But no, it was unlocked, and Gerard—who stood on the other

side of it—locked it behind them as soon as they were all through.

"The hackney is waiting," Gerard said, and sure enough, it was at the entry into the slightly wider street this alley met a dozen paces from the gate. It was cramped with five of them inside, but the driver must have recently cleaned it, for it did not have an overwhelming smell of poverty, perspiration, and piss, like so many.

Even so, Kemble had thought ahead and put a blanket he had been carrying over his arm down on the seat to protect her gown. He really was very thoughtful.

London's traffic was not yet at its peak. The morning deliveries were over and the upper classes had not yet begun their rounds of shopping, calls, and other outings. Nonetheless, it was busy enough that progress was slow.

"We could have walked just as fast," Kemble commented. Had he read Mel's thoughts? Probably. His amused smile hinted as much. "But this way, we are less likely to be seen and recognized. I do not want word of today's business to reach my father before we have Isaac and Jerome safely away."

About that! She had not yet had the chance to share the information about shipping. "I went to see the Satterthwaites last night because I know Christopher Satterthwaite has interests in shipping," she said.

"Can he find us a berth?" Jerome asked, eagerly. "When do we leave?"

"Where are we going?" Isaac inquired. "Do we have a choice?"

"To leave within the next few days, he suggests one of two ships. One in which he has a seventy-five percent share is leaving from Southampton in two days, bound initially for Gibraltar and then on through the Mediterranean to Egypt."

"Egypt," said Isaac, reverently.

"The other belongs to Kopet Dag Shipping, and is in the Pool of London. It sails on tomorrow's tide, and is bound for Venice, which is the home port of the Kopet Dag fleet. Mr. Satterthwaite is close friends with Lord Alexander Winderfield, whose brother is the head of Kopet Dag, and he is sure that the owner's cabin could be made available to you."

"Tomorrow!" Kemble made the word sound tragic, as if she had announced the sudden destruction of London by fire. He collected himself, and added, "Tomorrow is safer, and the distance to the Pool of London shorter. If Lord Alexander is able to arrange it, that would be the best ship."

"Venice would be very interesting," Jerome said to Isaac. "And once we are there, perhaps we can go on to Egypt."

"That is true," Isaac acknowledged. "And I am tired of never seeing daylight. Also, Italy is famous for its singers. Perhaps we shall be able to attend the opera."

The smile that trembled on Kemble's lips was a brave effort. "I daresay you shall enjoy your Grand Tour, my dear brothers. I only wish I had time to find an experienced man to be your guide. Mrs. Blackmore, we are in your debt again. May we rely on you to make the arrangements with Mr. Satterthwaite? We shall, of course, pay the cost of passage."

He really is a dear man. Mel nodded. "I shall visit the Satterthwaites after the wedding," she said.

The hackney stopped in front of the church and they descended, the men all being careful to wrap their mufflers around their mouths. They were just in time. Four of the couples were already waiting in the church porch, and the fifth couple's carriage drew up just as their hackney rolled away.

The wedding was a joint ceremony for all five couples, with few witnesses beyond the other brothers, Madam Hera, and one of the Golden Adonis's maids, the one who used the name Aedas.

When the service reached the point where each groom in turn was to make his vows while placing a ring on his bride's finger, Kemble came to each couple to present a gold ring, and shortly after that, the minister pronounced them all husband and wife.

The five couples signed the register, with Kemble and Mel as their witnesses, and they all shook hands with the minister. Kemble gave him an envelope. "A small token of our appreciation, sir," he said. "You understand, I believe, that this matter must be held in confidence for the next week."

"Yes, my lord," replied the minister. "Yes, indeed."

Distracted by this interaction, Mel suddenly realized that Gerard had been in intense conversation with Aedas. He now approached the minister. "Will you be available at half past seven tomorrow morning for a sixth wedding? My betrothed and I would like my brothers to attend, and two of them are leaving London later that morning."

"Gerard!" Kemble exclaimed.

"Amber, have you met my brother Allan?" Gerard said to the woman on his arm. "Allan, you may remember Miss Amber Spense, the daughter of our next-door neighbor at the Teign estate in Essex."

It was a rare delight to see Kemble, who prided himself on being always in control, so flummoxed that his jaw dropped. He collected himself rapidly, however. "Miss Spense? The Miss Spense the marquess arranged for you to marry two years ago? The one who ran?"

"Gerard and I arranged for me to disappear," said Miss Spense, looking pleased with herself. "I found work with Madam Hera. Imagine my delight when Gerard began working at the Golden Adonis." She hugged Gerard's arm and looked up into his eyes as he gazed back, both with that look of poleaxed pleasure that she had seen on the other couples around her.

Mel refused to countenance the twinge of jealousy, and chose to embrace pleasure in their obvious happiness, instead. "How wonderful you can now be free to marry," she said.

"My lord," said the minister. "If you can acquire a license by tomorrow, I should be happy to perform the ceremony."

HER FRIEND WINIFRED, now Lady Francis, insisted on taking Mrs. Blackmore to visit the Satterthwaites. "Yes, Lord Kemble," she assured Allan. "I shall have the carriage drop Frank and myself at our home, and return to convey Mrs. Blackmore wherever she pleases."

"I shall return to the tower as soon as I know the details of the arrangement," Mrs. Blackmore told him, and Allan had to be satisfied with that.

"Here is the key to the door from which I emerged earlier," he said. "We'll be in there."

She took it and smiled.

I would do a great deal for one of Mrs. Blackmore's smiles. Allan squelched the fleeting thought as she disappeared into Lady Francis's carriage, the footman closed the door, and the carriage drew away.

It was just the plethora of weddings that was turning his mind in such a direction. He'd been married once, and it was a disaster. In any case, despite his brothers' determination to defy fate and the marquess, he had no intention of bringing anyone else into the chaos that was their family.

Gerard was off to speak to the bishop, and would then return to the Golden Adonis to be with his intended bride. Most of Allan's other brothers had wives to return home with. "Come along, younglings," Allan said to Isaac and Jerome. "Let's go to the lower tower. There are several trunks lying around, and I'm sure we can find more items that will be useful for you in your travels."

And Allan would take a look at the space available, and choose a room to stay in. It would save money to remain in the tower, and if he stayed in the lower rooms, behind the hidden door to the tower steps and with the hidden door to the top two floors locked and bolted, he'd be perfectly safe.

In fact, it would be remarkably satisfying to be on the marquess's land but out of his reach.

By the time Melody joined the three remaining brothers, they had retrieved the luggage the youngest two would need—two large trunks to go in with the cargo and two cabin trunks that were fitted with drawers and partitions to carry what they needed for the trip and to be used as cabin furniture. A third smaller trunk was large enough to take a traveling desk so the brothers could write home and also the cases with Jerome's violin and Isaac's flute.

Allan had found each brother a money belt to carry the bank notes he intended to fetch on the way to the wharf. Although the savings account holding the brothers' earnings was at a bank the marquess didn't use and under a name the marquess would not recognize, there was no point in taking chances.

The detritus that had ended up in these unused rooms also included several travel shaving sets and some maps of countries around the Mediterranean. Isaac and Jerome were making their choices when Mrs. Blackmore arrived.

"We're just about to take these upstairs," Allan said. "My brothers will soon be packed and ready to go." He forced a smile. "What an adventure for them."

"I am sorry I was away so long," Mrs. Blackmore said, "but it is all arranged. You will need to go to the docks directly from the church tomorrow. You are sailing at ten in the morning on the Jamshid."

It was really happening. Allan's face was going to crack if he had to keep on smiling. "Let's get these trunks to your rooms, then try to get some sleep. We're still expected to work tonight, according to our agreement with Madam Hera."

Of course, he didn't expect Isaac and Jerome, excited as they were, to manage even a doze. He certainly didn't. His mind teemed with all the things that could go wrong, both before his youngest brothers embarked on their journey, and once the ship left London. A long sea voyage in winter, a foreign land where they did not speak the language, thieves, rogues, pirates, diseases.

Perhaps Mrs. Blackmore was able to rest her lovely head on her pillow and drift off into the arms of Morpheus, but Allan spent more than an hour tossing and turning in a bed that felt more and more uncomfortable by the minute until finally he gave up.

He must have been the only one haunted by visions of disaster, for the other bed chamber doors were firmly shut. Perhaps he should move his personal possessions down to the lower tower.

Other items, too. The brothers had long since chosen furniture, as well as mattresses and pillows, from the lower rooms to furnish the two levels the marquess knew about. Most of it could stay where it was, but there were a few items he'd like to keep secure from any rampage his lordship might instigate when he found them missing.

The living area he and his brothers had shared for so long looked strangely empty, though Allan tried to tell himself that it was the same every time the marquess's henchmen visited, and the brothers cleared away anything they didn't want the men to see. He could not convince himself.

Most of the brothers had removed their bits and pieces from the main room before they went to work last night. Allan had noticed but had thought nothing of it. Only when they had spoken to their respective brides did they drop their collective bombshell, but they must have been sure of the answer, for when he looked into their rooms, each of them had taken down any artwork from the walls or items from their shelves or drawers, packed a trunk or a box, and even stripped their bedclothes.

Zero, discomposed by the kerfuffle, had taken refuge on the wardrobe in Donald's chamber. Allan hoped that Donald would be able to catch him when he returned to collect the rest of his things.

Frank's chess set was no longer set up near their usual chairs. Cornelius had already moved all his personal possessions to the home of his aunts-in-law.

The travelers must have finished packing their own items, or at least taken them into their rooms, for the violin and flute were both gone, the harpsichord was shut in its box, and the box that held their sheet music had also disappeared.

Allan was going to be alone. So alone.

He couldn't stand the gibbering wreck he wanted to turn into. *You will have your daughter and your brother-in-law,* he told himself sternly. Not yet, though. He could not risk the marquess finding them. The plan called for him and those brothers who remained in London to take their battle with the old tyrant into the public eye, and the evil bastard would not hesitate to use Lydia as a weapon against Allan.

At least the eight of them would spend much of their time together—even Cornelius was determined to remain for the fight. His wife and her aunts agreed, Cornelius said. In fact, all the wives were indignant for their husbands' sake, and determined to help.

As long as Allan could keep them out of the line of fire. Mrs. Blackmore thought the public nature of their planned offensive would be some sort of protection. Allan could not quite believe it.

If only he could talk Mrs. Blackmore out of being involved, but she argued that the fight was hers, too. That those close to her had suffered at the marquess's hands. That her cousin's long separation from Cornelius could be directly attributed to his wickedness.

She was correct. And if she was determined to oppose the man, surely she was safer doing so as part of his team. He shuddered to think of the risks she had taken, facing him alone, protected only by her disguise, her charm, and her subtle threats.

You could protect her even better if you married her. It was not the first time the thought had occurred to him. *Melody.* Even her name was appealing.

She won't have me. While other women might chase him for his family and their fortune, Mrs. Blackmore—he was convinced—did not care about such things.

She, more than anyone, does not care about my empty rank, and she has every reason to hate my future title as much as I do.

As for Allan, the man, he was confident that Mrs. Blackmore

was not impressed by him. If anything, he annoyed her, though she schooled even that reaction in order to reach her goals. Except that, now and then, he had seen a spark of very female interest—eyes that lingered, a slight flush, a huskiness in the voice. Could he…

He gazed down at the floor, imagining he could see through it to her door, and beyond the door to the bed upon which Mrs. Blackmore currently slept, curled around herself, snuggled into her pillow and her blankets as he had seen her this morning.

He whispered a question that expressed both his objective and his new plan. Could he *seduce* Mrs. Blackmore into being his wife?

Chapter Twelve

ONCE AGAIN, MEL spent the night at the Golden Adonis, moving from room to room and group to group. This time, she was not there to listen, but to speak.

The members of the club were wealthy women whose independence came from their control over their own finances. Or over the men who controlled their finances. Many of them were wives, sisters, daughters, mothers, cousins and other relatives of England's most powerful families.

They were the ideal audience for the rumor she wanted to spread—that those in the Burlington Arcade at the fashionable hour tomorrow afternoon would be the first to know a particularly juicy item of gossip. "No, no. I was told in the strictest confidence. I could not possibly disclose details." At this point, she always lowered her voice. "But it involves several high-profile marriages, a deep rift in one of England's most prominent families, and a brewing scandal of the most appalling nature. I would not miss the occasion for any reason in the world."

Meanwhile, the brothers were all hinting at the same thing.

Before the night was half over, she began to hear new versions of the story, developed and expanded by people's imagination. The Deerhavens were planning to divorce. Or the Dellboroughs. Or the Stancrofts. The Versey family was feuding, two brothers siding against the other two. Or the Forsythes. Or the Redepennings.

One person even speculated that the little Haverford infant had been purchased in an orphanage and smuggled into the birthing room. Another was certain the prominent family in question was the royal family itself, although those rifts were so well known that her listeners assured the gossiper that could not possibly be the solution.

She was constantly aware of Lord Kemble. *Lord Apollo*, as he was known here at the club. A room changed when he entered it. Even if she was not looking in his direction, something in her recognized his presence, as if her body was tuned to his and vibrated at a tone outside of human hearing.

They had argued this afternoon. He had wanted her to move back home, and she had argued that it was too dangerous. She could not bring the wrath of the marquess down on her daughter or her sister and nephew.

"You cannot stay with me in the tower," he had insisted. "A woman living alone with an unrelated man? It is not proper. If anyone knew, it would destroy your reputation."

He wasn't wrong, but who was to know? Only his brothers, and they would not gossip. "I could, perhaps, rent a room," she had conceded.

She had expected him to object on grounds of safety, and she was not disappointed. "You might as well paint a bullseye on your back and stand in front of the marquess," he had scoffed. His solution was that she went to live with one of his brothers, preferably Cornelius, since Cornelius's wife was her cousin.

"They are newly reunited," she had objected. "Besides, their place in Spitalfields is tiny. And the others are newly-wed, and do not need a third party disturbing the early days of their marriage. The tower is convenient, it is safe, and it is free. And I am confident that I can trust you, Lord Kemble."

At that, he had turned away muttering. Even with her sharp hearing, she'd had to strain to pick up the words. "Not if you give me the least bit of encouragement, you cannot."

Excellent. Exactly what she was counting on.

She had been married for three years and widowed for seven. Marital intimacies had been a disagreeable chore, and she did not miss them. Since her husband's death, she'd discovered that other women found them pleasant—some said incredible, but she dismissed that as hyperbole.

Pleasant, though, she could believe. Otherwise, why would the Golden Adonis have private rooms? Not that she wanted to purchase the opportunity to share what was possible between a man and a woman. After all, looked at in one way, her marriage had been just such a cold-blooded transaction, her husband having the use of her body in return for the cost of her food and lodging.

She would not use another human being in such a way.

If Lord Kemble was willing though… Indeed, she could not imagine wanting anyone else. She trusted him—that, she thought, was at the core of her decision. Her desire for him, which she had at first found inconvenient, now struck her as a happy chance. But without trust, she would not have contemplated moving forward.

That afternoon—yesterday afternoon now, for it was well after midnight—they had set up bedrooms for themselves downstairs, and relocated their personal effects. When the Golden Adonis closed in the morning, the brothers were going to return to the upper tower and finish moving out.

After Gerard's wedding, the departure of the travelers, and the spectacle at the Burlington Arcade, she and Lord Kemble would return to the lower tower. The pair of them would be alone, for even the cat—after a brief struggle and much hissing and protest—had gone to join his owner in his new accommodations. It would be just the two of them. In the coming days, surely she would have the opportunity to make memories to take out and enjoy in her dwindling years.

THE BURLINGTON ARCADE was an exclusive shopping arcade. It had been built on the corner of his land by the Earl of Burlington, at least in part to mask his mansion and grounds from being overlooked by neighbors, who—or so it was said—were guilty of disposing of their rubbish by throwing it over his wall.

Be that as it may, the arcade was very new, very fashionable, and quite exclusive. It had its own force of beadles to keep out pickpockets and prostitutes, and maintain the atmosphere that drew those with money to spend to more than fifty single or double-width shops selling products such as hats, gloves, shoes, jewelry, lace, umbrellas, shawls, books, and music.

On entering through one of the three arched entrances at each end, a shopper found themselves in a long promenade lit from above by glazed roof lights, with ground-floor shops along both sides. The upper floor held residences and more shops, accessed by spiral stairs.

On the afternoon of the thirtieth day of December, though the weather was dreadful, the arcade was packed, with business booming in every shop, and conversation humming as those who came to see and be seen waited for the promised juicy story to unfold.

Mel had come early, on Lord Kemble's arm. He intended to have his own moment at center stage. Today, if they chanced to encounter the family of his father's bride for him. But the first act was to be the appearance of Cornelius and Thomasina.

Here they came, arm in arm, Cornelius holding the hand of a boy who looked much like he must have done when he was a child. The three aunts were there, too, an essential part of the scene, all dressed with that indefinable flair that marked French fashion. No one would know they had spent the last three decades working the vines and processing the grapes alongside their workers.

From the door of the bookshop, Mel saw Cornelius stop an acquaintance and introduce his wife, her aunts, and his son. The gentleman, in his turn, introduced the ladies with him. A mother, perhaps, and either a wife or a sister.

It could not have been the first such encounter, for the gossip had outrun the strolling family group, and all around her, Mel could hear people explaining to others that Lord Cornelius Sheppard, third son of the Marquess of Teign, had reunited with Lady Cornelius, and that the boy was their son.

"So, she isn't dead, after all," said one lady.

"I daresay she ran away from Teign," said another. "Horrid man. Everyone knows he chases every attractive female that comes within his orbit. Perhaps he tried it with Lady Cornelius."

From the Burlington Gardens' end of the arcade came the principals of the second scene of their little play—Lord and Lady Francis, Lord and Lady Gerard, and Lord and Lady Hudson, all still dressed in the garments they had worn for Gerard's and Amber's wedding.

Allan had suggested that today's newly-weds need not be part of the display, but the couple had insisted on joining what they called "the fun."

The brothers had been locked up since Thomasina's escape, so few realized who they were, until Cornelius saw them, and called out, "Well met, brothers and sisters."

Cornelius introduced the newly arrived group to the people he had been talking with, and once again, the buzz of conversation spread along the arcade as everyone expressed an opinion about where these three Sheppard brothers had been, when they had married, and what their appearance today presaged.

"It cannot have been long," said a lady who was standing near Mel and Kemble. "I know Winifred and Parthena. Their families were still trying to puff them off only last week.

"What is happening now?" asked another of their group, as there was a stir further up the arcade, in the direction of Piccadilly Street. She poked her escort, who responded by craning his neck as if that would give him the extra height needed to peer over the sea of tall hats and bonnets.

Once again, the murmurs arrived before the center of the disturbance. "It is three more Sheppard brothers, with ladies on their arms. One is Lord Baldwin, and the lady he is escorting is certainly *not* his betrothed."

"Lord Baldwin is with Mrs. Wickham, and Lady Verity Querrendale is with Lord Donald. I don't know who the lady is with Lord Ernest, but it is not the lady he is meant to be marrying next week."

"Did I not see the brides shopping here today, with their mothers?"

Mel grinned. She had spoken to Ernest's would-be mother-in-law herself, last night in the club. It was a bonus to hook all three mothers and their daughters with the same worm.

Perhaps news of the happenings in the hall reached into the recesses of the shops, for the crowd outside was growing, and among the new arrivals were the very ladies who most needed to hear the news of two of those weddings.

By some lucky chance, they were in the glover's, just opposite where the couples had stopped to exchange greetings. Act Two of the play was about to begin.

Baldwin's would-be mother-in-law glared at Clara on Baldwin's arm, muttered to her daughter, and attempted to march past with her nose in the air, and the other two mothers would have followed her lead.

However, the brothers and their ladies hadn't staged this display just to let these three go.

"Good day to you," said Baldwin, pitching his voice to be heard. "Lady Baldwin, may I make known to you these ladies, particularly Lady Atkinson, whom I have mentioned to you? With her husband, she joined Teign in attempting to bully me into marrying her daughter." He lifted his wife's hand to his lips and kissed it. "Fortunately, dearest, bigamy is against the law, so you have made me safe."

He sketched a mocking bow in the direction of the six ladies, all of whom stood gaping in his direction. "Please note, Lady Atkinson, I did not court your daughter. I did not propose. In fact, I did everything I safely could to discourage the marriage. I did not sign any agreement. If you object to my marrying someone else, I suggest you take it up with Teign."

Lady Atkinson shut her mouth, gave a decisive nod, and said, "We shall see about that. We are going to tell Lord Atkinson about this."

"Lord Ernest," said another of the mothers. "What do you have to say for yourself?"

"My brother has said it all, Lady Farringford-Smyth," said Ernest. He then deviated from the script. "Teign kept us imprisoned by threatening injury to our brothers. We have escaped his clutches, and will no longer do his will."

The hum of conversation became a thunder, and Mel could not hear what he said next, but he, like Baldwin, kissed his wife's hand. It was probably what they agreed. "I have chosen my own bride. Lady Ernest has made me the happiest of men."

The crowd had self-modulated, realizing that their own noise meant they were missing lines of dialogue, and Mel caught Ernest's next comment, again unscripted. He bowed to the daughter, saying, "I am sorry you have been inconvenienced, Miss Farringford-Smythe. The choices we brothers have made should not reflect badly on you or your friends. You were no more than a victim of Teign's machinations. If you knew all, you would be thanking all the powers that be for your lucky escape."

The third mother had been looking around, and had caught sight of Kemble. "Lord Kemble," she trumpeted, and surged toward him, drawing her daughter in her wake. "Lord Kemble, I suppose you are going to tell me that you, too, have married."

She looked Mel up and down with eyes that spat contempt. Had she the power, Mel felt, she would have burnt Mel to ashes where she stood.

"Mrs. Blackmore has not yet done me the honor of accepting

a proposal from me, Lady Spurfold. That, however, is not the reason I am refusing to wed your daughter. I was being forced into marriage by threats to my youngest brother. He is now on his way overseas, and will no longer be under our father's malignant guardianship by the time he returns to England."

He inclined in a shallow bow. "Be grateful. Coercion is grounds for annulment, which would have been far more embarrassing for your daughter than having me repudiate the agreement you made with Teign."

"Come along, Felicia," said Lady Farringford-Smyth. "We shall see about this. Lord Baldwin, we and our husbands shall be calling on Lord Teign."

The six of them, mothers and daughters, hurried off along the arcade, brushing off questions and comments from the bystanders.

"A flock of silly geese," said Kemble, with no sympathy at all. "They thought Teign would be their golden egg, but they should not have treated us as if we were of no account. Time for Act Three of our little drama."

The rest of the brothers and their wives approached. As organized earlier, a beadle hurried up with a wooden box. Kemble stepped out from the bookshop doorway, and climbed up on the box.

The brothers gathered around him, their wives on their arms. The audience stilled, waiting to find out what was about to happen.

"Ladies and gentlemen," Kemble said loudly. "The Sheppard brothers are no longer subject to Teign's tyranny, and he will no longer be deciding our social calendar, nor threatening our younger brothers to gain our compliance. Should you care to send invitations to any of us—my brothers, myself, our ladies— my sisters-in-law, Lady Baldwin and Lady Donald, have agreed to receive our mail. Thank you all for your attention."

He stepped down, and offered his arm to Mel. *Finis,* he said.

It was not, in fact, quite the end. Continuing Kemble's play analogy, Mel supposed she could compare the walk to a series of encores, as people claimed an acquaintance with one of the brothers, or one of their wives, and presumed on it to ask questions or offer an invitation to call.

They kept walking however, claiming another pressing engagement, which was true enough, for they all wanted to be somewhere else by the time Teign learned what had happened here this afternoon.

The people that Clara had hired—bodyguards from a firm called Moriarty Protection—closed around them as they left the arcade, and saw them to their carriages. The agency had assigned a team to each couple. One team followed Mel and Kemble when Winifred's carriage dropped them at the mouth of the alley that contained the gate to the tunnel.

"We shall be safe from here," Mel told them. "But I should like to reassign you, with Lord Kemble's permission, to guard my daughter, sister, and nephew."

"We could put another team on them, Mrs. Blackmore," said the senior of the two bodyguards.

"I need a team on my daughter and brother-in-law," said Kemble. "If Teign finds them, he will use them against me. But I agree that Mrs. Blackmore's family are also at risk. Talk to your employer and arrange for both addresses to be covered. As for Mrs. Blackmore and me, we are heading for our beds. We won't need guards until at least noon tomorrow, and can meet them here. I'll cover any extra costs."

The bodyguard peered at him with narrowed eyes and then nodded. "If I can have those addresses then, my lord, ma'am."

Mel felt in her reticule for a notebook and pencil. "I shall write a note for my sister, and put the address on it," she said.

"A good idea," Kemble approved. "If you would be so good as to spare me a sheet of your paper, I shall do likewise."

It took only a couple of minutes. Soon, the bodyguards had gone and Mel and Kemble were locked inside the gate and on their way down the tunnel and up the stairs.

✦

Chapter Thirteen

MEL WOKE UP in a warm cocoon of blankets, but when she ventured to get up, the cold beating in from the narrow windows hit her like a blow. The other rooms would be no warmer. There was no closed stove to warm any of the three lower levels, and Kemble had decreed they could not light any fires because the smoke would give away that someone was living in the tower.

She shrank back into the blankets, but it wouldn't do. Like it or not, she needed to get up. They had promised Madam Hera two more nights at the Golden Adonis, rather than leave her short staffed. Kemble would be handing over his responsibilities to his assistant. Rosina had already done the same with her manager duties, but Mel had promised to support the new Madam Thalia until after tomorrow night's New Year's Eve celebrations.

Mel grabbed her underthings and retreated back under the blankets until she was clad in at least her warmest stockings, her stays, and two layers of petticoats. As quickly as possible in the icy room, she put on her gown and walking boots, and wrapped herself in a shawl before venturing out into this level's sitting room.

It was not any warmer than the bedchamber, but her temper-

128

ature went up just seeing Kemble. The atmosphere between them was very different when the two of them were the only ones in the tower. Or perhaps it was just that she had decided to act on the attraction she had always felt for him. Perhaps it was that she had previously seen him as a possible enemy and then as an ally, and now she was viewing him as a potential lover.

She smiled at him, wondering how he would react if she put her cup down and asked him to take her to bed. Was she imagining the hint of wickedness in Kemble's return smile?

How did one seduce a man? She had spent her entire adult life—not excluding the three years of her marriage—trying to discourage male attention. She had no idea how to reverse course.

A series of rhythmic thumping sounds came from overhead.

"What is that noise?" she asked.

"I believe the marquess has heard that we have escaped, and his men are attempting to break into the tower." Kemble sounded very calm about it. "I heard the bell, and then shouting. I think they have given up and are taking an axe to the door. It is double layered, with the inner planks at right angles to the outer ones, so it is going to take them a while to chop through."

The pair of them had slept on the same level of the tower. Kemble had chosen a bedchamber on the same side as the bridge from the mansion, whereas Mel's room was on the other side, with several thick stone walls and a stone floor between her and the antechamber from which the sound came.

"I should like to have been a fly on the wall when the marquess was told about our performance in the Burlington Arcade," said Kemble.

"The plan is that none of us will fall into his hands until we have enough attention on us that touching us will be dangerous," Mel reminded him.

"I am well aware. At least Isaac and Jerome are now out of his reach. They must be down the Thames and out into the North Sea by now, heading for the open Atlantic."

"Tonight, I intend to hint that your youngest brothers are on their way to Liverpool, to take ship for the Americas," said Mel.

"Mrs. Blackmore," said Kemble, grinning, "I love how your mind works."

At least he loved something about her. In the recesses of her mind, she heard her parents' voices, her governess's, her husband's. *Melody, I do not understand. How can anyone think the way you do? The way your brain twists and turns. It is unnatural.*

"Misdirection will be useful in this case, Lord Kemble," she explained.

"Yes, I agree, and call me Allan," he invited, and then bent to pleading. "Would you? When it is only you and me?"

"Call me Mel, then," she said, suddenly shy. Which she had never been in her life. "Allan," she added.

"Not Melody? Such a pretty name."

"My sister is Harmony," Mel confided. "Her name suits her. She is a person who makes life easier for those around her. I have never felt that my name fitted at all. I am not musical, and I am more inclined to chaos than to sweet music."

"Have people told you that?" Allan asked. "If so, they are idiots. From what I understand, you have spent the past few years of your life solving problems and serving justice. Melodies are not always simple or sweet. But they are satisfying to the soul."

Is Allan flirting with me? If so, Mel liked it. "Thank you. I think."

He changed the subject. "Melody, let's put on our warmest coats and go out for a bite of dinner at the nearest cook shop."

⫸⫷

MRS. BLACKMORE—MELODY—WAS DIFFERENT today. Warmer. Softer somehow. Allan could swear that the expression in her eyes earlier had been at least interest, if not attraction, and she'd told him something personal about herself, and invited him to use her Christian name.

"Muffle up," he said, wrapping his own scarf around his neck and pulling it up around his chin. "We'll take the short tunnel out to the streets near the mansion, and it wouldn't do for either of us to be recognized."

"There's a nice place just north of the abbey," Melody suggested. "Do you know it?"

Allan shook his head. "Show me," he suggested. He offered her his arm. After days of drizzle and sleet, this evening was fine—or as fine as London got in the winter, when smoke from an uncounted number of chimneys clung to the rooftops and drifted through the streets. Coal smoke, too, most of it, scratching the throat and the lungs. The muffler at least filtered out some of the worst of the coal detritus.

The sun had set, but enough light lingered that their way was clear even before they reached the streets that had gas lamps. Other people were just muffled-up shapes in the dim light, so Allan had little doubt that he and Melody were as anonymous.

It was a ten-minute walk to the cook shop, which was on a narrow lane in a warren of modest homes and small shops. The contrast between the cold air outside and the warmth of the cook shop was remarkable.

"They keep a couple of tables with chairs for those who want to eat here rather than take their meal home," Melody told him. "Mrs. Pratchett, what is on the menu tonight? I've brought my friend Mr. Allan to sample your cooking."

The proprietress welcomed Melody with enthusiasm, and escorted them both to a table near the fire, chatting all the time. "I've a roast of lamb and a pie with steak and kidney, ducky," said the woman. "Take your coats and scarves off, Mrs. Black, Mr. Allan. You'll not get the benefit of them when you go outside if you don't take them off now."

She indicated a coat rack in a nearby corner, and bustled off to the other room, from which appetizing odors drifted.

"I've eaten in taverns and restaurants," Allan said, "but this is my first time in a cook shop. She doesn't seem very busy."

"She will be busier once the factories, offices, and shops close," Melody explained. "Most people bring containers, put the meal they buy into it, and take it home. And here is our meal."

The proprietress carried out a tray with two plates and two tankards, and offloaded it on to their table. As promised, each plate contained a portion of roast lamb and a slice of pie bursting with meat and gravy, the crust golden and flaky. The meal also included a mash of root vegetables and a spoonful of mushy peas."

"I've brought you a mug each of my mulled cider, Mrs. Black," said Mrs. Pratchett. "And I'll have a nice baked apple and custard for you for after."

"My treat," Allan said. "How much, Mrs. Pratchett?"

"Seven pence apiece, Mr. Allan, if you please. Four pence for the main, a penny for the apple and custard and tuppence for the cider."

Allan handed her a shilling and a six pence piece. "Thank you. It all smells delicious. Please keep the change."

"Thank you, Mr. Allan." She gave Melody a light punch on the arm. "You've got a right one here, ducky. Handsome, too."

Someone else entered the shop, and Mrs. Pratchett sailed away to serve this new customer.

"I am a right one, and handsome," Allan informed Melody.

"Eat your dinner while it is hot," she told him, but her eyes laughed into his.

The meal was delicious, the company more so, and Melody was obviously a favorite of the proprietress. "Do you come here often?" Allan said, only then realizing it sounded like the villain's line from one of those comic pieces that theatres put on to entertain early attendees before the main play.

Melody didn't see anything amiss with it, though, or was polite enough not to react. "My sister and her husband used to have rooms just around the corner. She moved after Mr. White died. It is not a safe street for a widow and a growing girl, and I could not always be there to protect them. While they were here, Harmony only had a fireplace for cooking on, but did wonders with a dutch oven and hot bricks. Still, whenever I had the money, I used to treat her and the children to a meal that Harmony did not have to cook or clean after."

"Not her husband, though," Allan noted.

Melody's lovely mouth twisted in a commentary of its own, but all she said was, "Mr. White was seldom at home." Her eyes darkened with memory, but the smile she pasted on was deliberately cheerful. "Without his incursions into the housekeeping, we were able to afford a whole floor in a safer area to the west of Mayfair, and a maid-of-all-work to do the heavy lifting."

"My brother-in-law also lives west of Mayfair. I pay for the house and the food, for he looks after my daughter. I owe him more than I can say." Phineas and his older brother had been horrified, not just at poor Alberta's ultimate fate, but her scandalous relationship with her father-in-law.

When Allan had gone to them, seeking a haven for Lydia, it had been Phineas who had given up his life at Oxford as a scholar of Greek to go into hiding with her. The older brother had the earldom of Nottwick to care for, but had secretly kept in touch with both Phineas and Allan over the years.

In fact, if Nottwick was in town, he'd be a good ally in the current campaign. Allan set the thought to one side. "Thanks to Phineas," he told Melody, "Lydia has been given a loving home, safely away from the marquess. I cannot see her as often as I would wish, but at least she knows me, and she loves her Uncle Phineas."

"Lydia?" Melody asked. "My daughter's dearest friend has the same name. They live in the same house, and share lessons, my Harriet, my sister's son, Benjamin, and Lydia Eastwood."

"Did you say Eastwood?" Allan said. It was too much of a coincidence, surely. "Does your sister live at 16 Jasmine Close?"

"16A," said Melody. "How did you know?"

He leaned close to keep his voice from carrying to any of the customers at the counter. "Because my Lydia and her Uncle Phineas live at 16B, downstairs from your family, and Eastwood is the surname they are using."

Her eyes widened. "Goodness me! Our daughters are best friends!" She laughed, then. "And, if I do not mistake the matter, your brother-in-law is courting my sister. When we win this war, Allan, we shall be seeing more of one another."

Allan took her hand, which was resting on the table, and lifted it to place a kiss on her palm. "So I hope," he said.

Melody blushed, looking down at her plate. "I, also."

"Here are your apples," said the proprietress, plunking them down on the table, while glaring at Allan. "Eat them while they're hot. A person can depend on apples. Men? Not so much."

Allan picked up his spoon with the hand that was not still holding Melody's. "Some of us are not so bad," he said. "And you said yourself that I was handsome. This apple smells wonderful, Mrs. Pratchett."

Mrs. Pratchett snorted, dismissively. "Handsome is as handsome does, Mr. Allan. Many a woman has mistaken glitter for gold, and ended up deserted or worse."

"But Mrs. Black is too smart to be tricked by fool's gold, Mrs. Pratchett," Allan pointed out. He smiled at the lady who was fast becoming essential to him. "If I am false, she will no doubt discover me, beat me to a pulp, and hang me out to dry."

That startled a chuckle out of the proprietress, and Melody, too, was smiling. "You have that right, handsome," said Mrs. Pratchett. "Perhaps you are not too bad after all."

"I am sorry about that," said Melody, when the woman had gone back to her cooking and her customers. "There are men who think widows and neglected wives must submit to their advances. Some tried to cozen us, some used force. If it had not been for Mrs. Pratchett and her friends, we could not have survived. She is still protective of me."

Then I owe Mrs. Pratchett my grateful thanks. "I am glad of it. That you were subject to such persecution makes me want to punch someone."

"I learned to defend myself," said Melody. She shrugged. "Men are vulnerable, if they are on their own and a person knows where to hit. But I always prefer to talk my way out of trouble, if I can."

Allan's admiration for the lady kicked up another notch. And his heart was hopeful. She had not snatched back her hand, though she now carefully disentangled her fingers from his so she could pick up her spoon. Still, he had a chance. She liked him. She was attracted to him.

Now all he had to do was convince her to give up her entire life, her independence, and every asset she had been able to accumulate to marry him. And look what he had to offer her in return for such a sacrifice? A lonely man, permanently twisted by his experiences, with a tyrannical father and next to no personal wealth.

His heart sank again. She'd be a fool to take him on as a husband. And Melody Blackmore was no fool.

❧

Chapter Fourteen

A T DAWN THE following morning, as they left the club, both tired and perhaps not as alert as they might be, the first direct attack came. As they walked down toward the docks, shapes appeared out of alleys on either side, resolving into men as they drew closer, batons raised and knives out.

Without consultation, they moved smoothly into a defensive position, back-to-back. Mel let her knives fall into her hands, trusting to Allan to produce whatever weapon he carried, and prepared to teach these bullies a lesson.

There were so many of them! They might not come out of this in one piece, but if they were to die in this place, on this last day of the year, Mel swore they would not go unaccompanied into the eternal night.

It took her a moment to realize that half those she believed to be opponents were Moriarty's guards, and they were laying about them with efficient and ruthless accuracy. Mel disabled one of those who managed to evade their allies. She cut his hand to make him drop his weapon, and hit him behind the ear with the hilt of her other knife to knock him to the ground.

As quickly as it had begun, it was over. Allan spun around to check on her. She had time to notice that he'd left two of the assailants groaning on the ground when he seized her and hugged her, so tightly that she could not get a breath.

"Melody! Are you hurt?" He drew back, gripping her upper arms to examine her, then hugging her again when she shook her head. Over her head, he spoke to one of Moriarty's men. "Are they all accounted for?"

"All six, Lord Kemble. One dead, five disabled. We shall tie them up and deliver them to the Southwark Watch House."

"After questioning," said Allan. "I want to know who told them we'd be here."

"It would not be hard to figure it out," Mel commented. "You have been masked, yes, but you've not changed your body shapes. Ten brothers work at the Golden Adonis. Eight of the Sheppard brothers appear in the Burlington Arcade and announce the other two have gone overseas. Ten brothers resign from the Golden Adonis, nine of them effective immediately."

"True," said the Moriarty man. "But we shall ask, anyway. And we'll ask who sent them, even if we think we know the answer to that. Be careful, my lord and madam. We cannot know whether this is the only ambush planned for this morning. Half my team shall escort you to the boats, and another team shall pick you up on the other bank of the river."

The leader of the three who formed their escort questioned the boatman and searched the boat before he would let Allan and Mel leave. "We would be wise to choose another form of transport for tonight's trip," said Allan.

Mel agreed. New Year's Eve. Their last night at the club. But if—as they assumed—the attack had been ordered by the marquess, then he would know where to find them. "We had better send a note to Madam Hera, telling her what happened," she said. "It might not be safe for her and the club if we put in an appearance tonight."

"If you will trust me with that message," said the Moriarty man, "I can let her know what happened."

"Tell her she can contact us through Lady Cornelius or Lady Ernest," said Mel.

The guards waiting for them reported no suspicious activity, and the lock on the tunnel gate was intact. They made their way cautiously up to the lower tower without incident, and Allan shut them in and barred the door from the inside.

"Let us try to get a good sleep," Mel suggested. "We are expected at Clara's at one o'clock this afternoon, and it must be nearly eight in the morning by now." Tired as she was, as soon as she put her head on her pillow, she fell asleep.

SHE WOKE TWO hours later from a deep sleep, not certain what had alerted her. The sounds were wrong. That was it. Accustomed to the background noise of the upper tower, she now had the deep stillness of the lower tower, with its thicker walls. The door of her chamber was thinner, though. Someone was moving around out in the center space.

When she wrapped herself in a shawl and went to investigate, she found that Allan was up, and was bending over a metal jug-like contraption that was heating over a spirit burner.

"Melody," he said, when he noticed her. "Did you smell the coffee?"

She did now. The pleasing odor was rising from the jug. "It's a Rumford percolator," Allan explained. "Little to no smoke, and we'll be able to drink fresh coffee in about ten minutes." After a quick look at her in her nightgown and the loosely-wrapped shawl, he had his eyes fixed on his coffee machine.

That won't do at all.

Mel dropped the shawl. "What shall we do for ten minutes?" she asked.

His head snapped around and his eyes devoured her for a moment before he said, in a hoarse voice, "My darling woman, if you mean what I think you mean, it shall take much longer than ten minutes."

He was not rejecting her out of hand. Mel gulped back the lump in her throat and said, boldly though with a quaking stomach, "Then I suggest you turn off the coffee pot until we are ready."

She watched in fascination but also disappointment as he jerked toward the pot as if moved by strings then stopped the motion, reasserted his iron control and replied to her, though his voice shook as he spoke. "I promised myself I would not take advantage of you when we are here alone."

Taking heart from the fact that his voice was not fully under his control, and nor was his gaze—it continued to heat her skin as his eyes roved her form—Mel said, "I made myself no such promise. Allan, may I take advantage of you?"

What could she say to persuade him? "We are alone together, and I want to be with you. I warn you. I have little experience. My husband was not much interested in me, and I suspect he was not very accomplished in the arts of the bed chamber."

That was what one of the women at The Golden Adonis had called them. *The arts of the bed chamber.* Mel had never seen much "art" in the messy, boring, uncomfortable process, but she was willing to learn.

"Your husband," responded Allan, his voice huskier still, "was a fool."

"Must I beg?" Mel asked.

Allan did not reply. Or perhaps his actions spoke for him, for he bent to the spirit lamp under the percolator and turned a wheel until the flame went out. Then he held out his hand, and she put hers into it.

"Are you certain?" Allan asked, and she assured him that she was.

"Your bed or mine?" That was the next question. She chose his, for it was larger. As he led her in that direction, he added, "You can stop me at any time. Just say 'stop', and I shall." That required no reply, but was good to know.

Allan was right about it taking more than ten minutes. And

those at The Golden Adonis who enjoyed the activity were right, too. It was neither boring nor uncomfortable. Her husband really had been a fool.

⫸⫷

THE MARQUESS HAD men watching Clara's. The leader of the guard assigned to Mel and Allan this afternoon had received a note from his colleagues explaining the likelihood of ambush and proposing a strategy for avoiding the risk points.

He sent notice of their arrival by one of the myriad street boys that Moriarty Protection used to run messages, and they waited for the planned commotion to draw the marquess's men away.

The plan worked like clockwork. They were climbing the steps at Clara's when they heard a shout from the roof above, followed by the sharp bark of a rifle. In the next moment, simultaneously, Allan shouted, "Get down!" and a yell of pain sounded across the street. Something fell to crash into the street. Feet scrabbled on tiles. A voice called from Clara's roof. "Sniper, sir. Neutralized."

Mel and Allan had both turned to look at the roof across the street. As her gaze fell to street-level, her eyes met Farnham's. Teign's steward was glaring at her as if attempting to incinerate her on the spot. She gave him a wave and a grin, just as Allan touched her arm and said, "It would ease my mind if you did not stay any longer on these steps, Melody."

She took his arm and allowed him to escort her inside as he scolded her, "I know we agreed that angering the marquess would encourage him to rash behavior, but you must not make a target of yourself. Farnham is a soulless bully, and you have already provoked him once."

"Twice, at least," Mel corrected. "I shall be careful not to go unprotected, Allan. I am not a fool. But I am not going to let him or anyone else frighten me into scurrying around like a mouse."

It was unusual for anyone to be concerned about her safety. Even her sister Harmony, who loved Mel and relied on her for protection, seemed to think that she was made of iron. Mel was torn between being annoyed at Allan for ordering her around and being touched by his evident concern.

At least he didn't compound his error by arguing. "I know you are competent, my dear lady. You know more than me about intrigue and derring-do, and I suppose you are going to tell me you have been shot at before. But please allow me to worry about you."

He was evidently teachable. "Very well, since you said 'please'," she said, smiling to indicate she was joking.

They had been escorted into the drawing room while they were talking, and most of the other couples were already there. "Has he been ordering you about, Mrs. Blackmore?" asked Donald. "He does that."

"He doesn't mean anything by it," Frank assured her. "It is just that he is the eldest, and used to being in charge."

"It is damned annoying, though," said Baldwin.

Their sidelong looks at their brother indicated that they were teasing, and he knew it, for his only reaction was to say, "Leave off, brats. I'm sorry, Melody. I tend to order, but I shall try to ask. Do you think you could be kind enough to just assume the 'please' if you are actually being shot at?"

The brothers and their wives gaped at Mel. "You were shot at?" Cornelius asked.

"Actually, the sniper could have been aiming at Allan," she told them. "Either way, Moriarty Protection had put a man on Clara's roof, and the sniper was shot before he could carry out his commission. Only wounded. He ran off. I don't know whether our guards caught him."

"Farnham was in the street," said Allan.

"We saw him, too." It was a group of four new arrivals, the twins Gerard and Hudson and their wives.

"Did you have trouble with him and his men?" Allan asked. He was leaning forward on the balls of his feet, his fists clenched, as if he was ready to rush to the rescue.

"Not at all," said Gerard.

Hudson continued the explanation. "The Moriarty bodyguard said the marquess's men had all rushed off to the way you came in, Allan."

"So, our carriage came straight down the most direct way," Gerard continued.

And Hudson finished. "Nobody knew it was us until we started up the steps to the front door."

"Our brothers and sisters may have some difficulties leaving, Clara," said Baldwin, seriously.

"I believe," said Mel, "that the street will be crawling with Bow Street Runners and constables from the other Magistrates' Courts. Someone took a shot at a marquess's heir, and others of the marquess's sons have been harassed on their way here. Nobody is going to want any harm to come to any of you on their patch. Nor is Farnham going to want his men caught and blabbing if the officers of the law are behind every brick, bush, and chimney pot."

"That makes sense," Clara said. "But also, Moriarty Protection's men have been efficient so far. We shall take their advice. First, though, we have a stack of invitations to consider. I have ordered tea…" she looked toward the door as it opened to let in a procession of maids and footmen. "And here it is. Please be seated, brothers and sisters—I include you as a sister, Melody, for you are as close as a sister to Thomasina and Winifred." She cast a sly look at Allan, but she was out in her thinking. Mel had no expectation of anything except heartbreak at the end of their affair. She was not marchioness material. Allan would have to marry one of his own kind. *Enjoy it while it lasts and don't fret about the future.*

The maids and footmen brought in all the paraphernalia for tea making, a couple of coffee pots, another two chocolate pots, and trays full of sandwiches, savories, and sweet cakes. A feast, in fact, though with sixteen of them in the room, they would probably devour much of it.

Once everyone had a plate of edibles and the beverage of their choice, Clara began. "Verity, Parthena, Winifred, and I have sorted these into three piles. I must say it was much easier than it would have been in the Season, when there are scores—perhaps even hundreds, if one counts the lesser entertainments—of possible invitations every day. Even if one only considers those from the top 500 families, it can be hard to choose."

"Some people remain in London all year round," said Winifred. "Some leave only in the worst of the heat. And some return for a few weeks over Christmas and the new year, so there are always a few events worth attending."

Verity pointed to the left-most of the three piles on the table. "We discarded those events with small numbers and those unlikely to attract guests whose opinions might matter to the marquess or those he still respects."

Parthena touched the smallest of the three piles—the one on the right. "These are the invitations most suited to our purpose."

"I suggest we discuss those first, and decide who is going to attend," Clara said. "Then we can go through the middle pile and use them to fill in available time."

"No fewer than three couples at any event, with their body-guards," Allan decreed. He looked at Mel, and though he kept his lips from smiling, his eyes danced. "I suppose you would like me to say, 'I suggest' and 'please'."

"Melody doesn't do that," Winifred observed. "She has a habit of handing down decrees."

Thomasina chuckled. "It comes of being the oldest," she said. "She grew up bossing Harmony and myself around, and it stuck."

Allan took Mel's hand. "We have insubordination in the ranks, fellow commander," he said. "We two shall need to stick together."

"If we could focus on the matter at hand," Clara reminded them, "we might be able to complete our responses to the invitations before it is time for our promenade in Hyde Park."

Chapter Fifteen

AFTER ALLAN, HIS lady, and his brothers and sisters had planned their assault on ton events and demolished the refreshments, they consulted Moriarty's lead bodyguard about their departure. He was of the same mind as Melody. The main street would be safest, because it was full of constables.

The man sent teams of bodyguards to inspect and accompany the four carriages from the stables behind the house to the front door, and to remain for the excursion to Hyde Park.

The family left the house without incident, and drove to the park, only a few streets away. There, they elected to walk together across the grounds while the carriages proceeded around the carriage way to meet them at the other end.

It was the last hour before sunset, with only a few clouds in the sky—even the ubiquitous smoke was clearer here in the park. As Verity had predicted when she suggested this excursion, the upper sort were out in force, though there were plenty of common people too, all taking advantage of the break in the weather.

Word must have traveled swiftly through the park about the presence of the Sheppard brothers and their wives, for soon onlookers crowded around them—or at least as close around them as the bodyguards would allow.

They only let people inside their perimeter if one of the wives—or, more rarely, one of the brothers—recognized someone and gave them an invitation.

With one exception. A girl who dove under the arms of two of the bodyguards, shouting, "Mama!"

Melody caught her in her arms. "Harriet! Darling!"

Allan nodded to the bodyguards and in doing so, saw who was beyond the barrier they formed with their bodies. "Damnation." The secret of his daughter's continued existence had just been exploded. Lydia was gazing at him with longing, and there, too, was Phineas, arm in arm with a pretty woman who looked like a pale copy of Melody. She had a boy by the hand, and was dissuading him from following the child Harriet. Benjie, Allan supposed.

They must have come after Harriet in haste. Phineas was holding an easel under one arm. Lydia had a drawing board and the boy was wearing an unbuckled satchel over one shoulder.

And four fit-looking people—two men and two women—who had that alert and slightly dangerous air of a Moriarty guard shadowed their steps, and were nodding at the brothers' guards.

With a beckoning motion, Allan indicated that the little group should approach. His family and Mel's entered the protected space, and those he supposed to be the bodyguards assigned to them spread out to join the defensive perimeter.

"I thought you were supposed to be in hiding," Allan said to Phineas even as he hugged his daughter with one arm while shaking Phineas's hand in greeting with the other.

It was unfair of him to make the accusation. After all, Phineas must have expected to be anonymous in the park. It was only Allan's own presence that had led to the encounter—or, to be more accurate—Melody's presence.

"Melody," he said to that lady, who was gently scolding her daughter for her impetuous action without letting her escape a loving embrace. "May I make known to you my brother-in-law and dear friend Phineas, and my daughter Lydia."

"Allow me to introduce my sister Harmony, my daughter Harriet, and my nephew Benjamin."

Of course, all the brothers wanted to meet their niece, too, and Cornelius's son, Elias, was charmed to meet Benjamin.

"I'm sorry, Melody, Lord Kemble," said Harmony. "I was distracted. I did not realize that Harriet had run off until she called out to you."

"Benjie had just completed a drawing of the swans," said Phineas, "and we were helping him put away his drawing things."

Lydia was still clutching the board, and now she showed it to him. "Uncle Phineas says that Benjie is exceptionally talented," she said.

Allan could only agree as he looked at the sketch of seven graceful swans, swimming across the Serpentine, the water—and the bank and trees on the other side—indicated in a few simple lines.

The artist, though, was not satisfied. "It would be better if that one is there," he said, pointing to another spot. His frown deepened. "And some of the necks are wrong."

Not to Allan's eye. The boy had caught the elegance and beauty of the bad-tempered birds, and even a hint—around the eyes—of their propensity for violence. Looking toward the Serpentine, he could see the originals, gliding in the direction of the reed beds where they nested.

"It is nearly sunset," said Thomasina. "We should be getting the children home into the warmth."

Melody nodded. "We have accomplished our goal, I think. And while I know your daughter's presence was not planned, Allan, I think we can count on it provoking the marquess still further. Harmony and Phineas—may I call you Phineas?—Allan and I have much to tell you."

"Go with them now," said Clara. "Take my carriage. Baldwin and I shall ride with Winifred and Frank. You are taking Cornelius and Thomasina, too, are you not? Everyone, remember we are attending the Dellborough New Year's Eve Ball tonight. We shall see you there. Then we shall meet in the afternoon at mine and Baldwin's house tomorrow, and two nights later is the Sutton Ball."

At both balls, they were to describe their situation to those Clara had selected as both highly influential and likely to be sympathetic to their plight. Allan was content to leave the Society maneuvering to the experts, and Clara and Verity seemed to know what they were doing.

They were almost at their transport. Allan assisted Melody and his daughter into the carriage, while Phineas did the same for Harmony and Harriet. Then Benjie climbed aboard, followed by Allan and Phineas. The seven bodyguards assured Allan that they'd manage to fit on the roof along with Clara's coachman and a groom.

"Very well," said Harmony, as soon as they were inside and the door was shut. "What is going on, Mel? Is Lord Kemble part of the job you couldn't tell me about? The one where you had to live in?"

"Yes," Phineas agreed. "I should like to know, too. But perhaps not in front of small pitchers."

"'Small pitchers have big ears'," Lydia quoted. "He means us, Harriet."

Harriet sighed. "I know. Auntie Harmony says the same thing. I'm not sure why, though. Pitchers don't have ears. Why don't they just say 'people'?"

"Well, small pitcher," said Allan, "I see no reason not to tell you that Papa and the uncles are not hiding anymore. That means the marquess will be very, very angry. I want all three of you children to promise you will stay close to your grownups."

Melody nodded her agreement. "That means no running off to see someone or something. Do not trust anyone, children, except the adults here in this carriage. If someone comes with a message from one of us, it could be a trick. Go straight away to one of your own grownups and let them know about the message. Especially if the people with the message say to tell no one."

"Are the color men our grownups?" Benjie asked.

A questioning look to Phineas elicited an explanation. "The guards you sent. They call themselves Green, Grey, Brown, Red—those are the ones with us today—and also, Black and Blue, who will be on duty later tonight."

"You were not even meant to know the guards were there," Melody complained.

Phineas shrugged. "We figured out we were being watched. I was worried the marquess had found us. Harmony asked them who employed them and invited them in for dinner."

His hand over Harmony's and the warm smile he gave her said more clearly than words how he felt about the widow. "She tries to look after everyone," he said.

"Well?" asked Lydia, returning to the point. "If we cannot find Uncle Phineas and Auntie Harmony, should we stay close to the color men?"

"Yes," Allan replied, and Melody added, "As long as it is one of the color men you know."

Once they were at home in Jasmine Close, the children were sent with the maid to change their outer clothing, leaving without complaint once Allan and Melody had promised to come and see Benjie's cage of pet mice, and the rag dolls that Harmony had made for Harriet and Lydia.

Once the door closed behind the children, Allan gave both adults a fuller explanation of their current situation and their intentions.

"So, you are staking yourselves out as bait," Phineas growled. "I do not like it, Allan."

"We are taking every precaution," said Melody, soothingly. "We have the guard from Moriarty Protection. We are eliciting the sympathies of the ton. We are being careful."

"I knew something was up when I saw the guard," grumbled Phineas.

"The marquess can be beaten," Allan pointed out. "We've beaten him before. You, your brother, and I rescued Lydia.

Cornelius and Thomasina fooled him with a fake suicide. We have been leaving the tower where he thought he had us imprisoned for years, and he has only recently become suspicious."

"All of those were defensive actions," Melody said. "He still made mistakes, mainly because he thinks he is all-seeing, all-knowing, and all-powerful, so he does not see the gaps in his own thinking. Now we are on the offensive, we shall push him into reacting without thought. We shall defeat him for once and for all, and all of you shall be free."

"Well then. I hope you are right," Phineas said.

AT THE BALL that night, they met so many people that Mel's head spun. They finished the evening with promises of a sympathetic audience from a glittering array of peers and their wives, and outright offers of support from the Earl of Nottwick, older brother to Phineas and to Allan's dead wife, and the Duchess of Kempbury, who had once been in the same line of work as Mel.

"Felix's sister-in-law is not in Town, though she and Somerville are expected," Adaline Kempbury said. "Nor are most of my former clients currently in London. "I shall visit those who are available. Have you considered drawing up a lawyer's brief on a charge of false imprisonment, and having it presented to the House of Lords? That might set fire to Teign's coat-tails."

It was a good idea, and a lawyer might be able to suggest other crimes they had evidence enough to prosecute, though a prosecution was not actually the point. Arousing the marquess's indignation until he lost his temper, that was the point, hopefully pushing him until he went after them in full view of witnesses, preferably witnesses with high rank and a solid reputation.

The feeling began as they were waiting for their carriage home to be brought to the steps. Mel was familiar with the uneasy sensation, as if something with many legs was crawling down the back of her neck. "We need to move out of the tower tonight," she said to Allan, as soon as they were in the carriage and alone, with only Baldwin and Clara to hear.

"Your reason?" Baldwin asked.

"The marquess will be stepping up his efforts to find the secret exit from the tower. Perhaps he never will. But perhaps someone will realize that the floor of the hidden room in the dining area is actually a hatch. Or perhaps someone will remember the barred and locked way into the courtyard, and investigate. The lock won't stand up to a determined assault, and I don't want to be trapped in the lower tower with no way out."

"I prefer being close enough to see what he is doing," Allan objected. "London is full of entrances to sewers and cellars and caves. No one has investigated the three that lead to the tower. Perhaps ever. Certainly not since we first discovered them from the other end."

"Moriarty Protection can keep watch from outside, and see nearly as much as you can from the tower," Baldwin argued. "It is foolish to take any extra risk."

"You can stay with us," said Clara. "Let us stop by the tower and collect your luggage."

"I don't agree." Allan narrowed his eyes to peer at Melody in the dim light of the carriage. "What makes you mention this now, Melody?"

"I can't explain," Mel said. "I get this feeling sometimes when danger is close. I've found that once I'm aware of it, I can usually work out what I must change to avoid the danger. Perhaps it is that I have noticed various things without realizing it, and my mind has put them together, or perhaps it is some kind of extra sense. But this time, all my instincts are telling me we need to be out of the tower. Sooner rather than later."

Allan's look at her was disbelieving, but they had arrived, and Baldwin was already opening the door.

Before anyone could descend, one of the bodyguards poked

his head in the door. "Bad news, Lord Kemble. According to the boot boy, the marquess's men have been combing the cellars for a secret way into the tower, and now they're going through the grounds. They're investigating the entry in the courtyard, trying to break the lock so they can get into the tunnel."

Both brothers cast Mel a look of mingled disbelief and respect.

"How close are they to getting in?" Mel asked.

"They sent for their blacksmith. Woke him up. He's claiming there's insufficient light to work. They're trying to set up torches, but the wind has picked up and is blowing the flames around. The blacksmith says he cannot do anything until dawn. They are trying to persuade him." Blacksmiths could always command a measure of respect, not only because their skills were essential, but because they were generally large and always strong.

"Dawn is at least four hours away," said Clara. "You'll have time to fetch your luggage. Baldwin, darling, let us go and help."

"Take the carriage slowly around the streets," said the Moriarty man to the coach driver, "and be back here in...." He raised a questioning brow, and Mel said, "Forty-five minutes." It was good thinking. A carriage parked in this street for any length of time would attract attention.

They made all the speed they could. As Baldwin said, how long the blacksmith could delay things would depend on whether the other servants managed to wake someone else who frightened them enough for them to force the blacksmith to his work.

However, Allan had unpacked little after their move from upstairs, and the two trunks Mel had brought back from her sister's—one of her own clothes and a smaller one of disguises— had not even been opened.

Teign's men must have found a way of persuading the blacksmith, for as the two couples came down the stairs to the tunnel, they could hear a rhythmic ringing clang—presumably the hammer on the lock. The two people with lamps shuttered them, and in the dark, they hurried their steps. They soon passed the short tunnel leading to the courtyard, distinguishing it by the glow of dozens of torches and oil lamps and the increased sound. Hidden by the darkness, they continued, those in front feeling the wall on the right for the next tunnel.

Seconds later, the curve of the passage hid them from sight, and then Mel, who was in the lead, said, "Here is the tunnel. Once we are within, we can afford to light one of the lamps."

Or perhaps not. A cheer from the direction of the courtyard confirmed that searchers might be coming this way shortly. They continued in darkness.

"I'll lock the gate," Allan said, once they were through it. Nobody had followed them so far, and they left the alley just as the carriage approached along the street.

"Good instincts," said Baldwin, as they continued their journey to Clara's.

Allan said nothing, but he had taken her hand and was holding it cradled in his own.

The point of contact soothed her, and she was nearly asleep when they pulled up outside the house. Whether Clara was keeping rooms prepared in case they were needed, or whether she had sent a groom ahead to warn the servants, Mel was shown to a warm room with a fire in the grate, a jug of hot water, and clean sheets that showed evidence of a recent encounter with a bed warmer.

She was grateful as she washed and prepared for bed, but she would have traded this lovely room for her cold room in the tower, if she was sharing it with Allan.

She was lying awake in bed, missing Allan, when there was a knock on the door. Clara, perhaps? Or a servant who had forgotten something?

She opened the door just a crack, and Allan—for it was he—pushed it further and slipped inside. "I cannot sleep without you by my side," he whispered. "May I stay?"

"Yes," she said. And in moments they were under the covers, Mel tucked in his arms, her back to his front. Comfortable at last, she slid into sleep.

ALLAN WAS WOKEN by Clara's voice. "Melody, I am sorry to wake you, but you are needed in the servants' hall." Melody struggled up through fathoms of sleep, shedding the fragments of a dream as she rose into wakefulness. Clara kept speaking. "Several women from the marquess's household have come to give their testimony. I've sent Baldwin to wake… Oh."

As she sat up, Melody had pushed back the covers, disclosing Allan, who was blinking his own way into the land of the living.

There was a knock on the door, but the person—his brother—did not wait for an answer, but burst in, saying, "Clara, Allan isn't there, and the bed doesn't look slept… Oh."

"Give them a cup of tea," Allan suggested. He was sitting up, now, making it perfectly obvious that his torso was naked. So, in fact, was the rest of him, for they had woken after several hours and come together, before falling back to sleep again. That was none of Clara's business. Nor Baldwin's. Allan's brother was keeping his eyes pointedly away from Mel's bare shoulders and his brother's even more disreputable state, and struggling to keep a straight face.

"If you will excuse us," Mel said, "we shall dress for the day and come down. What time is it?"

"Eleven o'clock, or close to," Baldwin told her without looking at her. "Right. I'll be off then. Coffee for you both, I take it? It will be ready for you when you come downstairs."

"Clara, would you mind making certain that the servants are all somewhere else for a minute or so?" Allan asked, sounding perfectly relaxed. Mel knew it was only an appearance, for she could feel, and see, the tension in him. "I do not wish to damage Melody's reputation by being seen emerging from her room," he added.

Clara gave him a narrow-eyed glare, but walked out of the room. Allan dived for his discarded banyan, picked up his nightshirt, and pressed a quick kiss to Mel's lips. "Not their business," he assured her, before hurrying off.

Mel had a sibling. She did not doubt that Allan's brothers would make it their business. So, for that matter, would Harmony. She sighed. There was no point in fretting about that now. She needed to wash, dress, and brush her hair. It was growing longer and beginning to curl. It was just as well she no longer had to be a convincing man.

Clara arrived back, as if on cue, while Mel was struggling to do up one of the fashionable dresses that Thomasina and the aunts had decreed for her. This time, she knocked, and only entered when Mel called, "Come."

"I thought you might need help with your buttons and your hair," said Clara, as she sailed across the room. "You and Allan, Melody? I thought something was going on. Baldwin thought it unlikely, but there you were."

"There we were," Mel agreed. *Where are we?* They had not discussed it. Mel had set out to have a casual affair. Or, at least, that was what she had told herself. It was a lie, though. Surely her feelings could not have deepened so quickly in fewer than twenty-four hours. She must have been falling in love with Allan almost from their first meeting.

Even if he was dictatorial and annoying. *Not really. He just bears the weight of being the first and feeling responsible.*

"Is that all you are going to say?" Clara was now making efficient work of threading ribbon through her curls to form a simple but elegant coiffure.

"Yes," Mel replied. She was a widow. Allan was a widower. They did not need to answer to anyone.

"Very well," said Clara. "I shall not tease you. There. You are ready for the day. No one would know you spent the night—"

"Clara!"

The other lady grinned and made a motion as sewing her lips together. Mel shook her head and led the way downstairs, and then had to step aside and let Clara show her the way to the servants' hall.

Allan was there already. Her eyes went to him as soon as she entered the long narrow room—as usual, she realized. He had become her lodestar, the point to which she turned at every moment.

He looked around and smiled, though she could have sworn neither she nor Clara had made a noise as they came in. "Mrs. Blackmore, please come and sit down. And Lady Baldwin, too. Please allow me to present my friends. Mrs. Palmer is the cook at Sheppard House, and has always been good to me and my brothers. Jenny is her assistant, and Polly is the head housemaid."

The three servants bowed in greeting.

Allan explained, "These good people have heard that Isaac and Jerome are now safely beyond the marquess's reach, and that we are rejecting his control. They wish to help us."

"There are five more, my lord," said the cook. "We couldn't all leave at once, but we shall send the others out on messages this afternoon. To market, and to buy ribbons and furniture polish, and the like. That is, if you want to see them all today."

Excellent. Who knows more about a household than its maids? Silent, invisible, and ubiquitous, maids saw far more than their masters ever knew. If these eight servants had chosen sides in this silent battle between the brothers and the marquess, the odds had changed decisively, and in Allan's and his brothers' favor.

"We do," Mel said. She sat down at the table, accepted the cup of coffee that Allan handed her, and prepared to milk this new source for every drop of information they could give her.

Chapter Sixteen

T HE DAY TURNED wet and cold as the afternoon drew on, which was a help in putting out the fire someone set in the wood stack against the back wall of Clara's house. Fortunately, one of the bodyguards noticed the smoke before the flames could take hold, and he used a rake to scatter the mess of twigs and straw that had been piled against the wood. Spread across the cobblestones in the rain, the embers soon gave up and went out.

Someone else must have made the same assumption as the maids—that Allan was living at the address he had given for correspondence. This theory was confirmed late in the afternoon when a thunderous knocking on the door—an attack rather than a request for entry—proved to be Farnham with a letter from the marquess.

He insisted on handing it to Allan in person. Baldwin left him in the cold bare parlor Clara only had heated on the days that she received petitioners from her estates, shops, and manufactories, and came to tell Allan and Melody, who were dressing for dinner.

"It's Farnham," said Baldwin.

"Threats?" Allan asked.

"Probably." Baldwin shrugged. "There is a certain way to find out, and that is to see him. I can always tell him you are not here and demand that he give me the marquess's letter."

"No need," said Allan. "I am here. It will be no secret by tomorrow, after all. I'll go down and see what he wants."

"His lordship demands that you return home or face retribution," Farnham said coldly, in the insolent voice he kept for his master's sons and disobedient servants.

Mel had insisted on coming to the parlor with Allan, and Baldwin and Clara were present, as well. It was Mel who spoke, her voice meditative. "The marquess is… what? Eighty years old? More? He shall be dead soon enough. Probably in the next ten years. Perhaps much sooner. He has led a dissolute life, after all. And then, Allan, you shall be Farnham's master."

"An interesting thought," Baldwin said. "Farnham, while you are thinking about that, remember that none of the marquess's sons like you. One of us—by rights it will be Lord Kemble—will inherit the title."

"Don't bother," Allan commented. "Farnham, tell the marquess that the answer is, and always will be, no."

Farnham sneered. "We know you sent your youngest brother away on the 30th. We knew yesterday that he and Lord Isaac were headed for Liverpool, and a ship to the Americas. The marquess has sent a veritable army after them, and by now they will be in custody and on their way back to London. Surrender now, and Lord Jerome's punishment will be lighter."

Good. That old villain believes the story we leaked to London's gossips. Mel managed not to smile.

Allan examined his cufflinks and then the set of his matching cravat pin, looking thoughtful. "That is a pity," he commented, after a while. "I trust his lordship does not intend to detain Lord Isaac? He is of age, and bringing him home against his will would be kidnapping. A capital offense, Farnham."

"He'll come along right enough when we drag Lord Jerome back," Farnham blustered.

"No." Allan looked at Farnham over his steepled fingers, his eyes as cold as the north wind. "No, he will not. And neither shall I nor any of the other brothers. We would, I grant you, have preferred to wait another five months, until Jerome was no longer under his lordship's legal authority."

He took a deep breath and let it out in a sigh. "However, your master made that impossible when he tried to force those ridiculous marriages. Tell the marquess that we are all agreed. If Jerome must be sacrificed, we shall not blame ourselves. We shall place the blame where it belongs, on the marquess. And we shall have our revenge."

"If that is all, Farnham," said Clara, "my butler shall see you out."

Farnham glowered. "Is that your final word, Lord Kemble?"

"I shall not enter any of the marquess's properties again until I am the marquess," Allan told him.

"You shall regret it," Farnham growled.

Clara clapped her hands for the butler. Mel turned her back on Farnham, though listening for his movements. She wanted to show her contempt, but she was certainly not going to allow such a violent, improvident man to step closer to her.

A pity this room was so plain. The contemptuous gesture was satisfying, but she would have liked a mirror to watch his reaction.

"My lady," said the butler.

"Show this person out," Clara said, refusing to refer to Farnham with an honorific, a term of respect, or even his name.

Mel longed for the absent mirror, but she held her pose as the footsteps of two men retreated into the hall. Only when she heard the front door close did she turn back to Clara, Allan, and Baldwin.

"That should put the cat among the pigeons," she said.

"Liverpool," said Baldwin, and snorted with laughter.

Allan stroked his chin. "We need to warn the others. His lordship will go after whomever he considers weakest."

"We shall see them at tonight's dinner," Mel reminded him. "Let us finish getting ready. It must be nearly time to leave."

Fifteen minutes later, they arrived downstairs to find there was a delay. The stable master had examined both horses and carriage, and had found sabotage of tracings, wheels, and axles. "He has brought out the alternative tack, my lady," said the groom he'd sent to the house. "And he is preparing the traveling coach to take you to dinner."

It didn't take long, but even so, Allan, Baldwin, Clara, and Mel were the last guests to arrive.

The Duke of Dellborough had invited some of the most influential people in the realm to meet the Sheppard brothers and their ladies. And Mel, who was what? Not Allan's wife, obviously, and not fit to be so, or so most of Society would say. She was gentry, not noble, and had fallen even from that level by earning her own living.

Not his mistress, certainly. She was not bedding him for payment in cash or in kind. His lover, of course, but she was not entering Dellborough's home in that guise. So, she was his ally. The woman whose knowledge, contacts, and experience would help him to defeat the marquess. She was satisfied with her analysis. As his ally, she had the right to stand beside him as they faced some of the great ones of their world.

She had to remind herself of that a short time later, when she faced the other ladies, with their pearls and their diamonds, their custom-made silks and their imported shawls. These were a cross-section of the great ladies of England, and most of them dressed accordingly.

In the gown that Harmony had made her, her cropped hair adorned only by the ribbon Clara had once again woven through the curls, her only jewelry the locket bequeathed to her by her grandmother, she felt like a common barnyard duck who had accidentally fallen among swans.

I am not here as a fashion doll or to puff off some man's status, she scolded herself. *I am Melody Blackmore, and I belong at Allan's side until the Marquess of Teign has been brought down.*

Melody was the most amazing woman Allan had ever met. Allan, though he was heir apparent to a marquess, felt inadequate in the illustrious company that the Duke of Dellborough had gathered under his roof. Yet Melody didn't turn a hair, but conducted herself as if she had walked with duchesses and marchionesses every day of her life.

He felt stronger and more capable just having her at his side. And he had not just her, but his brothers and their wives. With his family to protect, he could handle anything.

"Kemble," said the duke, after a round of introductions, "I'd like you to give the guests a quick summary of your situation, and what you are trying to do. We shall talk more seriously after dinner, but I know everyone has heard bits of gossip, and they shall not pay adequate attention to the delectable dishes my wife has selected for tonight without at least some idea of the facts behind the rumors."

Allan nodded, wondering what on earth he could say.

"You have already done this," Melody murmured. "At Burlington Arcade, you explained what had happened to you. All you need add is that we are collecting evidence of the marquess's crimes."

She was right. He squeezed the hand that rested on his arm as Dellborough clapped his hands to attract everyone's attention.

"Friends and family," the duke said, in a clear voice that carried easily through the large room. "I have asked you here this evening to hear the truth of the rumors that have been swirling about London regarding Teign's treatment of his sons, and their move away from his home. Lord Kemble shall give us a summary before dinner, and you shall have the opportunity to ask questions after dinner. Kemble?"

Melody, bless her, did not let go of his arm. Baldwin gave him a nod. Donald winked at him and Hudson grinned. They all believed in him. They needed him to speak for them.

"Your Graces," he said, "my lords, my ladies, gentlemen." That was the easy bit, but as he kept talking, he found the words came easily enough.

"You all know the Marquess of Teign, at least by reputation. My brothers and I are here tonight to say that what you have heard about the marquess is almost certainly true, and not the worst of it. Leaving aside what he has done to others, he has been a brutal tyrant to his sons, and our best memories are of those times that he ignored us."

They needed to hear something more specific. Enough to keep them satisfied until after dinner. "For many years, the marquess has enforced the obedience of each of us by threatening our brothers. He broke the leg of my seven-year-old brother when I refused the marriage he planned for me, and threatened to break the other one if I continued to refuse. He has beaten and injured each of us, time after time. My brothers Francis and Jerome have permanent limps because of his beatings."

He waited for the murmur of comment to die down and then continued. "He kept Jerome locked up for more than ten years to use him as a lever to control me. All ten of us have lived in the tower at his townhouse for the past seven years. At first, we were let out during the day," *except for Jerome. And Frank, after he was brought back from Spain.* "But for the past two years we have been let out—no more than three at a time, under the threat of beatings for the rest—only when he wanted to display us at some entertainment, or introduce us to a potential bride."

Was that enough? No. That was their past situation. Dellborough had asked him to summarize their current situation and their plans.

"We have been fortunate enough, with the help of our ladies, to escape the tower. Seven of my brothers have married, two have fled overseas—for Jerome will not be twenty-one for several months, and we want him out of the marquess's hands. We are free, and we intend to remain so, which means we need to find evidence of Teign's crimes and bring him to account."

There was one more matter he should mention. "Since he discovered our rebellion, there have been at least four attempts to kill or injure me or Mrs. Blackmore, and any person assisting us, including damage tonight to Lady Baldwin's carriage and the horses' tack. Fortunately, it was picked up by a sharp-eyed stable master, but that is what made us late this evening."

He bowed. "Your Graces, my lords, my ladies, gentlemen, my family and I shall be happy to answer any questions you might have after dinner."

The Duchess of Dellborough spoke into the buzz of conversation that followed Allan's statement, and the room hushed to listen. "Thank you, Lord Kemble, for giving us that explanation. Friends, shall we proceed to the dining room? Lord Kemble, I have placed you on my right. Would you be good enough to escort me in? Mrs. Blackmore, this is my brother Lancelot, who shall be your escort to dinner."

Lord Lancelot gave up the lady on his arm to another gentleman and winged his elbow at Melody. When she accepted it, Allan performed the same courtesy for the duchess and they went in to dinner.

The dining room table was large enough to seat the sixty guests and their host and hostess, and the meal was served *a la Russe*—that is, with all the dishes for one course already on the table. Allan, as he seated the duchess and took his place beside her, was the target of many curious glances.

So were his brothers and their wives, whom the duchess had, according to custom, split apart. Cunning lady. She had spread the Sheppards out around the table so that more than two thirds of the guests had a Sheppard on one side of them, and those who were not seated next to one of Allan's family were no more than one person away.

Melody was between Lord Lancelot and a lady Allan had been introduced to last night, the Duchess of Kempbury. The two ladies were deep in conversation. *I hope Melody is not being interrogated.*

Her Grace must have seen him looking. "I thought Mrs. Blackmore would appreciate sitting next to Adaline Kempbury," she said. "They are acquaintances from before the Kempburys' marriage."

That was a relief. She, at least, could enjoy the dinner. And Her Grace had also been thoughtful about seating Rosina and Amber, who might also feel out of their depth in the august company. Rosina was sitting between Dellborough's eldest son and the Countess of Stanford, who was a gentle lady and a champion for women. The son's wife was Amber's dinner companion, with the Earl of Nottwick, Phineas's brother, on her other side.

Allan relaxed and began to enjoy the dinner. His conversation with Her Grace was so interesting that they were halfway through the first course before he realized that, without mentioning the brother's plight, she was giving him a crash course into the personalities, alliances, and interests of major Society figures, and which side they were likely to take in the struggle with the marquess.

When the second course began, she turned her attention to the earl on her left. Obedient to social dictates, Allan was turning to Kempbury, who was sitting on his right, when the meal was interrupted.

They heard the shouting from outside the room, coming closer. Then the doors burst open and people scrambled into the room. First, two burly men in Teign livery, holding the Dellborough butler between them, his back facing the room as he protested, "My lord, Their Graces are at dinner. My lord, you cannot burst in this way."

Chapter Seventeen

T HE BURLY MEN were holding the poor butler by his arms so
his feet couldn't reach the ground, and after them came
several Dellborough and Teign footmen, shoving and pushing at
one another.

Finally, the instigator of this riot—Teign himself, with Farnham at his elbow—strode into the room, Teign's voice
thundering, "I shall see Dellborough now, and those scoundrelly
sons of mine. Dellborough, how dare you harbor these traitors!"

The Duke of Dellborough had risen to his feet. "Good evening, Lord Teign." He looked down the long table to where his
wife sat at the end. "My dear, are we harboring traitors?"

The duchess remained seated, regarding Teign with the expression of a householder who has found a cockroach in the flour
bin. "Lord Teign," she said. "What is the meaning of this
unseemly and violent invasion of our home?"

The marquess glared at her, looked around at the luminaries
gathered at the table, and made a visible effort to rein in his
temper. "My apologies, Your Grace," he snapped, with a
perfunctory nod in place of a bow. "I had to see your husband, to
tell him not to support my sons in their rebellion. I shall just be
taking them with me, and leave you to get on with your dinner."

"Lord Kemble?" said the duchess. "Do you wish to go with

your father?"

"I do not," Allan replied, managing to keep his voice calm, despite the anger and grief he always felt in his father's presence.

"And what of you other brothers?" said the duchess, managing to speak over Teign's angry retort.

All seven Sheppard brothers replied. Whether it was a "no", an "I do not", or "not likely", their answers amounted to the same.

"You have your answer, Lord Teign," said Her Grace of Dellborough. "If you wish to pursue any complaint you have against my husband, please have your secretary arrange an appointment with Dellborough's secretary."

Teign sneered. "What kind of a man are you, Dellborough? Letting a female speak for you?"

The duke chuckled. "A wise and happy one," he replied. He exchanged a warm glance with his duchess. *What an inspiration!* Thirty years or more, and their love for one another was palpable.

"A man who bows to a woman is no man at all," Teign announced. He added, "A woman should know her place—silent, obedient, and in a man's bed. If she forgets it, she should be beaten."

Good work, you old sinner. You have now alienated all the great ladies Dellborough and his wife had invited to dinner and most of the men.

Dellborough lifted an eyebrow at his wife, and she commented, "An interesting if primitive view. Tell me? How has it contributed to your domestic and marital happiness?"

The duke smirked.

Teign's sneer deepened, and he turned on his footmen. "Seize my sons, you fools. Have you forgotten what we came for?"

Allan clenched his fist and prepared to leap to his feet.

"The marksmen in the minstrels' gallery will shoot anyone who attempts to carry out that order," Dellborough drawled. "Up to and including Lord Teign."

Startled, Allan looked up. Sure enough, from the shadowy depths of the minstrel's gallery, several rifle barrels pointed at Teign's footmen, who were backing away despite the imprecations of their master.

Dellborough picked up his wine glass and leaned back in his seat. "My dear guests, I apologize in advance for the spilling of blood, but better to execute these invaders cleanly than to allow brawling in my wife's dining room. Teign, your language, sir! Please do remember that ladies are present." His drawl edged into insolence.

From a lifetime of observing the marquess, Allan could tell he was on the point of losing his temper. Could he be pushed over? He stood.

"You have no legal authority over us, Lord Teign. Your behavior toward us, our mothers, and our wives has destroyed any moral or filial responsibilities we might have toward you. None of us will ever live under your roof again, nor shall we obey your dictates. If you or your henchmen attempt to harm any of us, we shall seek recourse through the king's law. God save the King."

He sat down after the speech. His father would see it as further insolence, but truly it was because his knees were weak, as they always were, whenever he defied the old devil.

"And so say I," said Baldwin.

"And I," Cornelius echoed.

All of them spoke, one after another, in age order as if they had rehearsed it, while Teign exploded even more spectacularly than Allan had expected. Specks of foam flew from his lips as he ranted, then an apparent calm suddenly descended. This was the point at which he was most dangerous. Only by the most rigid self-control did Allan keep from flinching away from whatever torture Teign deemed a suitable punishment, and from the corner of his eye, he observed the same strain in his brothers.

In a low, grating voice, the marquess snarled, "You think you are so smart, Kemble. You think you've sent that little brat Jerome out of my reach. But think again. I have him, and his brother. If you don't return… if any one of you refuses to return, I'll start by breaking Jerome's other leg. Then I'll break his hands—he fancies himself on the piano, the useless molly boy. What sort of music can he make if I destroy his hands? I'll leave him one hand to write to you, shall I? To beg you to come home. Did you think I'd let you send him to the Americas?"

Kemble managed not to sigh his relief. "Isaac and Jerome sailed yesterday on the Beatitude, an American tea clipper. You have no authority over American ships."

With a curled lip, Teign took the bait. "Farnham caught them on the road to Liverpool. Did you think he wouldn't? And even if they had reached the ship, they could not have escaped. Farnham ordered the harbor closed down on my authority. Nothing was able to sail."

Honestly, the marquess is slipping. Farnham had been present in London yesterday and again today. Did the marquess think he had the power of translocation?

"I shall do my best to free my brothers," he said. "I shall not give you any more hostages. The answer is still no."

Teign wasn't expecting that answer. He gaped. And before he could gather himself, Dellborough spoke again. "You have your answer, Lord Teign. You and your bullies are not welcome in my home. Leave now, or be carried to the front door and tossed into the street."

After a look up at the minstrel's gallery and another look at the scores of footmen who had silently filed into the dining room, the marquess glared at him. "I shall be speaking to the king about your support for my rebellious sons," he threatened.

"I shall also be speaking to the king," Dellborough replied, calmly.

The marquess cast a fulminating glance around the room and then stormed out, his minions trailing behind him.

"Furness," said Dellborough to the butler. "That man is not permitted in any of my houses or on my estates. Pass the word. If refusal does not work, you are authorized to use force, and I shall defend you from any repercussions."

"Thank you, Your Grace," said his wife. "My dear guests, after that interlude, I do not feel I can do justice to this course. May I suggest we go immediately to the drawing room? I shall have tea and sweets served, and port or brandy for those who prefer, and we can ask our questions of Lord Kemble and his brothers."

LORD TEIGN COULD not have been more helpful to Allan and his brothers if Mel had written his script. The questions in the drawing room didn't bother with testing the brothers' truthfulness. Having observed the evidence of Teign's brutal bullying with their own eyes and ears, they questioned details, and considered possible ways to bring the man to book.

Before any of that, though, they responded to Teign's threats against Jerome. "Should we take constables to search his townhouse for the missing brothers?" one of them asked. "We can probably obtain a warrant based on who we are and what we have heard."

Another shook his head. "He could have them anywhere. And the man is a lunatic. If we invade his house, he might hurt one or both of the young men."

"We do not have to be concerned about Isaac and Jerome," Allan told them. "They did not go to Liverpool. At the time their ship sailed, the marquess thought we were all still locked up in the tower. We did not go out in public until they were safely on their way to somewhere that is not the Americas. We spread the news about Liverpool, hoping the marquess would hear and take the bait."

The chuckles and comments signaled that those present approved.

In light of that news, once they reached the point of discussing how to stop Teign, some were in favor of arresting him immediately, for undue violence against his sons. Others urged caution.

"There will be some," one of the earls said, "who would say the law should not interfere. A man is master of his own house, and has the right to discipline his wives, children, and servants."

"Discipline, yes," Nottwick growled. "Abuse, no."

"I quite agree," said the earl. "Proving abuse, especially now the bruises have faded, so to speak, is the issue. Remember, this is a marquess we are talking about. A sometime friend of the king, too. No, to convict the man—even to arrest him—we need more. Something that cannot be ignored. I do not suppose he has plotted against Crown and country, has he? Even the king won't brush over that."

"We have been thinking along the same lines," Allan explained. "Mrs. Blackmore suggested it." He inclined his head to Mel and went on, "Mrs. Blackmore believes that his violence and sense of self-entitlement will have led him to abuses of power against others, not only his wife and family—and we have found this to be true. Mrs. Blackmore, you were present during the interviews this afternoon and our discussions afterward. Would you like to summarize for our friends?"

"One moment," said someone. "What is Mrs. Blackmore's interest in Teign's crimes? What is her place here?"

Mel was taken aback by the question, and before she could marshal her thoughts to make an answer, Allan was speaking for her. "Mrs. Blackmore came to us while investigating the disappearance of her cousin, Lady Cornelius Sheppard. We were initially part of Mrs. Blackmore's group of suspects, but became her allies and then friends. I am currently courting Mrs. Blackmore in the hopes she will become my wife. Her interest in Teign's crimes is familial and personal. Her place here is with me."

Courting? His wife? Why was Allan making such an extravagant claim? Was it just to establish Mel's place within this lofty group? It must be. She had no illusion that she was important to him beyond the needs of the moment.

The Duchess of Kempbury was speaking. "I have known Melody Blackmore for some years. I consider her a friend, and would trust her with my life. She has successfully solved many puzzles for those who needed the discreet assistance of a person of integrity. Melody, I am glad you are here."

Kempbury took his cue from his wife. "Mrs. Blackmore, can you explain what interviews Kemble means, your discoveries, and your conclusions?"

Mel took a deep breath and began. "Today, eight servants from Teign's house came to speak to Lord Kemble. They wanted to tell him that, for a decade or more, Teign has purchased women, and hidden them in guarded chambers of his house."

"The servants have seen these women?" Kempbury protested. "Then why have they not reported it to the authorities?"

"They are servants, and he is a marquess," Mel pointed out, resisting the urge to sigh at Kempbury's naive expectation that the magistrates and their constables would make the slightest push to investigate a servant's claim against their master.

The Duchess of Kempbury explained it in clear terms. "They were afraid no one would listen to them, and that placing information would get them killed."

"Oh. I see," said her husband. "Very well, Mrs. Blackmore. I apologize for the interruption."

"In fact," Mel admitted, "The servants have seldom seen the women. However, for years, they have been expected to feed and clean up after men who seem to have no other task except to linger in one part of the mansion.

"It was the tower for a while, then an isolated wing of the house, and now it is the cellars. They provide more food than even hungry men can eat, and must clean twice as many rooms with beds as there are men."

Twenty or more men at present, the cook had told them. She could not be certain of the exact numbers, for they kept to themselves. But since the brothers had escaped the tower, she and the other servants who supported her had been counting those they saw when they cleaned or delivered food.

Mel continued, "The occasional glimpse of women who should not be there, being led from the guarded areas to the marquess's bedchamber has just confirmed their suspicions."

"The women must be aging after more than ten years," Dellborough commented.

"He replaces them regularly," Mel explained.

"What does that mean, 'replaces them'?" the Duchess of Dellborough asked, leaning forward. "Could we perhaps ask the retired women to tell what happened to them at Teign's hands?"

Mel shook her head. "According to what the servants have overheard, most women die within a few months. They are buried in the cellars. The survivors are sold to brothels when the marquess and his confederates have too many new women for the available space." *After their warders have had the use of them.*

"If we can prove any of this," said Kempbury, "we can demand that the king take action. But how?"

"We have the beginnings of an idea," said Baldwin. "We think we need to rescue the women, and we need to do it as secretly as possible, and with highly reputable witnesses, so that Teign is facing the accusations of his peers."

"The key to our plan is that Teign is currently keeping his victims in the cellars," Allan added. "And we have a hidden way into the cellars.

Chapter Eighteen

T HAT NIGHT, MEL could not resist prodding at Allan's casual remark about courting her. When they had slipped under the bedclothes and he reached for her, she said, "Thank you for supporting my right to be there this evening."

"Of course. You have the same right as my brothers' wives. More, because you are responsible for us fighting back."

The same right as the wives? What did he mean by that? She needed to be more direct. "You said you were courting me?"

"Of course, I am," said Allan. "If you have not noticed, I need to try harder," and he took her mouth with his own, stopping further discussion.

Surely, he did not intend marriage! Mel had far too much sense than to hope for any such thing.

THE FOLLOWING DAY was the second of the new year, and they had few plans—an outing in the afternoon, and dinner with all the brothers and their wives.

Tonight's chief topic would be thinking of a diversion or two to make certain that Teign and most of his bullies were not at home when Allan led the selected peers to make an assault on the cellars.

The dukes from last night were choosing the credible witnesses, who had to be young and fit enough to climb steep stairs and walk some distance along the maze of tunnels and corridors beneath the mansion.

And the Kempburys had taken responsibility for providing the professional fighters to protect those witnesses. In two days' time, both sides of the plan—diversion and assault team—needed to be ready.

Mel and Allan had breakfasted and were relaxing in the morning room when the butler came to tell them they had visitors. Mel braced herself for another encounter with Teign. It wasn't him, though it was his doing.

The butler returned with Harmony, Harriet, Benjie, Phineas, and Lydia. Also, the two leaders of their protection teams, who left it to Phineas to make their apologies.

"Our house was set on fire," Phineas explained. "Then, when we tried to escape the flames, we were attacked. They tried to carry off the two girls. Moriarty's men saved us and brought us here. They said if we were here, it would be easy to defend us. Do you think Lady Baldwin will mind?"

Clara declared she was delighted to have them, "Though horrified at the need, of course. And the men from Moriarty Protection saved the day again. We must be very grateful to them. Children, let us go and inspect the nursery. Mrs. White, Mr. Eastwood, I shall have bedrooms made up for you."

The children were soon settled at a table in the schoolroom, carrying on with their lessons as if nothing had happened. Indeed, the adults were more shaken than the children.

The bodyguards had managed to capture two of the assailants while driving off the others. One of the bodyguards had delivered the men to Mrs. Moriarty, their boss, while the others escorted their charges to Clara's house. Perhaps this would be their due cause—a provable offense for which they could have the marquess detained.

However, when Mrs. Moriarty reported a couple of hours after Harmony and the others arrived, the news was disappointing. Neither assailant knew anything about who had employed their gang. "I have a few leads to follow up, to find the person who took instructions for the job, and therefore what he knows about the man who paid him. We shall keep at it," she said.

Meanwhile, she agreed that the newcomers should stay in the household. "I shall leave all three teams in place. Teign will go after Lord Kemble first and foremost, as the leader of the brothers, and then his daughter, as a lever to move Kemble. It is convenient to have these two together, now we know the marquess has found where Miss Lydia was hiding."

After she left, Mel and Allan spent some time with the children, and then prepared to go out in public again, to keep Society talking.

The rain continued, so the brothers and their ladies met at the London Museum, and chatted as they strolled around, looking at the exhibits. "When this is over," Allan said to Mel, "we must come back with the children."

Quite apart from the attack on Harmony's home, two of the other coaches had been ambushed last night on their way home from the Dellboroughs. The assailants were driven off. Nothing else of significance had happened, at least to their knowledge.

They all went back to Clara's for a planning session and then dinner. That, at least, was the theory, but Harriet and Lydia each had their sole remaining parent close at hand for a change, and were waiting to pounce as Mel and Allan followed Baldwin and Clara in the door.

As the other six couples followed, Harriet drew back, suddenly shy, but Lydia had no such reservations. "Papa and Mrs. Blackmore, we need to show you the art we have been doing this afternoon. Also, Mrs. Blackmore, please will you tell us a story before bed? Your stories are so good."

"Are uncles permitted to come to see the art?" Baldwin asked, and Clara added, "And aunts?"

In fact, everyone wanted to come, and so the sixteen of them crowded into the school room. With the three children, plus Phineas and Harmony, there was not much space to move around, but the two girls were delighted to show their paintings.

Benjie, not to be left out, introduced everybody to his pet mice. "I had to bring them with me, Auntie Mel. I couldn't leave them in the burning house, and if I let them out, they might have been eaten by a cat."

Mel was impressed with how calmly Clara accepted this unusual addition to the household. "We have a cat in this house, Benjie," Clara said. "Make certain they stay shut in their cage at all times, for cats are very fast, and they do not understand the difference between tame mice and wild."

One could only hope that the boy obeyed, and that there was no carnage in the schoolroom.

"Can we come and watch the dancing later?" Lydia begged.

"We are not planning to dance later," Allan told her. "Are we, Clara?"

"Not tonight," Clara said, "but we have nine couples here. Why not go out into the long gallery now and dance?"

And so, they did, with the ladies and some of the gentlemen taking turns on the piano in the long hall that did sterling service as a place for children to play and adults to walk when the weather was inclement, as a picture gallery, and—as now—as a dance space.

It was ten couples, in fact, for the three children joined in, though the impromptu entertainment ended with the nine ladies—the seven wives plus Mel and Harmony—dancing a circle dance.

After that, the children returned to the nursery, and the adults to the drawing room. The discussion on the rescue mission to the cellars was enlivened by the teasing and camaraderie of the brothers. As Mel had observed over the days since she first met them, they were fast friends. Being men, they often expressed their affection for one another in insults, mocking comments, and even outbreaks of shoving and fisticuffs.

On the whole, Allan was immune from physical attacks, though he came in for his share of pointed comments. Baldwin, in particular, had a habit of producing embarrassing memories at apt moments. One example was a comment about not letting Allan take charge of any keys, which led to chortles and a story about their early days in the tower, after they had first discovered the hidden doors to the stairs and had begun the adaptations, such as the trapdoor, that hid their secrets still further. Apparently, it was they who had installed the lock on the door to the lower tower, and hidden it behind a brick. Allan had promptly lost the ring with two keys given to him by the locksmith. It had been discovered a week later, when they were on the point of blindfolding the locksmith and bringing him in to open his own lock.

"It was on the floor of the necessary," Hudson reported, with glee. "Kicked under the basket of rags. One can only guess how it got there."

By contrast, the ladies showed their growing friendships by sharing interests and life stories, supporting one another with encouraging remarks. Even those who had not previously known one another well were merging into a sisterhood through their loyalty to their husbands, and they willingly opened their community to Mel and even to Harmony, whose only connection to them was through Mel.

The ladies insisted on being part of the planning process, but said little until Mel declared that she would be part of the assault team.

"No," Allan said. "A fight is no place for a lady." Most of his brothers murmured their agreement.

"Allan, one or more ladies must be there. You will be dealing with an unknown number of women who have been repeatedly brutalized. If you want them to co-operate with their own rescue, you will need us."

"She is right, Allan," said Thomasina, and the ladies all nodded.

"I am willing to come," said Clara. "I can help if any of them need immediate medical care before being moved."

"I do not like it," Allan complained.

"I don't, either," said Baldwin. "But Melody is right. And the points she makes are ones none of the rest of us would have considered without her."

The clock was standing at thirty minutes past the hour of six when Clara called a halt so that people could change for dinner, which would be at half past seven. Mel went up to the nursery with Harmony and Allan and gave the children their promised story, then changed into a dinner gown.

One of the benefits of dressing as a man had been fewer changes, but she did enjoy seeing Allan's eyes drop to her chest when she returned downstairs. Her dress was one of several Harmony had made for her, and the bodice was lower than the gowns she usually wore, and another gown that she generally wore with a fichu.

Harmony had assured her that many ladies of high estate wore their gowns even lower, and the last week of socializing had confirmed the claim. Even so, Mel had avoided the gown until tonight, when the close familial environment gave her the confidence to give it an outing.

Appearing in public naked from just an inch above her nipples made her self-conscious, so Allan's burning look was a confidence booster. Even so, she was careful all evening not to lean forward. At least until she and Allan were alone. Perhaps she might leave the gown on and lean forward when he arrived to join her. It would be interesting to discover just what that look promised.

Chapter Nineteen

T HEY WOKE TO be told that a visitor awaited them downstairs. A maid brought the news, knocking on the door then putting her head around it to ask—blushing and stammering— whether Mrs. Blackmore knew where Lord Kemble might be.

Apparently, their nighttime liaisons were not as secret as they hoped. With their daughters living under the same roof, they were being particularly careful that their nocturnal activities did not become a matter of gossip. With that in mind, Allan stayed hidden under the sheets, while Melody left the bed. Since she had been wearing nothing, Allan would have liked to watch.

"You have a card?" Melody asked.

"Yes, Ma'am. Here, Ma'am."

"Madam Hera," Melody read aloud. "Please show her to the small parlor and tell her that we shall be down shortly. Would you be able to provide her with the beverage and refreshments of her choice while she waits? I do know where Lord Kemble might be, and shall pass on the message. Please send up a maid with warm water to my room and Lord Kemble's."

Allan raced back to his room as soon as the maid left, and washed and dressed in record time. The maid with her washing water must have helped Melody with her buttons, for she was ready at her door when he emerged from his chamber. They had been quick, but it was still thirty minutes before they arrived in the parlor to find Madam Hera sipping tea.

"Coffee for us both," Allan said to the maid, while Melody said to their guest, "Madam Hera, good morning. Thank you for coming to call. How may we help you?"

"By putting a stop to that fiend Teign," Madam Hera said, her face grim. "Lord Kemble, Mrs. Blackmore, I have now spoken to all my former colleagues from my days with Ramping Billy, and I have news to share. In private."

"I shall pour the coffee, Maudie," Melody said to the maid. "Please shut the door on your way out."

As soon as the girl was gone, Madam Hera told them her news. For years, the prostitutes of London had known that someone was buying the personal and exclusive services of a dozen or so of London's top whores each year.

Back before Madame Hera transferred her focus to the ladies' club, she, like the others in the profession, had believed those selected by the unknown buyer were the lucky ones, chosen to spend a year being pampered and richly paid, then able to retire on their newly earned wealth.

"By the time I retired from the brothel business," Madam Hera told them, "Some of us were beginning to have our doubts. Usually, when a girl does well, they come back at least once or twice to show off their clothing and their jewelry to the other girls, and to boast about how good their protector is to them."

She sighed, and took another sip of her tea. "Or, they waste their money, or the protector doesn't keep his promises, and they come looking for their old place back. In all the years this buyer took girls, I never heard of one coming back." She drained her cup.

"Let me pour you another," Melody said. Madam Hera passed her the cup and continued her tale. "When two of my girls were invited during that last year, I begged them not to accept. But they believed the promises of the buyer's agent, poor girls." She accepted the freshly poured cup of tea.

"Thank you, dear. I spent yesterday visiting different houses where I know the madam or the senior girls. I wanted to know if it was still happening, and if anyone had discovered who was behind it. Sure enough, my former colleagues have been watching, listening, and comparing notes."

After another deep breath was exhaled in a sigh, she said, "The buyer is only a middle-man, but he delivers the girls to a person who is an agent for a man named Farnham."

Allan must have reacted, for she nodded and commented, "I thought you would know the name."

"Teign's steward," Allan said.

"Indeed. Kemble, I don't know what has happened to those girls, but I am very afraid they are dead. Or most of them. There are rumors that a few discards are sold cheap to the worst hell holes in London or in other cities. The buyer purchased a new crop of girls a few weeks ago, but as to where they were taken, we do not know."

Allan exchanged a glance with Melody. They knew the location to which the girls were taken, and Madam Hera's information explained where they came from.

"Madam Hera," he said, "we think we know where Teign is holding those survivors. What you've told us might be the final nail in the villain's coffin. Would you be willing to write and sign a statement for the magistrates?"

He half expected her to refuse. Women who had pursued a career such as hers tried to avoid the notice of magistrates, except for those who came to them as customers, and who were therefore guaranteed to turn a blind eye to their illegal activities.

Madam Hera firmed her lips and nodded. "I owe it to those girls," she said. "What should I write?"

They settled that Melody should ask her questions and take notes, and then write out a statement that the club owner could copy and sign. Allan sent for more coffee and writing materials. By the time the rest of the family were awake, Madam Hera had told Melody all she knew about the girls who had been taken and the buyer, and had gone on her way.

Halfway through the morning came the news that Thomasina's house in Smithfield had been attacked in the night. The attackers had not reckoned on the resilience of three French aunts who had not only survived the revolution, the Terror, the directorate, Napoleon's years in power, and the return of the Bourbons, but had built a thriving wine export business out of the ashes of their former lives as aristocrats.

The aunts had gone into action while Cornelius was grappling with one of the intruders and Thomasina was taking their son to the attics, where a gap beneath the rafters connected the houses.

One had fetched a pistol, one a club, and the third had rung a large handbell that brought the rest of the neighbors out in their droves. With six men in custody, the community had awaited the arrival of the constables, celebrating with wine from the cellar, and baguettes, cheese, and olives produced by other merchants who had come to the rescue.

Several hours passed in revelry before Cornelius realized he should let his brothers know what had happened.

When Allan immediately declared his intention of going to Thomasina's place to make sure no one was harmed, Clara ordered him a carriage and Melody said she would go with him.

They found that both house and inhabitants were unharmed, though the same could not be said for the invaders. Apparently, while four people had entered the house meaning to kidnap or murder the family, two had stacked kindling along an internal wall in the basement and splashed it with gin so it would catch quickly despite the cold damp conditions.

They had been piling furniture onto the stack to give fuel to the proposed fire when the neighbors discovered them. The row of old terrace houses dated back nearly to the days that London was rebuilt after the Great Fire, and had been built in brick, but even so, had the fire caught, it might well have spread along the row.

Nothing and no one could have stopped the neighbors from expressing their anger on the bodies of the invaders. Two of them were still unconscious, and all six had bruises and broken bones from the beatings they had taken.

Under that treatment, those still conscious had spilled everything they knew. However, they had not been able to name the person who hired them. A man in a pub. A man who was muffled up against the cold and who wore a cap pulled down over his head. A man who kept to the shadows.

"The buyer paid half of the reward for the attack up front," Cornelius said. "He was to pay the other half after the job was done. The constables went to the rendezvous, but the buyer must have heard about his hirelings' failure, because he did not turn up."

Satisfied that Cornelius, Thomasina, their son, and the three aunts were all safe and well, Allan and Melody returned to Mayfair to find they had missed another attempted kidnapping.

"Papa," Lydia shouted in greeting, "we fooled the kidnappers!"

Kidnappers? Allan's immediate reaction was to grab his child and begin checking her for injuries. "Are you hurt, Lydia?" He looked wildly around and fixed his gaze on his brother-in-law. "Phineas, what happened?"

"An attempted kidnapping," Phineas said, baldly. "The two girls delayed the kidnappers while Benjie came to fetch us." He ruffled Benjie's hair. "They were all very brave."

There was more to it than that, of course. The girls, who rightfully regarded themselves as the heroines of the hour, claimed the right to tell the story.

"Cook gave us some bread to feed the sparrows, Papa," Lydia said.

"Aunt Harmony sent Uncle Hugo to guard us," Harriet explained. Hugo, who was hovering on the outskirts of Allan's family group, was one of the Moriarty men. The children had adopted their regular guards as honorary uncles and aunts.

"There was shouting in the mews, and Uncle Hugo went to see what was happening."

"I am sorry, my lord. I should have left it to my colleagues and stayed with the little ones," said Hugo. Allan nodded in acknowledgement, but most of his attention stayed with his daughter and Melody's Harriet.

"A man appeared in the gateway to the kitchen courtyard," said Lydia. "He said the cat had had kittens, and if we came with him, he would show us."

Harriet was lifting herself onto her tiptoes and back down, clearly unable to contain her excitement. "We told him that Uncle Hugo said we must stay where he left us."

Lydia nodded, and grinned at her friend. "We asked him to bring the kittens to us."

"He said they were too young to move." Harriet shrugged. "He stayed in the shadow of the gateway, and kept looking around as if he was afraid of being seen."

"The man hadn't seen Benjie. He was on his way back inside."

That was Lydia's contribution, and Harriet added, "Benjie doesn't like the cold."

"So, I thought of the code words," said Lydia.

The code words? Allan's face must have indicated he didn't understand, for Harriet explained. "Mama gave us a code to use if we were in danger. That way, if we had to send a message, such as if someone kidnapped us, we would just have to say purple pickled eggs, and she would know it was us."

"She told Harriet and Benjie, and Harriet told me." Lydia gave her friend a hug. "So, I said to Harriet, 'I love kittens more than purple pickled eggs. Do you think Uncle Hugo would understand if we went with the nice man?'"

"Benjie was so smart," said Harriet, casting her cousin an approving smile. "He rushed off inside. I argued with Lydia about staying where we were told, and she argued back, and the man just watched."

Lydia was bouncing now. "And then the guards came and caught the man and his friends, and Uncle Baldwin says it was because of us!" She hugged her friend.

Allan, his head teeming with all the ways things could have gone wrong, felt his legs grow weak with sheer relief, so he dropped onto his knees and held out his arms for his daughter.

Melody, he noticed, was doing the same with her daughter and nephew.

"I am so sorry, my lord," said Hugo, again, hanging his head and adding, in an undertone, "Mrs. Moriarty is going to kill me."

"Uncle Hugo told us to stay where the uncle who was at the window could see us," said Lydia. "So, we did. Do not blame Uncle Hugo, Papa." The Moriarty men had posted one of their number at an upper window to watch for assaults on the house, such as the one that drove Phineas and Harmony from their home and last night's one in Smithfield.

"Yes, and he punched the bad man very hard," Harriet pointed out.

That was some consolation. If the children had been seduced by the promise of kittens, Moriarty's men would have been on them before they could escape with their captives. Somewhat soothed, Allan decided to leave Hugo to the mercies of his employer. From the man's expression, he did not expect to get off lightly.

"All's well that ends well," said Phineas.

"Yes," said Melody, rather grimly. "But until we bring Teign down, it is not ended. Allan let us go and add this incident to our report for the group of lords that the Duke of Dellborough is coordinating." She closed her eyes, took a deep breath and let it out. Lifting her lashes again, she said, "It has been an interesting day."

LATE IN THE afternoon, they heard from Dellborough. His coterie of lords had been busy. Ten of them had been racing around town, leaping to the duke's command, visiting other influential peers. "We have the numbers to insist on an inquiry," Dellborough wrote, "even without evidence from tomorrow's expedition. As to that, I enclose a list of the four gentlemen I suggest for that little excursion. All four are peers or the heirs to peers and will be useful witnesses. All have military experience and will be useful in a fight."

A family connection of Kempbury's, the Earl of Somerville, brought Dellborough's message and was at the head of the list. He had been in the army during the wars with Napoleon, and seemed to think he would be in command this time, too.

"I know the cellars," Allan pointed out. "I shall lead the way." Besides, with the rest of the team being made up of three Moriarty guards, two of his brothers, himself and his lady, his seven outnumbered their four.

Somerville did not argue. "It is your family matter and is, or shall be, your townhouse," he acknowledged.

A man of reason. And, after all, Allan's battles had all been personal and familial. Somerville's experience would be useful. "I shall lead the way," Allan repeated, "but if it comes to a fight, I shall obey your commands."

"Where shall we meet?" Somerville asked.

"We need to get into the lower tower, which means going in through the tunnels," Allan said. "I suspect there'll be a watch on the entrances. After all, the marquess's men found their way into the tunnels, and only fools would not explore to find where they led."

"They may be fools," Baldwin commented. "But I would not suggest we count on it."

"We can't go in through the courtyard, and the riverbank will be busy in the daytime. We shall have to go in through the alley and overpower the guard before they have a chance to raise the alarm."

"As to that," said Mel, "I have an idea."

Chapter Twenty

"COME BACK TO bed," coaxed Allan.

By the evidence of the light seeping in around the edges of the drapes, it was full daylight outside, but they still had the rest of the morning to live through before the assault on the cellars.

"I cannot sleep," Mel replied.

Allan held out his arms. "Who said anything about sleeping?"

Although they had met less than two weeks ago, and had been lovers for only a few days, it seemed to Mel that she had loved Allan forever. She went easily into his embrace, and snuggled with him under the covers.

He slept naked, though she had not yet discovered whether that was a habit or a reaction to her presence, and he soon helped her out of the night rail she had donned before leaving the warm bed.

He yelped when she began to explore him with chilled hands, but grabbed them back when she drew away with an apology. "You'll warm up fast enough," he promised, and he was right.

Last night, they had coupled with frantic haste, needing to burn off all the anguish of the near kidnapping of their daughters and the threat to Cornelius and Thomasina, and their horror at the fates of so many poor prostitutes.

This morning, they came together at their leisure, taking their time to explore one another's bodies, murmuring words of encouragement and appreciation. Slowly, the passion built, until the tempo was not enough to meet the need spiraling outward from where they touched, belly to belly, chest to chest, hands roaming wherever they could reach. Rising in urgency and tension where they joined, the sweet agony that Mel had only learned in Allan's arms, though she had been a wife for three years long ago.

All too soon, Mel was as wordless as a newborn child, all language fled, begging for completion in gasps and moans. Allan's beloved face above her was distorted with the effort of holding back to wait for her.

His eyes met hers. He smiled and changed his angle and his pace, and in a few breaths the sweetness in her peaked and exploded. She managed to muffle her scream. Allan moved powerfully inside her and the explosion went on and on. As it faded, he stiffened and groaned.

In the tower, he had shouted. It was a pity they no longer had that privacy.

He lowered himself so most of his weight was on the bed, shifting her onto her side. Mel rested, treasuring their closeness. It might have been fifteen minutes later when he said, "Good morning, Melody."

"It has been so far," she replied, eliciting a chuckle.

"'Good morning' was my wish for you, my love. I hope you have a good morning."

My love. Allan had been dropping endearments like that into his private conversations with her. She tried not to take it seriously. The warmth, the longing for more—they would only make the inevitable end of the affair more painful. Her lectures to herself didn't help. She was head over heels in love with the man, and when he walked away, she was going to be devastated.

But that was a problem for another day. She intended to enjoy every moment of them being lovers, and let her broken heart wait for another day.

Allan, however, appeared to read her mind—as usual. "Melody, I need you to know something. It's about afterward. After this is over."

No! It is too soon. Mel fought the urge to put her hands over her ears and composed her face so it did not show her pain.

"What about after?" she said.

"I shall do it properly after," he said. "On bended knee, with flowers. But I need you to know now. Don't give me your answer, if you are not sure of it, but Melody, you are the beat of my heart and the fire in my veins, the breath in my lungs and the joy in my life. I want to go through life with you. I want to make babies with you—little brothers and sisters for Harriet and Lydia. I want to marry you and keep you forever by my side."

It was so much the opposite of what Mel expected that she simply stared at him. After a moment, he sighed and moved off her. "Not the reaction I was hoping for," he said, perhaps more to himself than to her.

Mel went to open her mouth and realized it was already gaping. "Allan," she said, "you cannot have thought. You are one of the highest born men in the land. I am gentry at best, and hardly that. I make a living snooping into other people's secrets. I am not a fit match for you."

Allan made an impatient gesture. "You mean you do not want to bind yourself to a penniless aristocrat who is nearing forty years and needed to be a male escort to buy food and clothing. You do not need to let me down easily, Mel. I know I am not worthy of a lady like you."

Am I hearing things? Mel shut her eyes tightly, gave her head a quick if miniature shake, and summoned all her courage. "I have fallen in love with you," she admitted. "But I never expected you to love me in return."

He pushed himself up on his elbow, hope lightening his expression. "Well," he said. "I do so love you. Melody, you are a wonderful woman. Of course I love you. And respect you, and admire you. I have been courting you all week. I have been arguing with myself for days about whether I ought to tell you how I feel."

"But I am poor," Mel protested. "And thirty-two. And a commoner."

"I do not care about any of that, and you don't need to care either. If you love me, and I love you, and we both love our daughters, then let's be a family. Will you marry me, Melody?" He grimaced, and made a cutting motion with his free hand. "No! I am not going to ask you yet. I want to propose to you properly."

She wasn't at all sure what her face was saying to him, but he must have been pleased with it, for he leaned closer and kissed her—a tender sweet kiss that brought tears to her eyes, for it promised a happy future that she had never believed possible for her.

The tears alarmed Allan. "You are crying," he accused.

"Because I am happy, dearest heart," she assured him.

"Oh. Very well, then. Melody, my darling, I don't know how it is, given I am no longer a young man, but…" He lay back on his pillow, took her hand, and put it down under the sheets to prove that he had recovered from his earlier exertions. "Shall we celebrate that we are courting?"

And so they did.

THE MOST IMPORTANT distraction set the time for everything else. Fortuitously, the king had returned to London, and the Duke of Dellborough had seen him yesterday, supported by the Duke of Kempbury and several other peers. They had presented the evidence collected so far and asked the king to summon the Marquess of Teign to answer questions arising from that evidence.

Since His Majesty did not rise before noon—and that was

early for him—the meeting was set for two in the afternoon, and the messenger from the king would arrive at Teign's house at noon. The summons commanded Teign's presence but did not give a reason.

Whether the interview would be of any use remained to be seen, but Teign would be away from his home from one in the afternoon until at least four.

The second distraction was for Farnham. They had been lucky enough to trace the agent that Madam Hera mentioned, and he was now locked up in Dellborough's cellars.

He was being very cooperative. He had handed over all his records, and had written a letter to Farnham offering "three prime whores, well-trained but still virgins, clean and in good condition." That letter would be delivered after Teign left to see the king.

The third distraction, a direct assault on the courtyard once Farnham was out of the way, should draw off most of the footmen and guard.

The brothers and their wives all arrived at Clara's house at noon. At ten minutes after one, a messenger arrived to say that Teign had left his townhouse. Ten minutes later, Mel, Allan, Baldwin, and Ernest were about to go out to the carriage that was ready for them, when another messenger reported that Farnham was on his way in the direction of the agent's warehouse.

The third distraction, the attack on the courtyard, was imminent, then. Set for thirty minutes after Farnham left, it would be active in twenty minutes, so they needed to quickly reach the Westminster Abbey grounds, where they were meeting the rest of the assault team.

They were in place with time to spare, half the team at each end of the alley where the tunnel emerged. Mel's group comprised herself, Allan, two bodyguards—both women—and a duke's son. Baldwin and Ernest were with Somerville, the other two bodyguards and two other earls. Three of the bodyguards were women.

Mel peered into the alley while being careful to stay mostly hidden behind the building on the corner. She could see two sentries. They had put up a brazier at the mouth of the tunnel, in front of the gate, but even so, they were marching back and forth, stomping their feet and rubbing their hands to counter the cold.

"Two men," she said. "I don't know if there are more in the tunnel, but if so, the distraction should move them." She hoped.

The assault group loitered in the street, doing their best to look as if they had just stopped for a conversation. The duke's son was keeping an eye on his watch. "Lord Kemble," he said after several minutes, "the distraction should begin in two minutes."

"It's time," Allan said to Mel, who unfastened the cloak she was wearing and handed it to Baldwin.

Beneath, she wore another of the costumes from her trunk of disguises—a gaudy but patched skirt and a patched and threadbare coat in an equally eye-watering color. She hung from Allan's arm as they strolled into the alley, patting his chest and looking invitingly up into his eyes.

As hoped, the two sentries dismissed them as harmless. Just a whore and her client looking for a little privacy. "Oy," shouted one. "Move along. You can't do that here."

"I know a place," Allan said to Mel. "This way, sweetie." He led her closer to the tunnel.

One of the sentries stepped into their path and held his arms out. "Go round," he demanded. "You can't come through here."

"Give us a break, mate," Allan begged. "The long way round'll take too long. I can't be late back to work, and Grace here won't wait till I'm off."

"Too cold after dark," Mel grumbled. "Too cold now."

"Tell you what," said the other sentry. "We'll let you through if she does us, too."

The suggestion had the first sentry stepping out of the way so she and Allan could move another few paces. The second man stepped out into the alley, trapping them, as he thought, directly outside the entrance to the tunnel.

It had turned out even better than Mel hoped. They were close enough now to see into the tunnel. If there were more men on the other side of the grill, they were in the darkness beyond where the light reached.

At that moment, they heard a cacophony rising from somewhere not far away. Clanging, banging, shouting, explosions, a scream. The sound was coming through the tunnels as well as over the buildings.

The two sentries turned to look in the direction of the noise, and at that moment, Mel and Allan moved. In seconds, Mel had hers trapped with a dagger against his neck and Allan had knocked the other unconscious. The rest of the assault team, in two groups, converged on them from each end of the alley, and took over tying and gagging the two sentries while Allan fished in his pouch for the key and opened the gate to the tunnel.

"We do not know whether there are sentries on the hidden door to the lower tower," Allan warned. "Be careful. But fast."

"Like rats up a drainpipe," said Ernest, cheerfully.

With the aid of a single lantern, carefully shuttered to throw a single pool of light ahead of the group, they hurried in single file along the tunnels. If Ernest thought these were like pipes, he would have to think again when he saw where they were going. Allan had described it to her last night—a long round hole, very much like a pipe, connected the tunnels under the tower with the cellars of the house.

The luck was running their way, or the diversion had worked. They saw no one in the tunnels, and when they reached the landing on the stairs where the hidden door into the lower tower was, there were no signs of disturbance. Allan moved the stone that hid the lock and used his key.

No ambush awaited them. The room felt as if it had been empty for days. Once everyone was inside, Allan locked the door again and worked the mechanism that replaced the stone.

"Downstairs," he said, and led the way. Mel passed the door of the room where she and Allan had first come together in bed.

At the time, she had wondered whether it was her seduction or his. She had never expected that he was serious about her—that he would want a future!

This was not the time to think about it, however. They were in the windowless ground-level part of the tower, and Allan and three more men were moving a heavy old desk and the mat it stood on to reveal a trap door in the floor.

Opened, the trap door revealed a ladder and below that a steep staircase. "Light the lanterns," Allan said, and Baldwin lit a spill from the lantern he carried and passed it to be used to light another lantern. The spill made the rounds until all the lanterns were alight.

Down into the tower cellar they all went, Baldwin coming last to close the trap door behind them. It was a big open space with a reservoir in the center, fed from an undergrown stream that flowed in through a pipe in the wall with the overflow running out through another pipe.

Surely the system dated back to when this tower was a defensive keep—a refuge in times of trouble for the people who lived nearby. Safe behind thick stone walls, with fresh water beneath their floor, they would have been able to outlast warring bands who attacked from the land or the river.

Allan led the group to a third hole in the wall. Round like the two pipes, it was much larger—big enough for even the largest of the men to crawl through, but not big enough to stand up or even kneel in.

They all stared at it. "This is the way?" Somerville said, after the silence had stretched for what felt like minutes.

"This is the way," Allan confirmed. "This pipe leads to the townhouse's cellars."

He sent Mel a quick smile. "I'll lead the way," he said. "The pipe is perhaps fifty meters long. Be careful with the lanterns when we get close to the cellars. I think the place we come out is deserted, but I don't want light to betray us."

"Lead on," said Ernest.

"Piping," said one of Dellborough's lords sourly. "Oh joy."

Mel had abandoned her gaudy skirts and petticoats in the tower, and just as well. Crawling through the pipe was much easier in the trousers she'd worn under her petticoats. She was near the middle of the group, with booted feet ahead of her, and Cornelius close on her heels.

She tried not to think about the weight of earth above her. Earth, and by now, surely, the townhouse itself? According to Allan, the cellars that were their destination were younger than the tower but older than the house, which had been rebuilt on the original site after the Great Fire.

The two were not quite contiguous, the cellars being bigger than the current house and at a different angle, so that parts of the cellars were not under the house, and in one or two places, parts of the house were not above the cellars.

Such ruminations distracted her from the sensation of being buried in a round hole in the ground. Distracted her long enough that she was surprised when the man in front of her suddenly disappeared and there was the outlet from the pipe to the cellar.

Her turn. She poked her head out into the cellar and two men stood, one on either side, ready to take her arms and swing her down to the ground.

She looked around as those behind her were being assisted in their turn. She was in a large cellar room with a low ceiling and a clay floor. There was no door—just a rectangular space in the walls with darkness beyond it.

"The place is still deserted," Allan said, keeping his voice low, his lips close to her ear. "We are under the old wing. The cells where I suspect they are keeping the women are under the main part of the house, near the exit from the cellar to the street that Cook says the warders use."

Baldwin whispered. "Let's go. But quietly. My part of the plan might not have worked."

It had, though, and better than they had expected.

When Baldwin had suggested giving laudanum to the marquess's cook to put in the warder's beer, they'd hoped to even the odds against them, at least ensuring that those not on duty would sleep through the noise of the invasion.

Instead, the cook had performed beyond all expectations. Men had dropped where they were, some still holding empty mugs. Had Cook added laudanum to the stew as well? "Lock them in one of the cells," Somerville ordered. "Choose two to take with us as witnesses."

"We brothers shall deal with the warders," Allan said. "Somerville, you and your friends go from cell to cell, and inspect the place for anything that might support the case against Teign. Mel, I'll leave you and the other women to follow Somerville and release the prisoners. Let us know if you find other warders. We'll collect them."

Moriarty's three women fell into step behind Mel as she followed Somerville. The place was a warren of tunnels with dozens of cells, some big enough for up to ten beds, some with as few as one or two.

They found eight women, locked in the dark in three of the rooms. The two women in the first room shrank away from the light, whimpering, but when they realized that Mel and the Moriarty guards were women, they ceased their noise and just waited, suspicious and frightened.

"My friends and I have come to save you," said Mel. "We shall take you out of here, away from Teign and his men."

"Is it true?" The woman who spoke straightened slightly.

"It is another of Farnham's tricks," said the other woman.

"No trick," Mel assured her. "Come. Your warders are all unconscious, and the men in our party are locking them up, except those we are taking to question."

The women remained huddled under the single blanket they shared. "What do you want us for?" demanded the woman who had suspected a trick.

"We want to rescue you," Mel said. "We intend to bring Teign to trial for his many crimes. We brought witnesses who can give evidence of what Teign was doing here. But we cannot leave you to suffer. Come with us to have your injuries tended, and after you are well, we shall help you find safe places to live."

The women exchanged glances. "If it is a trick," said the suspicious woman, "may you burn in Hell."

They got up from the bed on which they'd been sitting, and Mel realized something for which she and her friends had not planned. The women had no clothes. Each wore nothing but a grubby shift, spotted and striped with dark stains.

Mel went to the door. "Can you find these ladies some garments?" she asked Allan. She deputed one of the Moriarty women to stay with the two and help them dress, and took the others with her to the next locked room.

A similar scene played out. Before she had persuaded the three women in this room, the two from the first limped in, dressed in shirts, trousers, socks, and coats that must have been purloined from the warders.

"Might as well come along," said one of them to the three Mel was trying to convince. "At least they've given us something to wear. I'd risk a lot for clean clothes."

Mel left all five women with the one guard and went to the next room, where she was faced with a new challenge. The three women in that room had all been badly beaten.

"Allan," she said, when she emerged from the room, "these three are too badly injured to walk. Baldwin, can you come and see how we can safely move them?"

They were delayed a further ten minutes while Baldwin gave each of the three a drink of the doctored ale—a small one, since he was uncertain of the amount of laudanum in it—and prescribed temporary dressings and splints. "They will need a real doctor," he told Allan, Mel, and Lord Somerville. "But this will have to do for the journey. We cannot leave them here."

They had expected to have to fight their way out through the warder's exit, but the cook's reach had extended even to the guard post that prevented unauthorized entrances and exits. Two more warders joined the others, locked in a cell to sleep it off.

The transport Allan and Somerville had ordered was waiting, with a detachment of bodyguards on horseback. The five women who could still walk clambered aboard one carriage, clinging to one another and the Moriarty women. The men had made makeshift stretchers from doors, and they carried out the three with injuries too severe for walking. Baldwin climbed into a second carriage with them, to tend them on the journey. The rest of the men piled into the remaining two carriages, with the two warder prisoners, still unconscious but bound and gagged, thrown on the floor at their feet.

Mel mimed a kiss toward Allan and joined Baldwin in his carriage, to see what help she might be on the journey. It took only fifteen minutes, even at the slow pace they adopted to minimize the jolting. Mel and Baldwin tried to hold their patients still, but the trip could not help but cause further suffering. Fortunately, two of the three women were deeply unconscious, but the other moaned at every lurch. It was a relief when they finally turned into the stable-yard of Dellborough's townhouse.

The other carriages had arrived already, and a reception party waited with stretchers and a doctor for the injured. Baldwin went along with them to explain what he had done, and Allan, who had waited for Mel, escorted her to Dellborough's study, where a team of lawyers waited to take down everyone's statements.

"Dellborough and Kempbury were in the next room when His Majesty saw Teign," he told Mel. "Apparently, the King demanded that Teign answer to charges of abusing his power over his sons, sending assassins to set fires to kill his sons, buying and selling women, and keeping women prisoner. Teign lost his temper again and called the King a fat fool. The King is not pleased. He is currently determined to punish the marquess. One can only hope he does not waver."

"I have been told that King George has a kind heart," Mel replied. "If one of the lords were to tell him about the sad condition of those poor women, I am sure he would be touched."

"I'll suggest it," Allan promised.

"If His Majesty supports us, we cannot lose, Allan," Mel pointed out.

They were, for the moment, alone in a long passage. Allan tugged Mel into an alcove and kissed her until her head reeled. "Tomorrow," he promised in a whisper. "Tomorrow, this shall be over, and I shall be free to propose to you, my love.

Chapter Twenty-One

IT TOOK THE rest of the afternoon and long into the evening to take everyone's statements. Teign's warders were initially defiant, certain that, as one of them put it, "Ain't nobody can touch the master. And 'e'll send us to 'ell if'n we tell what we know."

"You fool," said one of the lawyers. "You see before you the Dukes of Dellborough and Kempbury. The Marquesses of Thornstead and Deerhaven. The Earls of Somerville, Sutton, and Trilby. Their Graces had an audience with the King yesterday afternoon to tell him about Teign's crimes. Even a marquess must answer to the King and the House of Lords. Teign's appointment with the devil is inevitable."

"In any case," Ernest pointed out, "we are witnesses to your own crimes, and we have enough evidence to convict you. You shall soon be dancing on the end of a rope. The question is whether what you tell us is worth a bucket of sand to weight your legs so you die quickly."

After that, the other warder broke and confessed, and his mate must have decided he was doomed either way, for he soon joined in.

At one point, Allan was called out to see Clara, who had visited with some unexpected company. The cook from Teign's townhouse and all her co-conspirators had turned up at Clara's house, escaping from Teign before he could figure out that they were involved in drugging the warders.

"We put laudanum in the stew as well as the beer, my lord," the cook explained. "And we made everything more salty than usual so they would be thirsty and drink more beer."

"It worked brilliantly," Allan told her. "Well done."

The Duchess of Dellborough agreed to offer the servants refuge, and Allan assured them that their positions would be restored to them after this was all over, if Allan had the power to make it so.

He might not. Allan had already considered—and discussed with his brothers—that Teign's crimes were so dreadful the title and all the estates might be forfeited. So be it. Teign had to be stopped, whatever the cost.

It was one of the reasons he wanted to wait to marry Melody. Although perhaps he should marry her before his future became clear, for she wanted to be a marchioness even less than he wanted to be marquess.

"Clara," he said to his sister-in-law as the duchess took the servants to hand over to her housekeeper, "Can you suggest where I might find flowers suitable to give to Melody when I propose?"

"Of course," said Clara. "Where do you plan to propose? I suppose you want privacy?"

Allan considered. "Actually," he said, after a moment, "I should like to make my formal proposal on bended knee in front of my family and hers."

Clara grinned at him. "Then," she said, "let us have a Twelfth Night party late tomorrow afternoon. I shall tell Harmony and all the wives."

"Warn them to say nothing to Melody," Allan cautioned.

"Of course. She will accept you, Allan. She loves you."

Allan hoped Clara was right. Melody *did* love him—she said so, and she was not a liar, despite her profession. But did she love him enough to take him scandal, marquisate, and all?

Tomorrow would tell the tale.

TEIGN MADE A break for it that night. His sons and their wives were all asleep and knew nothing about it until the morning, when Dellborough sent for Allan. Without preamble, the duke said, "After receiving our initial report on what you found in Teign's cellars, the king sent a detachment of his household guard to arrest Teign and convey him to the Tower of London. He was gone, and so was Farnham. The king has sent troops to each of Teign's estates, and more to the main ports."

"Troops!" Somerville snorted. He and the other peers who had joined in the assault on the cellars were together in Dellborough's study, dictating the final report. All four had been serving officers during the long war that ended nearly a decade ago. All four expressed their opinion of the royal component of the search in scathing terms.

"Parade-ground officers, all gilt and no substance," said Trilby.

"The troopers were as bad," Somerville claimed. "Shiny boots and feathers for brains."

"Who goes hunting for a miscreant in full dress uniform with a standard and a bloody drummer boy?" Trilby asked the room at large. He caught Melody's eye, flushed, and bowed. "Sorry, Mrs. Blackmore. Forgot. Ladies present."

"Twelve of them," Stanhope groaned. "Twelve troops of lummoxes in fancy uniforms on flashy horses, and every single one with a standard and drummer boy. The king wants us to keep the scandal quiet and sends out twelve drummer boys!"

"Useful for Farnham and Teign. They'd have been able to hear them a mile off," said one of the others, and the four of them sighed in unison.

"His Majesty wishes us to know he is taking matters seriously," Dellborough pointed out. "The real work will be done by the runners and thief takers. With luck, our fugitives will be watching the troops and will not notice who is coming up behind them."

"As for keeping the scandal out of the public eye," said Kempbury, "that horse has well and truly bolted. And I do not see the point, anyway. If a marquess has been breaking the law, surely the masses need to know that the royal family and the aristocracy will stand up for them and bring the villain to justice? This idea that the mob will descend on us if we do not hide the wrongs the wealthy commit, and pretend they do not exist…" He shook his head. "Ridiculous."

Allan thought that Dellborough underestimated Teign's devious nature. Who knew what the man might try, now he was cornered? The report writers had sent for all the Sheppards, to ask them a whole barrage of questions. The brothers spent the day trying to pretend they were not starting at shadows and flinching at loud noises.

If the various illustrious personages noticed, they were too polite to comment.

It was well into the afternoon before Allan, his brothers, and their wives could all gather at Clara's for Twelfth Night celebrations. Phineas and Harmony were there, too, of course, as were Harriet, Lydia and Benjie. Thomasina's aunts came, too, and so did Nottwick, Phineas's brother, and his wife and their two children.

All the children were delirious with excitement and joy. Not only did Lydia and Harriet have their respective parents with them, but every aunt and every uncle had bought or made each child a present.

The Twelfth Night cake was served first, with heated wassail to drink—sugar, nutmeg, orange juice, other spices, and cider. And a second version for the children, with apple juice substituted for cider, as Mel explained to Allan when he went to prevent Lydia from taking a third helping. Clara's kitchen had also produced a range of other edibles.

Phineas, who found the bean in his slice of cake, seemed nonplussed at being thus elected to be King for the night, but made a manful attempt to suggest silly games and even sillier forfeits, egged on by the other men.

The schoolroom party had come up with a play that involved the whole group. It featured the visit of the three kings to the baby Jesus, with Benjie, Lydia, and a cloth doll doing duty as the Holy Family, and Harriet providing commentary in the persona of the innkeeper's wife.

Allan, Phineas, and Cornelius were instructed to be the three kings, and the whole assembly was ordered to line up and think of a gift to bring to the baby. "It can be something real or something imaginary," Harriet said.

It took nearly an hour for everyone to present their gift. Most of them had chosen to amuse, and the company was often disabled with laughter, as when Harriet turned her nose up at the myrrh, because it was smelly, or when Allan solemnly presented a string of imaginary camels as being more versatile than a donkey.

Mel won acclaim from the ladies when she presented an invisible sack of clouts. "The sack never runs out, and the clouts in it are always clean. The discards will dissolve in water and never be seen again," she assured the very young Mary, who was not as impressed as the mothers in the room.

After that, the other ladies competed in presenting useful but extravagant gifts that could only be imagined. Baby clothes that grew with the infant. A self-replenishing dish of pottage. A baby carriage that was easy to push and pull, even over rough ground, and that also rocked on command. "Might as well give it a voice to sing lullabies," one of the brothers commented, and the lady who had suggested the device promptly added that to the list.

The children were allowed to stay up for dinner, though they had been snacking ever since the party started, and the littlest Nottwick was already sound asleep on her father's shoulder.

After that, parents began to make noises about bedtime. Allan, who wanted Lydia and Harriet to be present when he offered for Melody, signaled to Clara. This was the time.

SOMETHING WAS GOING on. Everyone kept looking at Mel. Did she have cake crumbs on her face? Surreptitiously, she peered into the glass on the cabinet doors. No. She could see nothing to explain the glances.

Allan was a target, too. Clara had just looked at him, then at Mel, then back at Allan. And there! Winifred was doing the same.

Mel sought to catch Allan's gaze. When he saw her looking and smiled at her, she became lost in his eyes. So much so, she was barely aware that he was closing the distance between them until he was directly before her.

There he stopped, and—without warning—went down on one knee. "Melody," he said, as her heart leapt and began to beat faster. "Melody, I never thought I would marry again. After my first wife, I was unwilling to risk such betrayal ever again, and why should I? I have a child who is the world to me. I even have an heir in my brother's son. Why marry?"

He smiled up at her. "But then I met a lady who made me reconsider. A lady who made me question my determination to spend my life alone. A lady of courage, integrity, and pride. You, Melody. You have filled the empty spaces in my heart and in my mind, and I can no longer imagine life without you. Your strength, your intelligence, your trust in me give me confidence that we shall never meet a challenge we cannot discuss and find our way through."

He took one of the hands that hung limp at her side. "Melody, my beloved, will you be my wife, my companion, my partner in life? Mother to our daughters and any other children God might grant us? My one and only love from this day until I take my final breath? Will you marry me?"

For a moment, Mel could not speak past the lump in her throat. His face dropped as he processed her silence. She shouldn't, couldn't bear his mistaken disappointment. "Yes," she croaked, forcing out the sound. "Yes, I will," she added, more normally, the one word having broken whatever blockage had disabled her.

Allan grabbed her other hand, grinning up at her, tears running down his cheeks. "You will?" He turned to glance over the gathering, grinning broadly, and shouted, "She will!"

Then Harriet and Lydia needed to be hugged and kissed, and assured that the family would all live together from now on. All those present had to assure one another they had seen this day coming, which was a surprise to Mel, for she had been certain it would never happen.

And finally, the children had their long-delayed bedtime, Allan and Mel escorting the group upstairs hand in hand with their two daughters.

Teign remained the only cloud on their horizon, and surely he would be captured soon?

Chapter Twenty-Two

F ARNHAM'S BLACK DEEDS came home to roost the following day. Allan and Mel had gone to visit the Bishop of London, to seek a license. They arrived back, mission accomplished, to the news that Farnham was in custody. In the prison infirmary, in fact. News of his crimes had filtered out, despite the king's prohibition on any details reaching the masses. He had been identified, and the citizens who enthusiastically apprehended him on behalf of the Crown had beaten him bloody.

"They say he will probably recover enough to be hanged," said Gerard, with great satisfaction.

The Teign butler, too, had been arrested, as had all the warders and some of the footmen. And the far reaches of the cellars at the Teign townhouse were being excavated under the supervision of a magistrate.

However, no one had seen hide nor hair of Teign.

And so it continued for the next two weeks, while those sent out of London to track the marquess down reported back, one by one, that they had found no trace of him. Meanwhile, Mel and Allan prepared for their wedding, and so did Phineas and Harmony. Phineas had proposed a few days after Allan, and he and Harmony planned to marry at the end of January, when Nottwick would be back in London after a lightning trip to his country estate.

Dellborough was continuing to take an interest in what the newssheets were calling "the Teign Affair". How much of an interest, Allan discovered the day before his wedding, when he received a visit from a royal herald with an invitation to wait upon the king that afternoon.

Fortunately, Dellborough was at home, and knew exactly what Allan should wear, how early he should arrive for the appointment, how he should enter and leave the room, and a dozen other things regarding etiquette when meeting royalty.

"Praise never goes amiss," Dellborough advised. "The king enjoys being admired."

"Do you know what this is about?" Allan asked, but the duke was not forthcoming, saying only, "It might be about a suggestion I made, but I shall say no more in case I am mistaken."

The king was vastly overweight and in poor health, but Allan caught flashes of the charm that had so enchanted the masses when the royal gentleman they called their Prince Florian was a young man. "Terrible business, this, with your father," the king said.

Allan agreed.

"Fathers can be the devil," the king mused. "Mind you, mine was mad—not saying yours is, Kemble, though one wonders." He shook his head. "Such elaborate schemes. Must be touched in the upper stories, don't you think?"

"He could not bear any kind of opposition, Your Majesty," Allan ventured. "I believe his wives showed too much backbone for him, though they had little enough, poor things. But those women we rescued had no chance to resist at all."

"*You* resisted," the king commented. "Dellborough told me all about it. His father was a friend of my father's, you know. Nice fellow, Dellborough. He tells me that Teign's title needs to be surrendered. Not attainted, you understand. Removed, so you can inherit and take on the responsibilities. Estates. House of Lords. All that. What do you think, Kemble?"

Allan realized he was gaping like a fish and shut his mouth while he tried to formulate an answer. "My father has disgraced the title and the British peerage, Your Majesty. His behavior is a smudge on your reign." The king frowned, and Allan hastened to add, "Though you removed it, of course, with your instant response, as soon as you knew what the man was doing."

"Yes, quite so," replied the king, with a smug smile. "Very well, Teign. It shall have to go before the House of Lords, of course, but I see no difficulty. Here. You shall need these." He gestured to the man who stood on his right and slightly to the rear, and the man stepped forward to hand Allan a card folder of papers, tied with ribbon.

"That shall be all, Teign," said the king. He sighed. "I have another meeting, but I am glad we have had this little chat."

Still unsteady after being called by his father's title twice in less than a minute, Allan backed away. After he was out of the room, he opened the folder. The covering sheet announced that it was for the lawyers, servants, and men of business employed by the Marquess of Teign.

Beyond was a letter to the senior partner of each group, the house steward or butler of each house, and the land steward of each estate, telling them that the king was taking steps to have Augustus Sheppard, Sixth Marquess of Teign, stripped of his title. Each letter then further instructed the recipient to treat Allan Sheppard, Earl of Kemble, as the Seventh Marquess of Teign until such time as he fully inherited the title.

"Of course," said Dellborough, who had been standing silently beside him as he read, "the king is a little beforehand addressing you as Teign, but the papers were drawn up by the Crown's best lawyers. You are in charge now, Kemble. And when the 'i's have all been dotted and the 't's crossed, you shall be the seventh marquess."

Dellborough seemed to think he was giving Allan good news, but to Allan, telling him he was about to receive the title seemed more like a curse.

Particularly when he arrived back and told Melody what had happened. She pointed out the positives, of course. "I know you didn't want this, Allan, but being wealthy and titled is a good thing. You will now have the power and the wealth to support your brothers, and to assist them in achieving their dreams."

Baldwin, too, could see the benefits. "Wherever Teign has gone, unless he has private assets, he no longer has wealth to hire bullies or lawyers."

And Phineas also had a suggestion to make the best of the current circumstances. "You should call the men of business and stewards together, as soon as possible, and tell them to give him nothing, and to let you know if he gets in touch."

All of which was true, but it didn't explain why Melody had resumed that bland expression that hid her thoughts. She had withdrawn from him, too, returning his smiles with an absent one of her own, and moving away from his touch.

He waited for privacy before he challenged her. "Melody, what is wrong? Do you not want the title? I don't have to be the marquess. I can leave Baldwin as my proxy and we shall run away with our daughters. Don't leave me, my love. I can give up everything else, but not you, and not Lydia."

Her mask slipped, and she gazed at him, her face expressing a mix of wonder and confusion. "But Allan, you cannot have thought. I cannot be your marchioness. My birth is barely acceptable, and I have been working for a living for years. Add to that, I am old. I might not be able to give you an heir."

In his relief that all her reasons were about social expectations and none about not wanting him, the first words that came to his tongue were, *Is that the maggot you have in your head?* Fortunately, he managed to trap the infelicitous words before he spoke them.

"If you cannot be my marchioness, I shall have no other, my dearest love," he said instead. "Your class is high enough to be acceptable to the Society hags who monitor such things. If it wasn't, I wouldn't care, except I should not like to see you being bullied by ladies who are not fit to kiss your slippers."

He thought of another point. "Besides, you have a duchess and at least two marchionesses on your side, and more than one countess. Also, your sisters-in-law. Together, the eight of you hardly need anyone else's approval, and only someone who is tired of living would dare to bully any of you. Can you imagine what Clara would do to them?"

To his relief, Melody giggled. Only a little splutter of a laugh, but a vast improvement.

"As to your age, you are thirty-two and I am thirty-eight. You are old enough and experienced enough to make a fit mate for me, and young enough to still give me more children, if God is kind. And if we have only daughters, or if our nurseries remain empty, I have one nephew and shall almost certainly have more in time."

His last argument brought a grin to his face when he thought of it. "As to your work, have you not solved many mysteries for fashionable families?"

"A dozen or more," Melody acknowledged. "They know how I have spent the past six years, and will tell their friends."

"Two points, heart of my heart. One. They cannot disclose what they know without also disclosing that Aunt Agnes stole the watch, or James Junior seduced the neighbor's daughter."

He had invented Aunt Agnes and James Junior, for she was discreet to a fault when talking about former cases. Still, from his expression, his point was made.

"Second, the Duchess of Kempbury was in the same line of work, and she is accepted everywhere."

Silence while he allowed her to digest his responses. After a while, she murmured, in a voice so quiet that he had to lean close to hear it, "Are you saying you do not mind?"

He took advantage of the closeness to kiss her, drawing away after an intense and passionate embrace just far enough to say, "Any other course of action, I would mind like hell. I love you, Melody Blackmore, and if you love me, we shall work out the rest."

"I love you," she told him. "That has never been the question."

"Then let us have our wedding so we can face this latest challenge together. Will you, darling? I cannot promise you peace and unsullied happiness, but I can promise you my loyal and unwavering love, from now until the day I meet my maker. Yes, and beyond."

He felt as if he could breathe again. He had been worried that she would not want to take him on. Certainly, she had good cause to reject him. Successive meetings with the men responsible for the marquisate—the lawyers, the stewards, and the men of business—showed that Teign had given up paying attention to his holdings a decade ago.

Fortunately, he had placed competent men in charge, but they were growing older, and some of them were beginning to lose control of the threads they held as part of the vast tapestry of the family's holdings.

The family was not in danger of bankruptcy, but the wealth was certainly not flowing as it should. Allan had years of hard work ahead of him to recover the situation, especially since he was determined to give each of his brothers a fully-functioning estate to provide them with both a home and an income.

He explained all this to Melody, believing she had the right to be informed so she could choose whether or not to stand by him. Her reply startled him.

"I suggest we hold a family meeting, beloved. I fully support your wish to see to the welfare of your family, but why not ask them what they want? For example, you own warehouses with wharves on the Thames. Cornelius plans to make his life in France, and may not want the trouble of an English estate, but warehouses for his wine business might suit him very well. Baldwin plans to study in Edinburgh to become a doctor, and you own a row of townhouses in Edinburgh, which would give his family a place to live, and income to live on."

Of course! She was brilliant! He grabbed her for a spontaneous hug. "We can show them the list of assets, and ask them to choose," he said. "I do not suppose we can gift the properties outright until I am officially the marquess, but we can give them the use and the income from them."

"We should ask for valuations where they haven't been provided," Melody mused. "That way, we can set an amount and give each brother equivalent value. We can tell them about it in the morning."

"We can leave them with the list and discuss it after we arrive back from our week at Barcliffe Priory," Allan proposed. All the brothers had spent most of their childhood at Barcliffe Priory, which was the Teign family seat on the coast in Hampshire. Allan had not been there in a decade, and looked forward to showing Melody the haunts of his boyhood.

He would do so under the unobtrusive watch of a team of Moriarty bodyguards, for Teign was still missing. Indeed, the news from all parts of the country was the same—nobody had heard anything from him since the morning of the fifth of January.

The Household Cavalry had searched the estate for Teign, and had questioned the servants and the tenants. After that, a couple of Bow Street runners did likewise. Mrs. Moriarty had also sent men to check.

The place was as safe as all those people could make it, and tomorrow night, Allan and Melody would spend the first night of their marriage there.

THE WEDDING THE following day was well attended, with the brothers and their wives, Harmony and Phineas, the French aunts, and the children. Mel worried, right up until the vows were made and his ring was on Melody's finger, that Allan would suddenly come to his senses and back out of the marriage.

He later told her that he had the same fear.

The wedding was only the beginning of a wonderful week. Mel and Allan set their duties and responsibilities—and their worries—to one side, and spent the week talking, playing chess, taking it in turn to read out loud, walking in the park, skating on the lake, and otherwise enjoying some rare leisure and one another's company.

And they explored one another's bodies. They went up to bed shortly after dinner, stayed under the covers in the morning, and often headed upstairs for an interlude during the day. Or they made good use of a nest of feather eiderdowns in the conservatory, or on the couch in front of the fire in the study, or in the room above the boathouse on the lake.

The physical side of marriage had been a revelation to Melody from their first time together.

Her previous husband was convinced that only scandalous women enjoyed such activities. He would not insult his lady wife, he had told her, by expecting her to get any pleasure from their coupling. "Lie still," he had said, on their wedding night. "I'll make this as quick as possible."

After that, he had come to her once a week, pulling down the blankets, throwing up her nightshirt, crawling on top of her, grunting and humping for a few minutes, then covering her again and leaving.

Once she announced she was with child, he had given up coming to her altogether until Harriet was weaned, at which point he resumed his weekly visits, except that now she had a child, he expected her to remain quietly at home while he made his frequent trips to race and hunt meetings in different parts of the country.

Mel had always assumed he had an arrangement with one or more scandalous women, and certainly he had spent few nights at home.

In the light of her new experience, she looked back with pity on her old self, and even on her first husband. Perhaps some of it was that she and Allan were in love, and their coupling was a physical expression of that love. In truth, she had never loved Blackmore, nor he her.

Mostly, though, it was Allan—kind and generous, masterful but respectful, adventurous, ever appreciative and encouraging. It was with deep regret that she allowed him to hand her up into the carriage for the journey back to London.

They had to return. Quite apart from all the work that awaited them in London, she and Allan were missing their daughters. His comment, as he took his seat beside her, showed that his thoughts were marching with hers. "Next time we come, we'll bring Lydia and Harriet."

"They will love it," Mel agreed. "What did Moriarty's man say?"

Allan had gone to speak to the team leader of their bodyguard as soon as they left the house. "He has had a daily report from Moriarty. No one has seen or heard from Teign. Nothing else of significance has happened."

They had agreed with family and friends that a messenger would be sent if Teign was found, if there were any more attacks, or if anything else important happened. Since they had heard nothing, they could assume there was nothing to hear. Except that they both became more and more on edge as the carriage drove closer and closer to London.

"They would have told us if anything was wrong." Allan made it a statement, but Mel knew it was truly a question.

"Yes, they would," she assured him, hoping she was right. "Or at least the Moriarty men would have heard." Her reason said it must be true, but she was still alert, waiting for something to go wrong and spoil her perfect happiness.

It was a relief to arrive at Clara's house, to confirm that the lack of messages meant merely that there was nothing to report.

It was late in the evening by the time they arrived, so Allan waited until the next day to raise the question of what each of his brothers wanted from the list of assets. He started with Baldwin and Clara, since he saw them first.

Baldwin immediately objected to the concept. "Clara and I have discussed it, Allan. We don't need you to do this. I'm a man grown, and my share of our savings is enough for me to look after my family until I have my medical degree." He patted his wife's hand. "And Clara is rich."

"The point isn't how much each of us need, it is what is fair." They were eating a casual meal at the table in the morning room, and Allan leaned forward over the table to emphasize his point. "Had our father been a decent man, he would have given each of us an allowance, and then, when we reached the age of looking for more out of life than leisure, a sum of money to buy a commission or shares in a business or an estate. That is all I am proposing, and it is long overdue."

"The Duke of Dellborough gave each of his sons the equivalent of the dowry he gave his daughters," Mel pointed out.

"I insist on this," Allan said. "If you won't say what suits you best, I'll do what Mel suggested, and put your name on the title deeds of the townhouses in Corrigan Place in Edinburgh. Since Clara has a house here in London, that will give you a home in both England and Scotland, and an income as well."

Baldwin and Clara exchanged glances. "Baldwin is concerned your generosity will leave you in difficulties, brother," said Clara. "We understand that the marquess's estates are not as productive as they should be, and that returns on his investments are down."

Allan shrugged. "That is true, but the books still balance and are in the black. When I inherit, even after giving you all your rightful share, I shall still have plenty of income to put some of it into improving performance, to live comfortably and with some grace, and to pay my wife's dressmaker bills."

The grin he sent Mel's way celebrated the shared joke—he had been trying to persuade Mel to buy a whole new wardrobe and she was resisting.

In revenge, and also to lighten the mood, Mel told Baldwin and Clara, "What my husband is trying to say is that he is currently merely as rich as a lord instead of as rich as Croesus."

"Truly," Allan assured Baldwin, "this will not hurt me at all, and I need to do it. I have not been able to protect you all in the last twenty years. This will make me feel I've made some sort of recompense."

"Balderdash," Baldwin responded. "No one could have been a better brother." After exchanging another speaking glance with Clara, he said, "Very well, then. If you insist. Clara and I shall take half the townhouses, and then, when I am qualified, a place in London suitable for consulting rooms."

The same conversation played out with each of the other couples as they called during the day. Phineas and Harmony, too, for Allan told Phineas he owed a debt he could not repay for Phineas giving up his own life to protect and raise Lydia, and Mel felt the same toward Harmony.

By the end of the day, each of the seven brothers had a home and an income, or at least the promise of it, once the legalities were completed.

It remained only to give Isaac and Jerome the same opportunity, but that could wait until they returned.

✦

Chapter Twenty-Three

BEFORE THE WEDDING, Allan and Melody had barely made a start at picking up the reins of the widespread Teign holdings. Throughout the rest of a cold and wet January, those responsibilities consumed much of their time.

At Melody's suggestion, Allan took one estate, one investment or one enterprise at a time, spending as much time as he needed to understand the potential, the problems, and the possible paths forward.

Dellborough's advice was invaluable. The duke became Allan's mentor, helping him with advice and practical recommendations. And the duchess was equally supportive of Melody.

Every day, Allan thanked God for Melody's presence at his side. Her common sense and her encouragement made it possible for him to tackle the Herculean task of cramming the lessons that he should have had three decades to learn, if the marquess had ever had any interest in training his heir to take over.

"We also need to find a place to live," Allan said to his wife one morning as they prepared for the day. "We cannot go on indefinitely living with Clara. Especially once she and Baldwin move up to Edinburgh."

"After today, it will just be us and the girls as visitors in their house," Melody mused.

They were dressing to attend the wedding of Phineas and Harmony, and that afternoon the newly married couple would be moving, with Benjie and the pet mice, to a house in Cheapside where Phineas planned to open a school for day pupils.

As many wealthy merchants lived in the vicinity, he was certain his school would be a success, and Harmony was gleefully planning to mother all the boys who came under her roof.

"Exactly," said Allan. "It is time for us to make our own home."

"What of the marquess's townhouse?" Melody asked.

Allan shuddered. *That hellhole?* He never wanted to set foot in it again.

But Melody hadn't finished. "From what you've told me of its history, it was a happy place once—a family home, as well as the London center from which previous marquesses had the kind of influence that Dellborough has now. It can be restored, Allan. Completely refurbished and redecorated. Rooms returned to their original purpose." She turned her back to him, silently asking him to do up the buttons on her fashionable day dress.

The buttons found the buttonholes, but Allan's gaze was inward, contemplating a grim reality. "They dug up the cellars, my love. They found more than fifty bodies in shallow graves. More than fifty women who ended their lives in pain and suffering. In that house." He cringed inside to think of it. All those murders and more at the hands of that awful man. *And I must have been living in the house when at least some of them took place!*

"Then what do you want to do?" Melody turned and slipped her arms around his waist. "I support whatever choice you make, my love. We can raze the buildings to the ground and build again. We can sell the townhouse and buy another one. We can ask the bishop for an exorcism."

"An exorcism?" Whatever Allan thought she might say, that wasn't it. Wasn't Melody one of the most level-headed people he knew? "Are you saying the place is haunted? Or infested with demons?" *This is the nineteenth century. Nobody of sense believes in such things.*

"Do you not want to avoid it because it reminds you of things you would rather forget?" asked his wife. "For you, the house is haunted by memories. As to the demon, he is gone. I would feel a great deal better if I knew where, but he is no longer in the house."

She slipped from his embrace and bent over the sparse collection in her jewelry case, took out the locket he had given her as a wedding present, and handed it to him.

Once again, she turned her back to him, presenting the nape of her neck as she said, "I only know that places have an atmosphere. I have entered a building and known people were happy there. Churches often feel peaceful and holy. Your townhouse is one where my skin crawled with discomfort from the moment I entered."

Allan obeyed the mute request, put the chain around his wife's neck, and fastened the catch.

Melody had not finished. "As the people are, so is the house. You are being too polite to scoff, beloved. But I have seen strange things enough to believe that an exorcism and blessing by the bishop will help to change the atmosphere, as will having servants who no longer live in fear, and owners who love one another."

She turned again and kissed his cheek. "Here I am, talking on and on when I have already said it is your decision, and I shall support you. I love you, Allan Sheppard."

"And I love you," Allan told her. He gathered her closer for a kiss that meant redoing her hair and changing the linen fichu they had crushed between them.

Later that day, after a long wrestle between his fear and his pride—he never wanted to enter that house again, but nor did he want his wife to pity him for a coward—he made a decision. "We shall keep the house," he told Melody. "Let us refurbish it and change it to our liking. And yes. Let us ask the bishop to come and bless it."

ALLAN AND MEL visited the bishop, who was not encouraging. "While I cannot deny the existence of malign influences, Lord Kemble, in general, I regard exorcisms as a relic of a more superstitious time. If you wish to dispel such influences, a simple prayer will generally do."

He nodded at his own wisdom. "In the first instance, I suggest you and your wife try sincere and faithful prayer. Perhaps do a careful examination of conscience, receive communion in your parish church, and then pray together for God to cleanse the house and free it from the pains and suffering of the past."

Mel pointed out how much evil had been committed in the house, and how difficult it had always been to retain servants. She did not mention her own reaction to the atmosphere—she had the impression that the bishop would discount her discomfort as womanly imagining.

The bishop would not change his mind, though he did agree to reconsider if his proposed approach did not work. He also gave them a little booklet with some prayers they could try.

They followed his prescription to the letter. Allan overcame his distaste for the house sufficiently to walk through it with her, reciting the prayers that the bishop had given them in each of the principal rooms. Room by room, Mel felt more and more oppressed. "I feel as if the house is glaring at me," she told Allan.

"I've heard that before," Allan told her. "One of the maids who resigned said much the same thing."

In fact, all the servants who had not been arrested as accomplices to the marquess and Farnham had either resigned or requested to be transferred elsewhere. The house was standing empty, with a pair of night watchmen patrolling the grounds at night, and a squad of maids from an agency coming in every second day to dust and sweep.

And even then, several of them had refused to return after

their first day of work, and one had walked out the door five minutes after walking in. Furthermore, they had hired a second night watchman because no one would stay even in the grounds at night if he was on his own.

"That was our last room," Mel told Allan. "Unless you want to do the kitchen?"

"Let's leave," said Allan. "We shall see whether that makes a difference to the maids. And us, for that matter, since we must be back here tomorrow to take the architect and the master builder on a tour to discuss what we want to have done."

The master builder only made it as far as the second floor before he told Allan he would not be taking the commission. "Some buildings just feel wrong, Lord Kemble. And I've learned over the years that working on them isn't worth it. Accidents happen. And fights, and other disturbances. People even lose their lives. This is that kind of building, and the worst of its sort I've ever seen."

The architect lasted the full tour, but he was clearly uncomfortable even before the builder's defection—pale and sweating, starting at the least sound, constantly looking over his shoulder. In the end, he, too, expressed his dislike of the building, though he prefaced his remarks with, "I know it is irrational, but…"

Before they even reached the tower, which they intended to reopen as overflow accommodation for the main house, he claimed another meeting. "I shall begin making concept drawings, Lord and Lady Kemble. I shall be in touch when they are ready. And you have told me enough about the tower for me to include a few ideas." His eyes darting from shadow to shadow, he hurried out of the building.

When the agency contacted them the following morning to say that the maid-team had threatened to quit if they were sent back to Teign Tower, Allan had had enough.

"We need to see the bishop again," he told Mel. "And if that doesn't work, the building will have to come down. If we can find someone willing to demolish it."

Hearing what had happened, the bishop reluctantly agreed to perform what he called "an exorcism and blessing. A deliverance, if you will." He and several priests whom he trusted would prepare, he said. It would require several days, and he had other engagements in the meantime. The date was set for the second Saturday in February.

"All those who are going to be present must also prepare with prayer and fasting," he warned. "We shall start in the main room of the house, and move through room by room."

He described the process in detail, his initial skepticism no longer in evidence. Mel wondered if he doubted her and Allan rather than the existence of inimical powers. That theory made sense, since—as a bishop—he presumably had a firm faith in spiritual beings beyond human imagining.

"I am relieved," she told Allan. "He is taking this seriously. It gives me hope that he knows what he is doing."

"I know what you mean," Allan agreed. "And yes, I have come round to your way of thinking, Mel. Something is wrong with the house beyond my own feelings about it. Something I can't explain. Best to leave it to the professionals." He twisted his mouth in a grimace. "I am not looking forward to telling my brothers. They'll be as skeptical as I was, and not as polite about it."

In the end, the brothers and their wives supported the exorcism. Baldwin was the one most inclined to scoff, but Clara told a couple of stories from her village about a house that was thought to be haunted, and Baldwin never liked disagreeing with his wife. Frank was wholeheartedly in favor, pointing out that the place had been oppressive all their lives and if what the bishop tried didn't work, they had lost nothing.

Even practical Thomasina thought it was a good idea.

So, on the second Saturday in February, those chosen to represent the rest of the family gathered in the drawing room at Teign Tower, all except for Allan and Mel, who waited by the door for the bishop and his assistants.

After a round of introductions in the drawing room, the bishop suggested that they begin immediately. "It is a big house," he said, "and I must repeat the exorcism in every room and closet."

He led them through the Lord's Prayer and the prayer of general confession, and then pronounced an absolution. After a Gospel reading came several prayers asking God to cleanse the house and deliver it from "all evil spirits; all vain imaginations, projections and phantasms; and all deceits of the evil one."

Then he sprinkled every corner of the room with water he'd brought with him, and pronounced a blessing on the room and all those within it. It might have been her imagination, but to Mel, the room felt better. Lighter, somehow, both in the sense of weight and of brightness. Though neither of those words were right, precisely. The sensation had nothing to do with normal senses.

"That's one," the bishop said. "Lord Kemble, let us proceed to the next room."

He and his assistants were very thorough. No room was missed, not the smallest attic bedroom, not the linen closet or the butler's pantry. In every room the bishop repeated the prayers of deliverance, the sprinkling of water—even into cupboards—and the blessing.

Since the house had grown over time, it was a bewildering maze, with corridors that apparently led nowhere or looped back on themselves, steps between levels, and another entire network of corridors to convey servants invisibly from one part of the house to another.

After an hour, they had visited fifteen rooms, blessing them and the corridors between them. They had almost completed the grandest floor of the house—the one designed for entertaining important guests and holding large gatherings.

On other floors, the rooms would be smaller and more numerous.

"How many rooms does the house have?" Mel whispered to Allan.

He shook his head. "I have never managed to count. Somewhere close to one hundred, I think."

"We are going to need to provide refreshments," Mel decided. One hundred rooms at this pace would take all day. And yet, already the rooms they had been in felt better.

Perhaps, as Baldwin insisted, it was her imagination. Still, it was worth continuing, whether the bishop was succeeding in driving malign influences out of the house, or whether she and Allan—and the other members of the family—were simply being deluded into imagining both the bad feelings and their expulsion.

Most of the family present for the ritual had stayed in the drawing room. "I shall find Clara, and ask her to organize food and drink," she told Allan, and he nodded his agreement before following the bishop's party into the next room.

Mel hurried her errand. The instinct that seldom failed her was nagging at her now, telling her that she needed to be at Allan's side as he went from room to room. There was danger in this house, and it was pointed firmly in the direction of Allan.

But it was not yet apparent where or when the danger would arise. She had time, and the immediate need was to make sure that those in the house for this exorcism were provided with food and drink as the day wore on. *We had better make a priority of cleansing the kitchen.*

Once Clara had promised to send for her own servants and food from her own kitchen, Mel returned to Allan, and tucked her hand into his. She was at his side, whatever the house had in store for them.

They completed the basement, with its kitchen, pantry, scullery, servants' hall, housekeeper's office, and all the other service rooms and moved on to the floor designed for family living and for hosting more intimate gatherings.

Once they had prayed in the family dining room on that floor, Clara escorted in a bevy of maids with trays and a couple of footmen with a tea urn, and they paused to eat and drink before continuing upstairs to the guest bedrooms and beyond that to the servants' rooms in the attics.

Hour by hour, as they progressed room by room, nothing went wrong and no danger made itself apparent. Mel began to wonder if she had allowed the history of the house to cloud her instincts.

Certainly, they finished the main block of the house, basement to attics, without anything disturbing their progress. There remained the family wing and the tower, and they repaired to the family wing after stopping to recruit their energies with a buffet meal.

All doubts fled as they passed through the double doors into the main corridor to the ground floor Mel had visited before. The marquess's study was here, as well as the stewards' office and visitor parlors in various sizes. Here, too, the sense of the danger that had been hovering at the back of her mind became suddenly present and piercing.

She and Allan were leading the way, with the quietest of the clerics who was assisting the bishop beside them. This man—he had been introduced as Beauclair—had been walking with his neck bent and his lips moving in prayer.

He stopped as they crossed in front of the side entrance used by the marquess's petitioners, his stewards, and other such visitors. In fact, he stopped so abruptly that Mel turned to see what had given him pause. She was in time to watch him lift his head and stretch it forward, his nostrils flared. He looked from side to side, for all the world like a hound attempting sight and sniffing out the prey.

"Your Grace," he said to the bishop, "this hall first, and then that room." He pointed to the door that opened into the marquess's study.

MR. BEAUCLAIR'S VOICE broke through the fog of dread and

despair that had been descending on Allan since they walked through the doors into the private wing. The emotions struggled to find expression in words. *It is hopeless. We can never win. We should just give in.*

He gripped Mel's hand as a point of reference in the storm, and fought the words back. She had come to him like a light in the darkness. She was his hope, his reason to fight until they won, his compass and his anchor.

Again, Mr. Beauclair spoke, his voice sharp with alarm. "Lord Kemble is under attack, Your Grace. And Lords Ernest and Hudson, too."

An attack. Is that what it is? From his father? The bishop's voice came to Allan as if at a distance, like voices heard on the threshold of sleep. "What do you recommend, Mr. Beauclair?"

"Let us pray for the safety of each of the Sheppard brothers, and send them back to the drawing room before we finish these rooms," proposed Mr. Beauclair. "And let Mr. Blasingstoke go with them, to pray with them for our success."

"I can… fight… it," Allan insisted.

The bishop was talking to Melody, and Allan was too busy to listen. He was trying not to succumb to the heavy weight of doom that pressed on his mind.

Then warm arms wrapped around him and pushed the weight back. Melody. It lightened still further at the light touch of hands on his shoulder—hands that drove back the dread while voices intoned the Lord's Prayer.

He joined in the *Amen.*

"Come," said Melody. "Let us leave it to the professionals for a while, and check on our brothers."

Allan let her lead him, back past the side door and through into the main house. The burden of dread lightened still further as soon as he was on the other side of the doors. Ernest and Rosina had come, too, and Hudson and Parthena.

Also, Mr. Blasingstoke, another of the bishop's assistants.

"What happened in there?" Hudson demanded. "I felt as if I

had no reason for living, as if every good thing had been leached of its virtue, as if fighting was pointless."

Ernest was nodding.

Mr. Blasingstoke quoted Shakespeare's Hamlet. "'There are more things in Heaven and Earth, Horatio, than are dreamt of in your philosophy.' My friend Mr. Beauclair understands these matters better than I. He says you were being attacked, Lord Hudson, and you too, Lord Kemble and Lord Ernest. A rationalist might suggest that you have been accustomed to such feelings in that part of the house, but the bishop has brought us here because the forces of evil are real, are able to produce—or perhaps merely to magnify—such feelings, and can be dispelled."

After the last five minutes, Allan had no argument with Mr. Blasingstoke's contention.

Back in the drawing room, the other brothers who had come to the house had also felt something—not to the same extent as the three who had accompanied the bishop, but enough that they didn't argue about Mr. Blasingstoke's explanation of what they had experienced.

Nor did they refuse to join Mr. Blasingstoke in prayer for the family and the house.

And throughout the wait for the bishop and his attendants, Allan clung to Mel's hand.

THE BISHOP AND his team didn't reach the tower or the cellars that day. They arranged to return the next day, and went home. They were all pale and looked exhausted, and Allan totally agreed. But his own weakness in the family wing was bothering him.

"Before we go," he said, "I want to go back to the marquess's study." *Want* was the wrong word. He wanted nothing less, but he was determined to do it, nonetheless.

Melody opened her mouth, and he could see from her expression that she was minded to argue. But she must have thought better of it, for what she said was, "I will come with you."

In the end, they all went. Five brothers and their wives. And the suffocating weight of despair was not waiting for them in the family wing. Allan stood outside the study examining his own feelings. He was tired. He was happy to have Melody and others of his family at his side. But none of that negative miasma remained.

"It is gone," said Ernest, sounding surprised.

"'More things in heaven and earth,'" quoted Hudson, and stepped forward to open the study door.

Allan braced himself and followed Hudson and Parthena into the room, to be assailed with memories. But that was all they were. In this room, he had experienced many things, most of them terrible. He didn't like remembering them, but it was not the devastating horror of that few minutes earlier today.

"A complete redecoration," Melody said. "In fact, we should make another room into your study, Allan, and turn this one into a visitor parlor, since it is just inside the side door."

"We did it," said Ernest. "We showed each other how brave we all are. Now let's go home."

IT TOOK TWO more days for the bishop and his team to go over every room, closet, and passage in the house, but the gruesome discovery on the second day overshadowed the third day, which was benign by comparison.

Allan and Melody were showing the men around the tower. Several of the other brothers went ahead of them, opening the hidden rooms and hiding places. One could only hope that five clerical gentlemen could be trusted to keep the secret of their existence. However, even if one or more had loose lips, sending the brothers ahead meant none of them knew where the catches were.

They had prayed for the deliverance of each room in both upper and lower tower, and in the stairwells and tunnels, and were about to leave the tower dungeon when Ernest said, "What about the oubliette?"

After his experiences yesterday, Allan was more than half inclined to tear the house down and not leave one stone on another, but Ernest was right. Best to be thorough.

He nodded to Ernest to open the hidden door, and said to everyone else, "There's a hidden door on the right-hand side of the dining space on the fourth level. At first sight, it looks just like the one we came down by. The door lets on to stairs much like those behind the left-hand side, but certain steps will trigger ambushes—weights from the ceiling to drop on people's heads, steps that drop away, arrows that fire from the walls. At the bottom is an oubliette—a bottle dungeon. Anyone caught in one of the traps drops down to end up in the oubliette, and there's no way out except for the hole twelve or fifteen feet above an unfortunate prisoner's head, with sheer walls all around."

"We shall stand in the doorway for our prayers," said the bishop. "Will that be safe, my lord?"

"Yes, Your Grace, but I warn everyone to go no further. The oubliette itself is covered with a thin piece of card, and the stairs are treacherous."

"Allan, the traps have been triggered," Ernest exclaimed. Sure enough, the hole to the oubliette was uncovered.

And worse, a foul smell rose from within.

At that moment, something happened. An attack, Mr. Beauclair had called it yesterday, when they approached the marquess's study. This one was so much worse that Allan never for a moment thought that the emotions that surged out of the gloom had their origin in himself. Despair, envy, spite, anger, and surpassing all the rest, the tide on which they rose, hate—they battered at him with such force that his knees sagged, and only the grip Mel had on his hand kept him upright.

Dear Mel, once again keeping him sane in the insanity that boiled up from the oubliette, so strong that Ernest had fallen to his knees and was bent over, supporting himself on his hands.

And wonderful Mr. Beauclair had stepped forward to help Ernest to his feet and passed him backward to be supported by Rosina, and was standing in the entrance, holding up a cross and reciting the prayers with which they were all now so familiar. The weight on Allan was already lighter, and as the other clerics joined Mr. Beauclair, the gale of emotions lessened and finally whisped into nothing.

"Is anybody there?" called the bishop down into the hole in the floor.

There was no reply. Allan had not expected one. Perhaps the person who had triggered the traps and fallen into the oubliette had survived the fall, but surely not for long. And the similarity of the recent storm to the emotions that had infested the house for so long identified the person.

"We have found Teign," Allan said.

IT WAS, INDEED, the Marquess of Teign and he was dead. The coroner had to send someone down a ladder to tie the corpse to a stretcher so it could be hauled out of the oubliette on a rope.

The brothers left that matter to the coroner and the runners from the nearest magistrate's court, and only learned at the coronial inquiry that the marquess had survived his fall for many days, and eventually died of thirst.

When the door at the top of the fatal stairs had been opened, they'd found food, drink, books and other supplies—the marquess had clearly planned to wait in hiding until the furor over his disappearance died down.

Reconstructing the man's fall and subsequent death from the available evidence, the officer in charge of the recovery and investigation hypothesized that Teign had been carrying a box containing bottles of wine and a lamp when he reached the first trap.

The lamp had not survived the fall intact. The box and most of its contents landed in the oubliette with the marquess, all but a couple of bottles shattered and their contents lost into the cracks between the cobbles of the floor.

Allan stared at the sheet that covered the marquess's remains and imagined the man at the bottom of the oubliette, in pain from two broken legs, a cracked rib, multiple scrapes and bruises, a dislocated shoulder, and more. In the dark. Alone. Cradling the surviving bottles of wine and taking a miserly sip from time to time, to make the liquid last. Hoping that someone would come in time. Knowing he would die if he was not rescued.

The end was inevitable. Farnham, the only man who might have known where the marquess was hiding, had not recovered consciousness and had eventually died from his injuries.

The coroner ruled the marquess's death accidental but in Allan's mind, and perhaps those of his brothers'—it was an appropriate ending, for he suffered, even as his sons and the women he'd abused had suffered.

Most importantly, the evil man's reign was finally over—Teign was gone and Allan's brothers were safe.

"May I express my condolences, Lord Teign," said the coroner, and for an awful moment, Allan thought the man was talking to the dead marquess. But of course, he was addressing the living marquess—Allan himself. *I shall never get used to wearing that name.*

Melody squeezed his hand, and Allan managed to respond with a semblance of composure. "Thank you," he said. *How would the man react if I said what I was thinking? Don't be sorry. I am not, and nor are any of his family.*

"The body will be released to you whenever you are ready, my lord," the coroner continued. "I know you shall wish to arrange burial."

"Thank you," Allan said again. He considered telling the

coroner that the marquess could be thrown into a common grave with whatever other anonymous or pauper bodies required burial, but he supposed it wouldn't be fair to the paupers.

Once he was free of the rooms where the inquest had been held, he shared that thought with his family. "I don't want him put in the family tomb at Barcliffe Priory, though. Buried with all honors? He doesn't deserve it."

"We should plant him at a crossroads with a stake through his heart," Cornelius grumbled.

"Given what you all experienced in the house," said Baldwin, "consecrated ground would probably spit him out." *Strong words from a rationalist.*

"Given what you experienced in the house," Clara corrected, "burying his remains in consecrated ground might be a wise, defensive measure." She added, "And may he burn in Hell," which was surprising, from such a kind and composed woman.

In the end, Melody and Clara arranged for the man to be buried without fanfare, in a grave in the corner of the burial ground of St. John's church, with a simple wooden marker that recorded his name and nothing else.

Even the interred corpses from the cellar had more dignity in the cemetery of St. Brides—a joint tombstone listing as many names as they could discover and the catchall phrase "and other women who could not be identified." Underneath was a verse from the Book of Psalms: "Yea, though I walk through the valley of the shadow of death, I will fear no evil: for thou art with me; thy rod and thy staff they comfort me."

Now the Sheppard brothers could all pick up the pieces of their lives and be happy. Baldwin and Clara were off to Edinburgh in the spring, where Baldwin would be attending the medical school at the university. Cornelius and Thomasina had purchased tickets to cross the channel and would be taking their family to France as soon as weather allowed. Donald and Verity had decided to live chiefly on her country estate, where they had an engineering workshop and a breeding kennel for dogs.

The next two brothers and their wives would live closest to Allan and Melody. They were moving to cottages on the Barcliffe Priory estate, where Ernest would study with the steward, so he could take over when the man retired, and where Frank would become Allan's secretary while Winifred and her father continued their studies.

The twins Gerard and Hudson, with their wives Amber and Parthena, had chosen an estate near the Priory that was big enough to comfortably support two families, and that could be split in two for their future heirs.

And, to judge by their letters, Isaac and Jerome were thoroughly enjoying their grand tour.

As for Allan and Melody, they gave the architect and builder their approval to begin planning the reconstruction and refurbishment of the townhouse, and left for the country with Harriet and Lydia.

Allan would be perfectly happy, except he did not want to go through life wearing the Teign title. At least none of his family used the hated name, and even some of the fashionable people he had met through Dellborough were content to call him *Allan*, whereas in the country, once they arrived, the servants soon learned to call him "my lord" and "his lordship."

If there was occasional confusion over the generic form of address, the reward was not having to hear himself addressed by the title that had always meant pain and humiliation for him or someone he loved.

Melody, of course, called him many things. "Husband" was one of his favorites. "Beloved," "darling," "my heart," "dearest love," and so many other endearments. She, at least, never addressed him as Lord Teign. And it was she who came up with the solution.

Chapter Twenty-Four

MEL CHOSE A moment when she and Allan were alone together, in their private sitting room at Barcliffe Priory. She was not certain how he would feel about her going behind his back. She had had the best of intentions, of course, but they had promised to be open and honest with one another and to have no secrets.

Except, said a later amendment to the promise, they could keep a secret regarding a present or other surprise, intended to bring pleasure to the other person. Surely that provision applied here?

"Allan," she said, "I have a confession to make. I have done something in secret."

Her darling husband took her by the waist and pulled her into his arms. "Will I like it?" he murmured, between kisses.

"I certainly hope so," she said.

He stopped his kisses, lifted his head, and examined her face. "You are frowning, darling. I will love whatever you have got me, I am certain."

"It is a new title," Mel blurted, rushing her fences. "Or, at least, it will be, if you apply, and if the king approves. And Dellborough thinks he will, only it will then go to the College of Heralds, and it is unlikely to happen overnight. But probably no more than a year, Allan. Eighteen months at the most."

After a bewildered blink or two, Allan backed her into her chair and took his own. "Can you start at the beginning, please, my lady? What new title? What do you mean?"

A deep breath allowed Mel to compose herself. "Allan, I wrote to the Duke of Dellborough to ask him how to go about retiring the name the former marquess disgraced so badly, and replacing it with another. I thought you might wish to use your grandfather's name, Arlesley."

He was gaping at her, as if she was speaking a language he didn't understand.

"I wasn't sure if it was possible, but other peers have applied to change their name. Dellborough agrees that you can, too. His Grace says it might mean new Letters Patent, which is why it might take a while. He has consulted the king, and he will look favorably on a request."

"Change the name of the title, you mean," Allan said, in a carefully neutral voice.

"Yes. If you want to, that is."

"The Marquess of Arlesley," said Allan, a smile dawning in his eyes and spreading across his face. In the next breath he caught her up in his arms and swung her around, laughing with delight. "Arlesley," he repeated. "Melody, my love, you are a marvel. Change the title! Brilliant."

His exultant dance ended in another hug, this one so fierce she could manage only the shallowest of breaths. She hugged him back, thrilled with his response. "I love you, Allan," she told him.

"I love you, Melody. The day you swaggered into my tower and announced that you were there to uncover my secrets was the day my life began. And every day I live, heart of my heart, I shall live for you."

Epilogue

Eighteen months later

IT WAS FINALLY done. Dellborough and the king might have thought changing the name of Allan's title would be simple, but the College of Arms and the palace staff had agonized over the implications and possible processes to avoid adverse consequences.

Melody was here today, sitting at the back of the House of Lords with all of her brothers-in-law and most of their wives, as a result of their solution. The Marquess of Teign had become the Marquess of Arlesley, but with a new patent and writ of summons, which the king's advisers had decided meant a formal presentation to the House of Lords as if Allan's peerage were entirely new.

He would be here any moment. His mentor, the Duke of Dellborough, had just walked into the chamber, and Melody knew that he would have stayed with Allan to the door of the chamber. Yes, and here came the Garter King of Arms in all the glory of his traditional costume, with Allan after him, the Marquess of Deerhaven on one side, and the Marquess of Winchester on the other. All three of them wore the ceremonial parliamentary robes of a marquess, made of red wool and marked with the three and a half bars of white fur, edged with gold lace that designated their rank.

As Allan bowed to the Lord Chancellor, Melody leaned forward as much as she could, given her pregnancy. She watched intently as the Lord Chancellor ordered the Garter to read the patent and the writ of summons. Next came Allan's oath of allegiance to the king, and finally, Allan was led to his place in the chamber, where he took off his cap and bowed to the Lord Chancellor.

She had heard his maiden speech over and over. He had been practicing bits of it for weeks, and had said the whole of it for her twice yesterday. "I shall be so nervous that I shall forget it entirely," he said, and took a written copy of it with him, in the pocket of the breeches he wore under his robes.

He didn't need it, however. As Allan always did, he rose to the needs of the moment, thanking the lords for their support, reaffirming his support for the king and "this great country that we all love", and promising to serve both to the best of his ability.

It was done. Though those in the know had been calling Allan by his new title ever since the decision was finally made, today marked a watershed moment. Teign was gone forever, and only Arlesley remained. Melody hoped that Allan's long-deceased mother somehow knew that her father's heritage lived on in her son, and was pleased.

The Sheppards did not stay for long after Allan had finished his speech. They filed from the chamber and made their way out to Old Palace Yard, to wait for Allan.

"We'll meet you back at Arlesley House," said Isaac to Mel. He and Jerome had arrived a few days ago, back from their travels. They had matured in their time away, and gained confidence. Like the other Sheppard brothers, they were men of substance, and it showed. The two of them, and a couple of the other brothers, set off to walk to the mansion, which was only a few streets away.

Several of the wives took the barouche that was waiting, with their husbands walking alongside, but Thomasina and Winifred stayed with Mel to wait for Allan. Baldwin and Frank were talking to the journalists. The newspapers were painting the renaming of the title as Teign's final defeat at the hands of his heir, and were eager to resurrect the scandals of Teign's life and death.

They had a point about the occasion. The sons of the former marquess would never forget the torments they had suffered at their father's hands, but they all agreed that Allan's acceptance of the Arlesley title put Teign's evil heritage firmly in the past.

There was a stir among the journalists when Allan walked out of the palace, accompanied by Dellborough. They abandoned Baldwin and Frank and rushed Allan, but a few terse words from Dellborough scattered them again, and cowed them enough to keep them from crowding the family while each husband handed his own wife into one of the two remaining carriages.

Their carriages rolled on to Arlesley House—the former Teign Tower—which had been utterly transformed by the renovations. They entered through the main doors into a restored great hall that had once been broken up into an entrance hall and two levels of reception rooms.

The great hall was now the grandest reception room of all, with a magnificent curving staircase on one side, a minstrel's gallery on the other, and enough space in between, under the arching roof thirty feet above, to accommodate eight sofas, four couches, a couple of dozen chairs, a score of occasional and side tables, a dance floor, a grand piano, and more.

It was currently serving the family as a gathering room. Isaac and Jerome were playing a duet on the piano. Several of the brothers were standing by the sideboard that contained the decanters, engaged in a debate that clearly required glasses to be waved, their contents sloshing dangerously.

Cornelius sat with Thomasina, their baby daughter in asleep in his arms. In one corner, the toddling infants played under the supervision of their nurses. Four of them must have been conceived at The Golden Adonis, for they arrived between six and seven months after the weddings.

Lydia and Harriet, who had had a joyful reunion yesterday

afternoon, were hand in hand and deep in conversation on one of the couches. Elias was sitting next to his father, with Benjie next to him, leafing through a book.

Allan and Baldwin were welcomed into the group by the decanters, while Frank went to sit by Winifred, who had not come to Parliament today, as her second baby was expected at any time.

Mel handed her bonnet, gloves, and coat to the butler. "Please tell Mrs. Parker to serve luncheon," she said. It would be a casual meal, with the food laid out on one or more of the side tables and everyone welcome to help themselves.

She took a seat by Thomasina, ready to admire the newest Sheppard baby. Or, at least, the newest at the moment. With eight of the brothers increasing their families, the title of youngest baby seldom remained long with one holder.

Much of the attention today was on the six adults who had traveled farthest to be here with Allan on the day he finally shed the burden of his father's title—two from Edinburgh, two from France, and two from further afield, most recently Egypt.

There was enough interest to spare for the three ladies, including Mel, who were with child. Mel was certain that the brothers had a bet or two on whether the ladies were carrying sons or daughters, and on the birth date for each, for a couple of them had asked her questions about her food preferences and what side she chose for sleeping. She'd also seen some assessing glances at the shape of her belly, for the grandmothers said that boys were carried low and girls were carried high.

Allan had threatened to clip his brothers' ears for their impertinence, but Mel knew it was all in good humor. It was such a joy to be part of a large family.

It was hard to believe they were living in the same house that Mel had first entered more than two years ago. In fact, perhaps they were not. Every room had changed, from the attics to the cellars. Some had required little more than redecoration. Some had had walls demolished, and even, in some cases, parts of floors or ceilings, so that rooms disappeared and new ones were built in their place.

After more than a year of work, only the least-used spaces still had workmen beavering away to finish them. And the tower, which was being fully restored as rooms for the eventual heir to the marquisate, and would in the meantime, act as overflow space for guests.

It seemed unlikely that they would ever have enough guests to require the space, but given the way the family was growing, perhaps it might happen.

The biggest change in the house was not the building renovations, however. It was the atmosphere. People enjoyed being here. Mel knew it, and so, she fancied, did the house. Even skeptical Baldwin waxed poetical on the topic, saying that the house had woken from a nightmare and now remembered how to be a happy family home, for all its ridiculous size.

The two youngest brothers had been assigned a bedroom suite each here in Arlesley House when they'd arrived two days ago. They had been polite enough to try to hide their reluctance, until they saw how different the house was now. They had now settled in, and that initial distaste was gone as surely as Teign Tower.

The Sheppard family, plus Phineas and Harmony, spent the afternoon together, those with London homes being reluctant to leave the gathering. They even stayed for dinner, and most of the family who lived elsewhere would be remaining in London for at least another two days, so the family reunion would continue tomorrow. After all, it had been two years since they had seen Isaac and Jerome.

Mel enjoyed the whole day, but when Clara announced that she was tired, and that she and Baldwin would be heading home, and Winifred and Thomasina both declared their intention of going up to bed, Mel's own weariness seemed to crash in on her.

"I must beg you to excuse me," she said. "I feel I should stay, since I am your hostess, but…"

"You are tired and you want your bed," said Harmony.

"We are family," said Ernest. "Do not worry, sister. We shall not swing from the chandeliers or take pot shots at the vases."

Allan sent his brother a scathing glance, but his words were for Mel. "I shall retire, too, my lady," and he offered her his arm.

"I shall be your maid," he said, and he sent Mel's maid away. "How tired are you?"

"Not too tired," Mel replied, interest in Allan's intentions driving back the weariness.

It was the perfect end to a perfect day, rejoicing in one another's love, repeating once again the ancient dance of love that celebrated and reaffirmed their marriage.

"I love you, Lady Arlesley," said Allan, as they lay in one another's arms, replete and content.

Sleepily, Mel took Allan's hand and placed it on her belly. "Your child is restless, Lord Arlesley." Like him, she was enjoying the sound of their new title.

"A new house, a new title, a new child," Allan said. "Was ever a man so fortunate?"

"I am the lucky one," Mel insisted, around a yawn, and she drifted off to sleep to the touch of his kiss to her forehead. Allan. Lord Arlesley. Her love, her partner, her marquess, her lord, her very own night dancer.

THE END

The band of supporters who helped Mel and the brothers to bring Teign down included several characters from others of my stories. In particular, Clem and Chris were hero and heroine of *The Secret Word* (A Twist Upon a Regency Tale Book 10)

This book was inspired by the story *The Twelve Dancing Princesses* (with my usual twists—a female investigator shut in with the heroes, who are escaping at night to dance, the Regency setting, and real-world reasons for what appears to be magic). But when I realized I would have ten dancing lords, I could not resist singing the Christmas song, The Twelve Days of Christmas. And so Christmas became the season for the story, and as my characters lived through the days from Christmas Day to Twelfth Night Eve, I had fun reinterpreting the lyrics in the song, one for each day. Did you catch them all?

A partridge in a pear tree: See Chapter Six

Two turtledoves: See Chapter Six

Three French hens: See Chapter Eight

Four calling birds: or, originally, four colly (black) birds, which was a slang term for clergymen. See Chapter Ten

Five golden rings: See Chapter Eleven

Six geese a-laying: See Chapter Twelve

Seven swans a-swimming: See Chapter Fifteen

Eight maids a-milking: See Chapter Fifteen

Nine ladies dancing: See Chapter Eighteen

Ten lords a-leaping: See Chapter Nineteen

Eleven pipers piping: See Chapter Twenty

Twelve drummers drumming: See Chapter Twenty-one

Burlington Arcade

The Burlington Arcade exists to this very day, and Londoners and visitors to London still shop there. It was, indeed, built by the Earl of Burlington, purportedly for the reasons given in my story—to mask his mansion and grounds and to stop neighbors from throwing their rubbish over the fence. And it still has its own force of beadles.

Changing a title

From what I could discover, this was theoretically possible. Peerages are created by the monarch, who is considered the "fount of honor"—that is, the source of every peerage. From time to time in history, monarchs have revoked titles for great crimes or for acts of treason. Today, revoking a title requires an Act of Parliament, as it has since the early twentieth century.

It is technically possible that the reigning monarch could extinguish a peerage and grant a new one to the title holder, which is what I have written here. Which is another way of saying that I made this part of the story up.

I've based Allan's presentation to the House of Lords on the ceremony used at the time for a newly created peer. A peer who had inherited a title rather than being granted a new one, merely entered the house, bowed to the Lord Chancellor, and took his seat.

English coinage in the 1820s

British currency was based on pounds, shillings, and pence. A pound had the value of twenty shillings, and a shilling the value of twelve pennies.

Coins in circulation included the two-pound coin, guinea (twenty-one shillings), sovereign (one pound), half sovereign (half a pound), crown (five shillings), half-crown (two shillings and six pence), shilling, sixpence, threepence, and twopence, penny, halfpenny, and farthing (one quarter of a penny). In the reign of George III, there was also a coin worth a third of a guinea, or seven shillings. This had the slang name of a "sparkle".

What is an oubliette

An oubliette, as mentioned in the story, is a bottle dungeon—that is, a hole in the ground, with no exit or entry except through the hole at the top. The name is French, and comes from the word *oublier*, to forget. It is a particularly nasty place to imprison people. Teign deserved it.

Exorcism

From the seventeenth century until toward the end of the nineteenth century, the Church of England appears to have had a rather disapproving attitude to exorcism. From 1604, Anglican canon law, and specifically Canon 72, forbade exorcism without a license from the local bishop.

Some have taken this to mean that there were no exorcisms until spiritualism became a popular fad in the second half of the nineteenth century. Others assume that exorcisms continued, but were rare, private, and not documented, which is the view I've taken. I've based my procedure on the appendices in the Exeter Report of 1972 (*"Exorcism: the Findings of a Commission Convened by the Bishop of Exeter,"* edited by Dom Robert Petitpierre, O.S.B., 1972), making the possibly unwarranted assumption that the practices of that time would have been based on earlier practices.

Have you ever wanted something so much you were afraid to even try? That was Jude ten years ago.

For as long as she can remember, she's wanted to be a novelist. She even started dozens of stories, over the years.

But life kept getting in the way. A seriously ill child who required years of therapy; a rising mortgage that led to a full-time job; six children, her own chronic illness... the writing took a back seat.

As the years passed, the fear grew. If she didn't put her stories out there in the market, she wouldn't risk making a fool of herself. She could keep the dream alive if she never put it to the test.

Then her mother died. That great lady had waited her whole life to read a novel of Jude's, and now it would never happen.

So Jude faced her fear and changed it—told everyone she knew she was writing a novel. Now she'd make a fool of herself for certain if she didn't finish.

Her first book came out to excellent reviews in December 2014, and the rest is history. Many books, lots of positive reviews, and a few awards later, she feels foolish for not starting earlier.

Jude write historical fiction with a large helping of romance, a splash of Regency, and a twist of suspense. She then tries to figure out how to slot the story into a genre category. She's mad keen on history, enjoys what happens to people in the crucible of a passionate relationship, and loves to use a good mystery and some real danger as mechanisms to torture her characters.

Dip your toe into her world with one of her lunch-time reads collections or a novella, or dive into a novel. And let her know what you think.

Website and blog:
judeknightauthor.com

Subscribe to newsletter:
judeknightauthor.com/newsletter

Bookshop:
judeknight.selz.com

Facebook:
facebook.com/JudeKnightAuthor

Twitter:
twitter.com/JudeKnightBooks

Pinterest:
nz.pinterest.com/jknight1033

Bookbub:
bookbub.com/profile/jude-knight

Books + Main Bites:
bookandmainbites.com/JudeKnightAuthor

Amazon author page:
amazon.com/Jude-Knight/e/B00RG3SG7I

Goodreads:
goodreads.com/author/show/8603586.Jude_Knight

LinkedIn:
linkedin.com/in/jude-knight-465557166